Readers love
AMBERLY SMITH

Marriage Most Convenient

"…a nice friends-to-lovers story line with some hot sex mixed in."
—Gay Book Reviews

"…I loved the way Smith handled the roadblocks she put up for the characters. It was really well done and believable."
—Joyfully Jay

"The dialogue between the characters was candid and distinctive. The characters' voices matched not only the setting but fit their overall personality."
—Hearts on Fire

Rinse & Repeat

"I really liked this book. I thought the interesting plotline was addictive to read and very easy to follow."
—Night Owl Erotica

"The writing is instantly engaging and very entertaining. This is perfect for a light and enjoyable afternoon read."
—Long and Short Reviews

By AMBERLY SMITH

Closet Case
Higher Learning (Dreamspinner Anthology)
Marriage Most Convenient
Rinse & Repeat
Waking Jamal

Published by DREAMSPINNER PRESS
www.dreamspinnerpress.com

Waking Jamal

AMBERLY SMITH

DREAMSPINNER PRESS

Published by
DREAMSPINNER PRESS

5032 Capital Circle SW, Suite 2, PMB# 279, Tallahassee, FL 32305-7886 USA
www.dreamspinnerpress.com

Waking Jamal
© 2016 Amberly Smith.

Cover Art
© 2016 Maria Fanning.
Cover content is for illustrative purposes only and any person depicted on the cover is a model.

ISBN: 978-1-63477-133-7
Digital ISBN: 978-1-63477-134-4
Library of Congress Control Number: 2015920422
Published March 2016
v. 1.0

Printed in the United States of America

This paper meets the requirements of
ANSI/NISO Z39.48-1992 (Permanence of Paper).

A special thank-you for James who answered my many questions on qualifying for Special Forces and the military's current ranking system.

Glossary of Terms for
the Valhalla Initiative

ASVAB—Armed Services Vocational Aptitude Battery. Testing the United States military uses to measure aptitude for different positions in the military or MOS.

Bloom Energy Server—Created by K.R. Sridhar in 2001. Technology once used only by large corporations like Google, Amazon, and Microsoft is now used commonly as a clean energy source.

cadre—An instructor or trainer; someone who belongs to a cadre.

Dios Provee—A Christian extremist group that originated in South America. They believe that what God created should not be tampered with and are against modifying food and people. This includes Hamra and medication. They are highly volatile, and their bases are spread across many continents.

duds—Hamrammr that have been trained in the activation program but did not successfully activate.

Hamask—A Norse word meaning bear, used by military forces to describe a specific type of warrior. Modified supersoldier with heightened strength and enhanced senses—both watchman and warrior.

Hamra—Short for Hamrammr.

Hamra Pair—the ultimate supersoldier team made up of a bonded pair: one a Vargr, the other a Hamask.

Hamrammr—Norse for shapeshifter or with the ability to change, they are the potential Hamask and Vargr. The term is also used to refer to active members of the USHP and is sometimes shortened to Hamra.

HAVOC—Hamask and Vargr Operational Center—also the call name of the military base that houses the HAVOC program. Though the USHP has other active locations, only HAVOC's location is secret.

MOS—Military Occupational Specialty code, also referred to as the day job or task assignment of military personnel.

ROTC—Reserve Officer Training Corps. A program that allows students to gain military experience while in college.

static—Acceptable, normal.

Team Leader—In charge of WREAC teams.

teltom towers—An advancement in communication and data processing that replaced cell towers and fiber optics in the late 2050s.

The Mountain—Department of Defense and Homeland Security Joint Operation base in the mountains of Colorado.

UH-90 Ghost Chinook—High-grade, fully combat-ready transport helicopters that are powered by a bloom box.

USHP—United States Hamrammr Program, which is tasked with activating, training, and utilizing soldiers that have become Vargr or Hamask.

Vargr—A Norse word meaning wolf, used by military forces to describe a specific type of warrior. Modified supersoldier with the abilities of superfast reflexes and mental cognition—walking supercomputer.

WREAC—War Reconnaissance Extraction Assault Corps. Teams of five to seven men and women. They are recruited out of the dud pile and from other elite teams like Navy SEALs and Army Rangers.

Supporting Documentation of the United States Hamrammr Program

Section 5: Increased Sensations of Sight, Hearing, and Taste

Rather than hallucinations and paranoia, the activation process increases sensory abilities in the Hamask, including heightened sight, hearing, taste, and touch....

With initial fury, the candidate does not have an anchor to his training. Furthermore, evidence suggests that the sedatives used to calm the candidate instead further aggravate the sensory overload, and the brain shuts down to protect the candidate, inducing hibernation.

Introduction of an anchor, or Vargr, restores the candidate to preberserk levels. (Bur, Brad S., PhD, [New Tokyo Military Academy, 2093], AAT NX722718)

Chapter 1

HAVOC Class, 2097

ACTIVATION FOR Jamal Zumati started on a Thursday morning. He ate with the others, then gathered his rations and gear and hiked to the farthest shed. The US military insisted on some of the antiquated practices of the early aboriginal tribes in order to bring his abilities online; isolation, little to no food or sleep, and meditation. The hardest part of his training had been the goddamn meditation.

You want a former Adderall-dependent guy to focus by sitting quietly and not thinking about anything? So not going to happen. One of the cadre had finally suggested yoga. The poses allowed him to focus on the strain, the heat generating from each muscle, rather than the mind-numbing silence.

The military either ignored the other historical aspects or felt they went a bit too far, voodoo and wives' tales. So no eating mushrooms, bloodletting, or purging. Which was all fine and good, except being the farthest out meant he went last, and those mushrooms would have at least kept him from being bored.

He spent the week stretching his mind and body.

Some couldn't handle being alone this many days. For Jamal, it felt like the first couple of weeks at a new group home. You got your bearings, established which of the kids were the bully, the narc, and the druggie, and then you shored up and tried to make it to school each day. There was always food at school.

Jamal kept to himself until the second time the foster had to enforce a rule. *The first time they're on their best behavior, so you don't get the real picture. Second time, though, when they go apeshit, vein pulsing in their neck, that's when you see the real them.*

Wednesday morning, the sweat dried on Jamal's chest as he held his sun pose then eased down to upward-facing dog. He heard them activating someone just down the hill: the sound of stomping boots and tears instead of the buzz of insects and the occasional rustle of an animal scurrying past. Maybe it was one of the girls, or a guy who had hung his masculinity on being a bear and knew instantly that he was a wolf. Bear or wolf—it made no difference to Jamal. He had a duty to his country. It had supported him through his whole life: paid his medical, bought his food, provided for his schooling. Now he would pay with his muscles or his mind. He'd act honorably and serve the people.

He placed his forehead to the smooth wooden plank and let the tension wash out the tips of his fingers as he took the *balasana* or child pose. It was finally silent again outside. Jamal's ribs slid around loosely, his chest full of liquid heat, revved up to take on this vital step.

As the activation team entered his shed, Jamal stood and saluted his senior officers, no longer self-conscious about his nudity.

"At ease."

He moved to a parade rest and surveyed the team: four military police, a nurse, a doctor, and Captain Chakosky. Chakosky was a Vargr and would be on hand to help with grounding Jamal if he activated as a Hamask. Chakosky was round of face, his size equivalent with Jamal's broad shoulders, but Chakosky was rather soft for Special Forces. Genetics could still snuff gym effort.

"Are you ready?" The doctor's eyes were bloodshot, his clothes creased in odd places.

They must have worked through the night and had one more to activate before they could call it a day. *What, they couldn't be bothered to dress up for the occasion?* Jamal had on his birthday suit, so dress blues should at least be required for everyone else.

"Sir, yes sir." Jamal sat on a wooden chair—the solitary piece of furniture was older than the shed—and stared straight ahead while they prepared his skin.

As he activated, Chakosky was the first thing he was aware of. The man stood in front of Jamal and had his hands clasped as if in prayer.

Wrong. Gross.

Jamal pushed the sickness in his stomach down.

There was a medical tray holding the empty vials and the thirty acupuncture needles, a few tipped with red. Jamal's eyes felt dry and he reached up to rub at his eyelashes. His nails felt like metal files tearing at wooden lashes. *Shit, what have they done to my eyes?* He flattened his palm against his cheek and eye socket to gently, slowly rub away the debris. His dry, coarse fingertips shredded his skin like a cheese grater. Tears poured down his cheeks.

God, this is embarrassing. Fuck, yes, it hurts, but I've had worse.

Tears were a sign of weakness. Tears made you a target. He just needed to pull himself together. Just give him a minute to calm down, to process.

Chakosky took a step toward him. *No.* He held up a hand to ward the man off. He just needed another minute.

That wolf shouldn't be touching me. Shouldn't be in my territory.

The abraded skin itched, and Jamal staggered to his feet as he scrubbed with his fingernails. He was definitely a Hamask, could even feel the increased power in his arms and thigh muscles. His touch was all haywire, but realization felt distant, almost separate of self.

Chakosky took another step toward him and Jamal raised both hands to hold the Vargr off. "Just give me a minute."

Something was wrong—his hearing was normal. Not all his senses had come online. That would be okay, no surprise to learn he was subpar at even this.

The nurse pulled out a brown bottle, and as she unscrewed the lid, the smell—lavender and rice starch in rancid water—made Jamal jerk his head back and stumble toward the wall, bile rising in his throat. He bumped into someone and his skin recoiled and shot with pain. "Stay the fuck back," he whispered to the MP. Stupid jock was going to mess this all up.

They needed to clean the activation away. Left unattended, the chemicals would fry his neural synapses. Shit, he couldn't focus around the pain. As the nurse advanced, an MP and Chakosky stepped up to take hold of his arms. Caustic bile churned in Jamal's throat at their repulsive touch and he dry-heaved.

Hold on, you can do this. They'd clean him up, give him fresh water, and then he'd head back to the base with Chakosky keeping him grounded. That was how all activations were supposed to go. Except, even with the Vargr touching him, he wasn't leveling out. Physical contact should help. "What's happening?"

He tried to push Chakosky away and realized his fingers were smeared with blood. Had he cut himself on the wooden chair? Moisture dripped from his chin, and a red splotch smeared like oil over water on his chest. Not tears. Blood.

His hearing kicked in at the same time that a deep feeling of hatred, so hot and bright that he closed his eyes, poured through his bones. They had done this to him. Come in with their bullshit B game, used crap chemicals, and blundered around like idiots. *Damn them.* "Stop. Don't."

"Stand down."

"Attention!"

No.

LT. RYAN "Rum" Walker could tell the men and women filing down the aisles of the lecture hall were ensigns, privates, cadets, and seamen. They looked like kids, and they had yet to develop that ramrod posture that came with any service past basic. The uniforms—standard issue and for the most part unadorned—told the same story. But being faced with their youth was another slap to his recently demoted face.

He waited for the creak of wooden seats and the quiet murmurs to settle down. His psych and anthropology training divided the room into Myers-Briggs subtypes and recognized those whose body language showed either confidence or secrets. A human map stretched across the tiered rows of wooden seats. With 78 percent accuracy, he could identify those who would be good wolves or bears, who had lied to get here, and who would kill to stay. Those were the things he should be teaching. How to read people. If they were going to pull him from the field because of insubordination, let him teach candidates actual battle-ready techniques, something useful. Instead they assigned him this propaganda bullshit they spoon-fed all the newbies.

Rum had a lesson planned, just not the one the brass were expecting.

As he stepped into view, someone called out "Attention!" They jumped to their feet, and Rum returned their salute. "As you were." They settled back in their chairs and he let his voice fill the hall.

"My name is Lieutenant Walker. Welcome to HAVOC." He then clicked the old-fashioned wireless remote in his palm.

"Hamask and Vargr Operations Center" projected on the forward wall. There were a few murmurs, and a girl in the front row, her hair tightly braided, shifted in her seat. Her eyes weren't the only ones that gleamed.

"This morning I will give you a *brief* summary of what we do at HAVOC and answer any general questions you may have. You will then be divided into groups, where you will watch an in-depth video on the Hamrammr initiative, and then you'll choose."

He let the silence draw out. "Choose to be activated or... choose the blue pill. Choose to return to your current posting."

When they got a Hamask to do the morning introduction for potentials, it turned into parlor tricks. Who used which soap that morning? Which male had masturbated in the last twelve hours? They'd have the class write something down at the room's farthest corner and then the Hamask would read it. The instructor might even tell you the type of fabric you were wearing. *Hello! We're in uniform.* The last one even Rum could do.

Rum squinted at them, glaring the murmurs back to quiet. He tilted his head to one side, leaning his right ear toward the noise, and took an audible sniff.

As a Vargr, his enhanced skills didn't involve his senses, but his abilities were always in play. Hard to turn off, in fact. If there was a sleep mode for his brain, he sure hadn't found it yet.

Rum clicked the remote again. Pictures of men and women, often in uniform, always in pairs, slid by on the screen. There was official verbiage on what, exactly, he was supposed to say. However, if he were any good at following orders, he wouldn't be here.

He lowered his voice, knowing the microphones around the stage would carry to the full room just fine. "You are each here because you have potential. Your ASVAB scores and DNA indicate that you could be activated as a Bear or a Wolf. 'You're a wizard, Harry.'" He wasn't surprised when no one laughed. Sometimes it took people a minute to warm up to him. "Half of an elite fighting pair. Pairs like—" He paused the screen on two female doctors. "—Dr. Janis McCarthy and Dr. Lynn Ladd. Hamask McCarthy is a renowned heart surgeon and Vargr Ladd has revolutionized the organ transplant process."

He liked using this particular example because it showed possible endgames for those who wouldn't become career military, and because McCarthy and Ladd weren't in a traditional bonded relationship.

It would have been nice to include a picture of the FBI pair Bur-Longwei, but that suggestion had been nixed pretty damn high up the food chain.

He clicked the remote again and the screen displayed a new pair. The man and woman stood in front of their WREAC team—War

Reconnaissance Extraction Assault Corps. "WREAC and HAVOC. Hamask Tidsdale and Vargr Lange are in the foreground with WREAC Team 3, instrumental in saving thousands during last year's tsunami in Hawaii."

A dark-skinned airman with soft eyes scoffed.

Rum snapped an index finger in his direction. "Skepticism. Good. But tell me, Airman…?"

The airman was slightly older than average, tall, broad shouldered. He stood upon being addressed. "Sir, Adayo, sir."

"Airman Adayo. Why did you assume the woman was Vargr Lange?"

Adayo's eyes widened, and then he swallowed. "Sir, I—"

Gawd, I love bein' right. "Unvarnished truth, please."

"Sir, I reacted to my programmed cultural expectations on gender roles. I assumed that the woman would be the Vargr and the man would be the Hamask. I know that is not always the case."

And that was why Adayo was here. Because he was smart enough to see his own shortcomings. Rum nodded in acknowledgment, and Adayo reclaimed his seat.

"Less than 25 percent of Hamrammr initiates are women. Though when they make it through training, women have a slightly higher success rate of activation." Which meant the most common Hamra Pair was two guys. He'd let them do the math.

He clicked to the next picture, a more stereotypical pairing. "This Hamra Pair both specialize in weapons and demolition." The picture showed the two out in the field and heavily camouflaged, the Hamask distinctive with his bare hands. "A more… traditional team. Currently in deep assignment tracking Christian extremists in South America."

He explained that those who stayed would face twelve intense weeks of physical and mental training. He highlighted the different military occupational specialties each successful Pair could be assigned to. He sprinkled in a few obscure references to old cultural evidence of Hamrammrs or those with the potential to change into Hamask and Vargr, including how the pair became two halves of a superserum soldier, i.e., Captain America.

"By the end of today, once you make the second-toughest decision, you'll be housed in coed barracks with your fellow potentials."

Rum did not talk about bonding, though he identified five of them who practically quivered to ask about it. He did not cover the activation process, though he strongly believed it was something they should know before making the decision to stay. He didn't warn them of the political bullshit that came with activation. Only a third of the candidates would make it through training, and only half of those would successfully activate. Maybe ten people in this room would become part of a sanctioned, bonded pair.

He turned off the old projector. Military budget restrictions had curtailed the crazy spending that was so rampant fifty years ago, but this ancient tech was sad. At least the mission rooms had holo sets.

"Things you probably all know, but just to be thorough. Hamask and Vargr always work in pairs. Hamask, also called bears, learn to use their senses and strength. Vargr, the wolves, act as a guide, provide a baseline for the chaos bears live in." That was an oversimplification if he ever spouted one, plus it didn't explain the heightened speed Vargrs gained in reflexes and mental processing. "Feel free to ask questions, but for the sake of time, *please* do not stand."

There were a few chuckles at this. Now to see if the seeds he'd planted would generate the questions he wanted them to ask.

The female marine with the braid raised a hand. He nodded to acknowledge her. "Is it true what they say about the bonding process?"

Rum raised his eyebrows and gave her an incredulous look. *Seriously?* That wasn't going to give her the information she wanted. "True that a bonded pair is stronger than an unbonded one? Absolutely. Bonding isn't a requirement and plenty of pairs never bond."

Yes, I'm going to make you work for it. Try again.

"Sir, why are only officers activated?" asked a hesitant seaman with more freckles than hair.

"Good eye. Yes, all Hamra, short, of course, for Hamrammr, are designated officers. Upon activation Hamra roll over to an M-rank system, similar to noncommissioned officers. They use officer designations, and though not all of you are officers currently, you all have completed the required college degrees for that status or you wouldn't be here."

Which made the two seventeen-year-olds present even more impressive.

A private, so rosy-cheeked that he would probably be carded until he was in his midthirties, raised his hand and asked, "Are Hamrammrs allowed to choose their partner?"

"Yes. Let me emphasize that. *Yes*." He nodded and then gestured to communicate exactly how important this was. "The military will make suggestions. If the partner you choose does not qualify for some of the advanced options, that may limit you. Thus the suggested pairings. But you get to choose. *You*, bear or wolf, get a choice." A few heads shook in the negative, and Rum immediately labeled and categorized them as American-born, second generation, military service. Military brats.

They came in thinking that the wolves led the bears around by the nose; that the only way to keep a bear in check was to form a sexual bond and manipulate their own pheromones to keep the wolf as the dominant in the relationship. Total military-culture bullshit. Rum memorized each face. By the end of training, either they'd be gone or they would darn well have a new perspective on partnerships.

The next question was from a female airman with the palest blonde hair Rum had ever seen. "Sir, why wolf and bear? I mean, the transformation rumors have been disproved and the abilities of each don't really match actual bears and wolves. So…?"

"The words hamask and vargr are from Old Norse. Viking mythology, legend, stories, whichever you prefer, tell tales of sending berserkers into battle. Changed men, fierce as bears and cloaked in wolf skin." He raised his finger to draw their attention even tighter. Giddy warmth filled his chest even as his shoulders tightened.

"There have always been such people. The aboriginal people of North Sentinel Island. Celtic lore. Even Native American vision quests. When the United States discovered a way to fully activate these abilities, shortly after the September 11 attacks in New York, the first Vargr held a doctorate in Norse history. He chose the terms. Don't worry. You'll get more of a history lesson during training."

A few arms shot up, and Rum indicated a tiny guy from the Coast Guard. Rum wouldn't be surprised if he was one of those two seventeen-year-olds on the list of candidates.

"Can you explain the bonding process and specifically the sexual aspects?"

Better question. "This is the United States military. We are not known for our sexual acceptance." It was his first use of "we," and like most of what he said, it was a strategic decision. "Yes, sexually active pairs are bonded pairs. Do all Hamra Pairs have sex? In my opinion, that's their business, and no one else's. Bonding does not require sex." The military strongly disagreed with him, but he wasn't about to disillusion potentials. That was more of a week-three activity. "Next question."

Adayo's hand was the first one up. "What is the hardest decision?"

Bingo. Now to reel them in. "Good question." He gestured to indicate the whole conference hall. They'd put in their time and deserved his best performance. "If you believe that I am a Hamask, raise your right hand. Starboard for the seamen in the room." He smiled. "If you believe I am a Vargr, raise your left hand. Okay, keep your hands up." He looked through the crowd and watched them look at each other. The training cadre were watching to see who would change their answer, and who were right.

"Adayo."

"Yes, sir?"

"Why did you choose Vargr?"

Adayo smiled. "At first I thought you were Hamask. You fed that belief by emphasizing your use of senses. Squinting, cocking your head to hear better."

Rum had also crafted each response and kept a tight lid on his accent. He'd teach them how to pick up on those clues eventually. "But?"

Adayo tilted his head and looked back at him with a critical eye. "Well"—he shrugged—"if you're not Hamask, then only Vargr is left."

"That is how most people see the Hamrammr initiative. If you're not a bear then you're a wolf. A second choice, less than. Despite the wolf being the leader in the pairing."

Hell, a lot of what was broken in this program surrounded that inferiority complex.

"Toughest decision that you each need to make before deciding if you'll stay: does it matter if I'm a wolf or a bear? Until we try to activate you, we don't know which you are." He scanned the room. "All of you are Hamrammr, but potential *what*? If you've got your heart set on being a Hamask, can you live with being *only* a Vargr?"

He checked his watch. 1122. Eight minutes to spare. Perfect. He tapped the watch's face to bring up the group lists and sent it to the candidates' smartwatches. "I'm sending each of you an itinerary and group list for the remainder of the day."

"Lieutenant Walker?" Tiny Coast Guard had his hand up.

Rum blinked at the boy, genuinely surprised at the additional question and the gold bar indicating the seventeen-year-old was an ensign—college degree and officer training completion. "Yes, Ensign—?"

"Sir, Kramer, sir. Are there any potential side effects of being activated?"

Bastian Gero Kramer. Rum's memory supplied the information. The ensign's voice spoke of New Orleans and his Latino upbringing.

Damn, he was good. Rum had specifically asked General Khan whether he could cover this and had been shot down. Khan's exact words were "don't bring it up," but he'd also told Rum to answer all their questions.

Rum smiled, and based on a few of their responses, he knew the grin looked evil. "You could fury."

Chapter 2

"YOU LITTLE shit." General Khan, Commander of the HAVOC program, watched the video feed from the lecture hall. When the ensign asked about potential side effects, Khan groaned. Walker had manipulated the room and gone against his directions. Not that the general had expected Walker to toe the line, but with the ensign's question he realized this could go wrong in several ways.

Over thirty years ago, when the general went through Indoc to join the Rangers, they didn't have an orientation day. Instead the cadre had used flash and bangs to create a controlled chaos. No talking about *feelings* or future options; instead he'd had a cadre yelling at him, "Just quit and this goes away." Yet, being a Hamra Pair was more about head games, so the general didn't begrudge the soft approach.

The initial weeks of physiological indoctrination built the mental space soldiers needed to activate as Hamra. Sitting to Khan's right, Colonel Browning, the head of Indoc training, watched Walker's performance with a smirk. The colonel was rather pleased with himself, the bastard. As if he could take credit for a Vargr who had been trained before his stint at HAVOC. Walker could easily teach Browning how to be a better Vargr.

Let him smirk. Browning was a short, stubby fool. Yes, Khan had told the lieutenant not to talk about the risks involved—and specifically fury. But Khan had run out of options to get Walker paired with a Hamask. He was the most talented, caring, unpaired Vargr Khan had ever seen. And they were going to lose him. Putting him in front of a group of Hamrammrs, ones that might one day recognize him as a Vargr, was worth the possible fallout and obvious manipulation.

Vargr became self-destructive and eventually suicidal the longer they were active without pairing. The military kept a very tight lid on that little piece of intel. Hell, polls indicated that most Americans thought bears and wolves were battalion mascots. People thought the men and women in each group received additional training. Reports of special abilities were seen as propaganda, a way to scare the enemy. Recruitment numbers would take a serious blow if more people knew of the activation risks.

Walker was already showing signs of instability. Intelligent before activation, his new skill set had tipped him into crazy smart. He had quickly become an expert in Hamask history and tactical training. He spoke three languages fluently, wrote articles for psychology magazines, and had a chilling ability to manipulate people into doing whatever the hell he wanted. But the caring was turning into rabid self-destruction, disobeying orders, and outright insubordination.

All of which Khan would deny until his dying breath. There was no way that prick Browning was getting any leverage or further reaction from Khan. If there was a good fit for Walker in this class or the one they'd just finished activating, Khan was going to make sure the man had a chance. They needed Walker for Valhalla.

On screen, Walker had finished describing the fury state and the ensign had a follow-up question about fury. Really, the proper term was "berserk," but the brass in the Pentagon hated that word.

"That's rare, right? I mean, sir, when was the last time that happened?"

"Fifty-six days ago," Khan said and leaned toward the screen when he heard Walker say the same thing. How did the lieutenant know about Jamal Zumati?

Khan cocked an eyebrow at the colonel. The class was filing out. Khan could see them through the panel of glass on one side of his office. "Explain."

"Sir." Though the man was always completely professional, he left Khan feeling chafed, his nerves dried to the consistency of leather. Browning slid his palm over the top of his bald head. "We plan to use Hamask Zumati's activation and fury as a training video, sir."

"And Walker has seen this video?"

"Yes, sir."

The first time Khan had met Walker, they'd talked about waking a feral Hamask, pulling someone from a fury state. Walker had recently made the rank of captain and Khan was new to his current position. He'd heard of Walker, seen his very impressive stats, and had hoped to groom him to be lead cadre. Instead he'd received a thorough verbal report on Dr. Brad Bur's doctoral thesis and Walker's firm conviction that the United States Hamra Program—USHP—and specifically HAVOC, was doing it all wrong. Like Khan couldn't see it for himself?

It was the main reason he'd been appointed—a nonactivated career-military infantryman—to command a training division. They needed tactical eyes from an outsider to steer them back into alignment with the rest of SOCOM—Special Operations Command. But the closed society had deep-seated issues and he'd only made slow progress. If he could get Walker to help Zumati, not only would they be proving Dr. Bur's theory, but he'd have a powerful Hamra Pair on his side. The perfect pair to lead HAVOC's Valhalla.

"You'll need Kirkham with Intel Security to sign off on the video usage."

"Already done, sir."

"Add either commentary from the med ward or have Major Sanderson available to answer questions. I don't want candidates assuming sedation is part of the activation process."

"Yes, sir."

Khan considered pulling Walker in now to talk with him. He'd spent the morning in a holo meeting with the Commander of US Special Operations and Khan's boss, the head of Joint Special Operations. Throw in a presidential advisor and a few gentlemen he suspected were part of the CIA, and it made for one hell of a briefing. They were seeing serious stockpiling in South America by the Christian extremist group Dios Provee.

There hadn't been a successful attack on a US military base in over fifty years. Yet Dios Provee had successfully hunted and killed nearly a dozen Hamask and Vargr in the last eighteen months. Then three months ago they had attacked Kamadel Outpost, killing twenty service members before the base was able to stop the assault.

The briefing was all rehashing of speculation. Did Dios Provee have inside knowledge? Maybe even actual Hamask and Vargr members? All three other operational Hamrammr initiatives—Germany, Jerusalem, and Russia—kept strict track of all those they activated. Intel did not indicate that Dios Provee had their own Hamrammr, not with their obvious hatred and targeting of the military pairs.

The pressure fell to training. They'd increased recruitment and tried to manipulate activation numbers with little success. Khan knew they needed better soldiers, not more fodder. So far Command was in agreement. But it was hard to tell how long they would wait to see results.

Khan would take another look at this Zumati. Walker could be killed if he tried to pull the berserk Hamask from hibernation. Or it might save both their lives.

"Colonel, I want a copy of Zumati's video by the end of the day."

Bur, Brad S., PhD, National Center for the Analysis of Violent Crime, Critical Incident Response Agent, Federal Bureau of Investigation. Personal Journal, Collected 4/5/2097, South Chicago. Evidence for case number 572092-Longwei.
Page 1

AS AN agent of the FBI, I made sure my report was professional, fact-based, and thorough, but it doesn't tell my story.

Longwei and I? Shit biscuits, it was nothing like they said it would be and exactly as described. I'm writing this second account because one day, after we're both dead, I want there to be a record. One that isn't the neutralized, diluted nonsense of any official version. Plus someone else out there will need this to guide them through the bureaucratic bullshit.

So here is how it really happened.

"The FBI thinks you're some white male, midthirties, from the backwaters of Washington State, with sexual performance issues."

I did my best to chat up my captor. Long story somewhat shorter, I'd been taken hostage while working my first serial killer case. Not like my first case ever. Come on. They don't let greenies take lead. I'd put in the sixty-hour weeks long enough to finally pull this case involving a fast-food-joint-robbing serial killer. I refuse to give it some cool name, because the man's ego was already an issue. "Statistically those traits are very common among serial killers, but we both know you aren't typical."

I have this way of talking, when I want to at least, that holds a lot of warm regard. Pop calls it my pastor voice, to which I always reply, "Being ordained wouldn't have kept me from being gay."

So I'm sitting on the hard tile floor of a burger joint in South Chicago, a scrawny Hispanic guy standing over me with a gun, and I'm using the Voice. "You've got the robbing down pretty fucking smooth. You know when the drawers will be flush with cash, when the traffic will be low. You always pick joints with good... parking lots." The Voice is saying I'm awed, inspired even. If I have to keep this up much longer, I'll run out of things to say and start complimenting his taste in shoes.

The dickhead has been pretty easy to figure out. Five other known robberies, a total of seven deaths counting today's. I've had the case less than two days and I've figured out the basics to the point that I came to this burger mecca because it is on my short list of possible future targets. I just hadn't considered that today would be the day. Seems to be a recurring theme for my life: I don't always think things through. I'd like to say that's the Vargr-powered brain, but that's bullshit. My two previous FBI partners thought me dangerously rash. My current partner will probably agree, especially since she is currently locked in the back office with the manager and two other employees.

The third employee is dead. Gunshot wound. That'll never get static. Doesn't matter how many crime scenes I see, that isn't ever going to be okay. With war zones, first they smell different and you expect to see bullets flying when you flak up and head out fully loaded. Wearing a suit makes me feel academic. Also, this kid dying is a total waste. He left home this morning, dressed in his own kind of uniform, prepared to serve food to a bunch of ingrates.

Dickhead stands at just the right angle to avoid the FBI shooters outside. I could provoke him, get him to step into a line of sight. I'm good at poking people. The right words, body language, tone, and you can get the most Zen pacifist to 'roid out. That's what I did for the military—provoked fights. People will tell you all kinds of things when they're pissed and think they're about to kill you. Plus, if they swing first, it's easier for your commanding officer to sell the kill to their bosses.

But I'm not doing that today. See, I like to at least be armed when I tell someone to bring it. Also, my Hamask, Daire Viano, isn't here to protect me. Hasn't been since being killed by the Dios Provee in Columbia. Honorable discharge from the USHP, a Doctorate in Criminology, and four years with the FBI later, and I'm sitting on the floor with Richard Dickerson mumbling in Spanish behind me. Not his real name, but it plays well with the dickhead theme, so I'm going to go with it.

Dicky Dickerman had worked at a fast-food joint that was held up, and he was so scared he pissed himself. That's the perp's hidden backstory. Of course I can't prove any of that, but he has inside knowledge of the places he robs and his kills always involve scare tactics to make an employee evacuate before he shoots them. Yep, I'm pretty damn sure on this one.

I'm not supposed to make deals with criminals. There is some pretty stringent wording on not offering reduced sentences or making promises to your captors, but I'm getting bored. I don't know how long I've been his hostage—I'm not good with time—but enough for the coppers to get into place outside. I can see SWAT gear, both local and feds. I'm wearing my smartwatch, an ingrained habit to know what time it is and to record situations like this. But looking at my watch is part of the provoking body language mentioned earlier. I keep my arms on top of my head, grasping opposite elbows as ordered. My arms are getting tired and my back is sore.

And that's what decides it. Those damn hard floor tiles. Give me a chair and I'd go another hour. In that split moment of decision, I consider a lot of factors. Though there had been no bullhorn or contact with a negotiator, I know there are shooters in place. My captor has ignored any attempts from me or the guys outside to move this along. Pop and Ma love me and will take care of my cat, Little Shit. Mr. Peckerwood, said captor, has only used ten of his possible fifteen rounds. My own weapon was dropped in the deep fryer. I have more hand-to-hand experience than the perp, but he will gladly add "FBI agent" to his kill list.

"*Nadie más tiene que morir.*" I slide toward the window, away from Schlong Face, stretching my legs out and then using my ankles to pull myself forward. "*Podemos llegar a un acuerdo.*" Which all means "no one else has to die, and we can negotiate." Basically. That and "Adios, motherfucker," are all I know in Spanish. I roll to my back and kick out with my legs as he yells at me. I land a kick to his knee, but he doesn't even flinch. He fires his gun and then two holes bloom in his forehead. Excellent shot, very fast and tight cluster. *A pair of snipers or just one?*

Yes, that *is* what I'm thinking. Sure, he shot me, but it just nicked my arm. My mind turns that all off as I scan the room. I apply pressure as I roll to my feet and step back to get out of the Feds' way. This roar, like a shit-on-a-shingle scary *boom* of a noise, shakes the room. I distinctly see bullet shells bounce around on the floor. Like, literally dinosaur-level vibrations.

Then a man in body armor, FBI in yellow lettering across his chest, charges in and....

This part is hard to describe. I'll first say that I firmly believe it was a justified kill. The man saved my life. Also, the serial killer was already dead. But yeah, it makes my stomach churn even now thinking about what happened next.

He rips Dick's arm off by pressing a foot to his chest and pulling. For the rest of my life the sound of cracking knuckles is going to make me nauseous, trigger this memory and that sound of the bone popping. I'm not too worried about the sound of tearing flesh. Nothing else sounds like tearing flesh.

He takes the bloody arm and smashes it against Dick's head, which is surprisingly clean and blank until the bloody stump sprays it. He drops the arm and turns his head to look right at me. He's this hunched, heaving predator, and he focuses straight on me. It sends chills down my back.

I've done my homework here, folks. I know the blue face paint of the Norse berserkers is just part of the legend. I've lost a bit of blood, and I'm sure if I go back to that restaurant I'd find blue-tinted lights. My judgment and mental capabilities are in question. Yet, for a moment, his face looks ice blue. His crazy eyes are filled with heat and his sharp cheekbones look primitive. He takes a breath through his nose and his pupils go wide.

I feel heat flood toward my gut. Bonding heat or lust or maybe recognition. *Hamask.* There is a lot of yelling and maybe some rookie puking in the bushes. All of that fades to static because I know they will have to put him down. Even if they have tranquilizers available, that only delays the inevitable. The Hamask is dead; he just hasn't realized it yet.

Looking back, maybe I should have been afraid, but instead I was determined. Before he finishes taking that breath, I have considered my top five options and chosen this path: *save the Hamask.*

I turn up my pheromones to, like, a ten, and then I clock him. I turn my hips and put all the momentum I can into that swing, hitting him as hard as I can. He has his guard down, maybe feeling the bonding heat or from the intentional pheromone overload, I don't know. I'm simply glad it works. He stumbles to one knee.

"I can't let them have you," I say as I hit him again. He falls back, hits his head against the counter, and drops into unconsciousness.

When Daire died, they told me I would never bond with another Hamask; no one is capable of a true bond twice. Yet even after that gruesome display, I know we can make a go of it. Which is idiotic. He was in a fury, and I was already renting a U-Haul.

Not an ideal way to meet a potential lover, true. Proper introductions or maybe an official assignment to work together would be better.

But in Longwei's defense, he didn't know he was still a Hamask.

Chapter 3

RUM, AS an activated Vargr, knew all about missions—establishing objectives, planning for all possible contingencies. The USHP were still trying to figure out where to send him once he left HAVOC. For now he was exactly where he wanted and needed to be for his current mission. He was likely to get shot, or at the very least, court-martialed and then shot. So, cakewalk.

Really important cake, because Rum knew the hollow echo in his chest wasn't loneliness. Something was wrong with him, and just because he couldn't find supporting documentation, similar case studies, that didn't make it simply paranoia. He needed to fix this before it got worse, and it made sense to finally pair with a Hamask.

He wanted to put his training to actual work. Paired and bonded to a full-fledged Hamask, he would qualify for fieldwork again. He'd done profile assignments with the FBI, run recon in Columbia. Having an impact like that again, that was the goal. That would silence the echo in his chest.

But no Hamask would have him. Rum was short, only five six, his hair was past thinning, and he had the bad habit of squinting while thinking, an unconscious reflex from wearing eyeglasses for twenty years. Most Hamask with their near superhuman abilities sneered at those flaws. Then add the two charges of insubordination, and he'd been permanently taken off the dance card.

If he didn't have such impressive reflexes and mental stats, plus the commendation for saving that Hamra Pair in New Tokyo, he would have reached limbo a lot sooner. He'd burned some major bridges. Pun intended.

He was grateful to have one last chance with a Hamask. Yes, he recognized that Khan must have an ulterior motive, but no matter what it was, Rum would figure out a way to make it work in *his* favor. Or, if this mission were successful, to the favor of his new Hamask.

He'd picked his timing carefully, coordinating the plan with General Khan. And why did the general need a covert mission on his own base to get anything done? Because the Hamask in question had gone into a complete fury state. At least that was the story Khan kept angling. Rum didn't know why the general would help him, but all the possibilities had played center stage for the last several sleepless nights.

The cement road reflected the harsh sunlight heating him from both sides as he jogged at a steady clip. Across the compound he could spot a group of eight-weeks being trained in advanced hand-to-hand combat and a group completing PT.

Sweat ran down Rum's body in rivulets. Hopefully it would be enough. He detoured around the mess hall to the large water station. A Hamask and his Vargr stood under the overhang out of the sun. Rum slowed as he approached, greeting them with a proper salute. He kept his feet moving in place as he got water from the spigot. He tipped his head back and heard a growl.

The Hamask, a tall farm boy from Iowa, had sharpened his sight until his pupils blacked out the irises. His nose flared, and his Vargr, a slightly older female, stepped forward and turned to block the Hamask's vision. From his recent paper-pushing days, Rum knew the pair—Lisa Naylor and Tony Travers—had yet to bond, and he was not surprised that it was the Vargr who'd growled at him. He'd had that same effect on Bur whenever he got too close to Hamask Longwei. Special Agent Longwei was an FBI sharpshooter, and Dr. Bur worked as a profiler. Rum had studied Bur's work for years and had worked with the bonded pair out in the field in a joint action.

He backed away with his eyes averted, then tossed his plastic cup into the recycling bin.

The Hamask's response had given Rum hope. He needed to have some kind of effect on Jamal Zumati. Dr. Bur had hypothesized that providing sensory anchors and creating a safe place would allow a Vargr to pull a Hamask out of fury.

Jamal was currently sedated and contained in the med ward's long-term care section. He'd been there for the last four months since his botched activation when he had kicked into instinct mode. Or that's how Dr. Bur saw it. The USHP saw it as "breaking regulations and having a psychotic episode." *Fury.* He hoped for Jamal's sake Bur was right and that better activation conditions would have prevented the Hamask from feeling cornered.

Rum had seen the video, the way Zumati had tried to peel off his own skin, tried to kick Chakosky's balls into the wall. He'd then had an anaphylactic reaction to the tranquilizer, died, and roared like a bear when they used adrenaline to stabilize him. *Morons.* Then things had got really wrecked when they tried to restrain him. Two of the MPs were still doing physical therapy to repair the damage.

Rum kept his pace slow to allow his heart rate to even out now that he had reached the target zone. He wanted the pheromones rolling off him.

If this went badly, Khan would deny all knowledge of his actions. If it went well, though, Jamal would wake from his coma and allow Rum to be his Vargr.

Rum had no illusions here. He didn't expect it to be a perfect match like his parents—a bonded Hamask and Vargr—and nowhere near as powerful as Longwei and Bur. But to finally get to work as a Vargr, helping people, protecting a Hamask—that would be enough. He had wisely put aside his other grand dreams. Bonding would be totally unrealistic. He needed to feel useful and productive, and he'd sleep at night knowing he was doing the right thing. The echo in his chest would quiet once he found purpose.

If it was true about the pheromones, he was practically forcing himself into Jamal's life. But he assuaged his conscience with the alternative: Jamal's body would deteriorate and die. The military kept soldiers on life support until their bodies gave out. No one had ever come back from hibernation.

Rum used his ID to slide into a rear entrance. Never looking anywhere but forward, he went through a series of doors to the elevators purposefully, with no hesitation or suspicious, darting looks.

Doctors and nurses were standing for inspection at the front of the building. Rum couldn't see them but knew they were there. He had ten minutes and one guard on the third floor to avoid.

Rum slipped through the sliding electric door into Jamal's room and pushed the Close button, locking himself in. He knew the immense damage a psychotic Hamask could cause, and felt a small amount of fear roll through him. He didn't want Jamal's first scent of him to be chickenshit, so he concentrated on calming his breathing. He could smell his own sweat and adrenaline and the clean flat smell of the hospital, but nothing else. The lights were dim in deference to the Hamask's enhanced sight.

Rum approached the bed, glancing at the door and around the room, unsure how much time he had left. Finally he looked at Jamal.

Jamal looked back at him.

Rum jerked in surprise, then realized Jamal actually stared into space, his vision between focus, so deeply immersed in the void that he saw nothing. Then, as Rum stood staring, Jamal's nostrils expanded and his pupils contracted.

Damn. Rum took a short, quick breath. The man hadn't responded to any stimuli for months, and Rum was in the room for less than a minute and there was a reaction. Definitely good. It supported Bur's thesis and was proof for Khan that more could be done to help these Hamask.

Not wanting to send Jamal into a painful sensory spike or drown him in too many stimuli, Rum kept his hands and voice to himself. He fidgeted and glanced toward the door. Hopefully, Jamal was adjusting to his scent.

Jamal tipped his head toward him. Rum smiled, feeling the sultry siren of hope spread through him. He pulled it back, trying to stay realistic, on guard. The general had arranged for Jamal to be taken off most of his medical equipment and the last dose of sedatives had not been given. Hamask in fury always woke and returned to that moment before they were sedated, fully raging mad and bent on destruction. The general made sure Rum knew where they kept the approved sedatives and the guard on the floor was armed. Jamal's response could be his system surfacing further than it had in months and not Rum specifically.

Jamal was tall, six two according to his file. He had deep brown eyes and brown hair. His brown skin looked waxy compared to his file photo, from the lack of sun. He had strong, full lips, and Rum stopped his hand before he could run a rough thumb over the bottom one. Jamal's nose flared again as he took a deep breath.

He should have had enough time to adjust to the scent. When Rum spoke, he wanted his voice to be instantly distinguishable from the medical staff, and he did so softly, avoiding the high tones of a whisper. He also used every bit of Southern twang he usually kept buried.

"Lieutenant Zumati. I'm Ryan Michael Walker—Lieutenant Walker. My call name is Rum." What else should he say? "I'd be right grateful if you'd take a moment to listen to my sweet ramblins."

It wasn't the words, his mother had often said, but the tone that was important. It provided the Hamask with a base line, an anchor. "You've been right rude ignoring all the folks that come through here. People think you don't like us none." Jamal opened his mouth and took a shuddering breath, rattling his shoulders and flexing his chest.

Perhaps a bit early to crow victory over, but the security camera that recorded everything would show what had happened, and he could get permission to work Jamal out of his coma.

A flash of movement at the clear-glass door caught Rum's eye. *Guard.* She would be armed with a Taser, since tranquilizers had proved dangerous, and backup would be on its way.

"Looks like my time's up, Zumati. I'm leavin'."

He stepped around the bed, but before he could reach the door, Jamal grabbed and pushed him back into a wall. His head smacked with a dull *thump* against the cabinet, but he ignored it. Jamal stood in front of him inside his personal space. His body shook from lack of use.

Jamal was *standing*. Fast, strong, upright. *Whoa.*

Time for the crowing. "Zumati?" Jamal turned his head toward the sound but his eyes remained overfocused. "Let's work on those pretty brown eyes. They're far too focused. Just edge back a bit." He spoke slowly, drawing the words out, focused on Jamal. "Nice and slow. You can alter both distance and light. Do you see me?"

Jamal blinked and nodded, and Rum's heart clenched with happiness. He was sending a bottle of scotch to Longwei and Bur. They'd convinced him this could be done, laid the groundwork. And perhaps when he saw Khan next, he'd forgo the derisive snort.

Jamal's head turned toward the door and he growled, the rumbling deep and animalistic.

"Sugar?" Rum said the term of endearment without thought or strategy. A simple response to the beautiful man before him.

Strong hands gripped his arms and pushed and shuffled them away from the door. Everything the military had drilled into Rum said this was bad. His training screamed danger. As the fear rose up inside him, Rum fought against his own panic. The scent of his fear would only worsen the Hamask's anxiety over defending him.

Jamal pushed him back into a far corner, using his long frame to shield Rum.

See—protecting him, not hurting him.

Jamal kept at a distance, touching only Rum's fabric-covered upper arms. He sniffed Rum's shoulder. The exhale brushed the stubble and fine hairs on Rum's cheek. "Vargr."

Rum was speechless.

Jamal stepped back and reached for the window, checked the joints with his fingers. He had a rolling, easy gait, so different from the precise, steady march of the military. Rum must have made some sound because Jamal was immediately back, leaning over him; his hands slapped against the wall with a high-pitched *smack*. Jamal breathed sharply through his nose in hot snorts like an angry stallion. He shook his head and scented Rum again.

Rum's fear was gone, replaced instead by curiosity and a heat similar to awe. Jamal growled, and Rum realized he was waiting for some kind of response. "Staying. I'm staying," he assured him.

Jamal turned and headed for the door. He lifted a tray off of a side table and, with a nasty *scrunch*, jammed it into the doorjamb.

"Crap. They'll come now for sure. They'll see that as aggression. They'll take me."

Jamal pushed the tray in tighter. He walked the perimeter of the room, ran his fingers along the walls, and checked the cabinets.

That was when Rum saw the broken IV hanging from his arm. It dripped blood onto the soft blue cotton of Jamal's thin pants. The end caught against his clothing as he turned and Jamal flinched.

"Hey, let me help you with that." Rum stepped away from his corner, and Jamal was instantly on him, using his height and presence to back Rum into place. It still got Jamal close, so Rum didn't care. "Let me take that out."

He took a hold of Jamal's wrist and turned the arm over to get a better look at the IV. Jamal jerked his arm away, and something oily and slick clenched in Rum's chest.

Rum grabbed Jamal's hand as he tried to yank the IV out on his own. "No. You'll hurt yourself. Let me?"

Jamal stilled. Rum raised his head to return his gaze. Jamal looked normal. His eyes were peaceful, his body no longer hunched; the predatory edge was gone. He stood straight, his shoulders relaxed, his chest barely rising as he breathed.

"Do you see me?"

"Yes," Jamal whispered. His posture was back to military rest.

"Let me take this out. Okay?"

"Yes."

Rum tried to step around Jamal, looking for alcohol swabs and cotton balls.

Jamal blocked his way. "Not yet."

"Ah, we've graduated to two words at once. Tight." He tried to step around again.

Jamal placed a hand on his chest and firmly pressed him back to the wall. Rum took a breath, allowed himself to seethe as the anger filled him, and then took Jamal's wrist again. He pressed down at the insertion point and pulled the needle free. When Jamal didn't even flinch, Rum knew the Hamask had turned down his sense of touch.

Keeping pressure on the small wound, he pulled the medical tape off with a yank. "You all right?"

Jamal didn't answer but cocked his head to the side, his face turned toward the door.

Satisfied that the blood flow had stopped, Rum let go. Jamal still pressed against Rum's chest.

"What happened?" Jamal asked.

"Officially?" Rum leaned his head back and looked toward the ceiling. "You broke formation during training. When they tried to reprimand you, you picked a fight. It took four of them to take you out. Psychosis." As he spoke the military words, he used their voice without the twang.

He tilted his head to look at Jamal. Jamal, who was staring at Rum's throat. *Creepy.* Or at least it should have been. Instead, it made Rum flush with warmth.

"Unofficially?" Jamal asked.

"I've seen the vid. The team had just finished your activation and… things went south." He couldn't say Khan's name or explain Bur's theory. He wouldn't let any of the deep shit he was wading through track back to them, and this room was definitely under surveillance.

"They wanted to wash me with that filthy—" Jamal tilted his head again and stopped speaking. His eyes got vague and his hand slackened. He was slipping back into darkness. Probably had tried to overuse his hearing.

"Zumati." Nothing. "Jamal!" Still nothing, and as Jamal's breathing became even shallower, Rum felt desperation and dread roll through him. He needed to keep this man from retreating into his partially self-inflicted hibernation. In his most commanding voice, he said, "Lieutenant Zumati. *Stand down.*" Nothing.

Oh shit. Rum rubbed back and forth along Jamal's bare forearm. With his other hand, he brushed Jamal's cheek. Soft as rain, he said, "Sugar?"

With a shudder that caused Jamal's body to flex painfully into Rum's chest, Jamal resurfaced. "I zoned."

"Got that."

"I'm sorry."

"It's tight," Rum assured him.

"They're listening."

"Figured as much, since they haven't come to drag me off to the stockade."

Jamal started his rolling gait, checking the window and door. Pacing, restless. Then he turned and looked at Rum. "You're here without permission. Against orders." They were accusations, not questions.

Just Rum's luck that his Hamask would be a rule follower. "Yes." He might as well air his other faults now. "I'm short and older than you. And I'm not liked by certain authority figures."

Jamal continued to stare at him.

"You needed help." Rum's plan had been to get proof that Jamal would respond to him. He'd only partially believed it would work. And he was being… well, not exactly held hostage but… what? How did Jamal see the situation? What did they do next?

"How long?"

Rum looked at Jamal, waiting for him to elaborate on his question.

"How long have I…?" He gestured at the room.

"Four months."

"What about my family?"

How new was this guy? Didn't he realize what they did to Hamask who'd gone berserk? Rum had taken Bur's advice and not read past Jamal's stats in his file. Surely Jamal knew that family was not allowed contact with an injured Hamask. It was too dangerous. *Please God, let this be okay.* "I don't know. Typically they advise the family that you are missing in action until—" Rum's own family would have known what really happened, but Jamal's parents, would they have known what it meant when a Hamrammr went MIA? "Eventually those in comas die, and then the body is returned to the family. Sorry. Are you… married?"

Jamal snorted his disbelief and shook his head.

"Are you going to let the guards in?" Rum asked.

Jamal studied him for a while, looked him over from shoes to bare head. Rum let him. Jamal had stopped in the middle of the room, a strategic place where he could see Rum and the door. "Not yet." Jamal swayed in place.

"I'm here to help you, and it isn't going to help you if you drop from exhaustion."

"I've been asleep—well, at least in bed—for four months."

"Right. Your body isn't used to the movement. That's why you're trembling. Fatigue."

Jamal shook his head, then ran a hand over his hair and stopped in obvious surprise as he felt how long it had grown. "Four months," he whispered.

The shaking increased. Perhaps his touch was out of whack to the point he couldn't feel it.

Rum took a step toward Jamal, and when Jamal's eyes darkened and he growled, Rum scoffed. "Safe," Rum said. He extended his arms out to his sides, opening his stance as he slowly approached. "It's important that we work together. You'll keep me safe. I'll be your wolf skin, your Vargr. Your senses are out of whack. Let's get them back to normal. You've done nothing for four months but let them run wild."

He worked Jamal through each sense, standing close. Sight, sound, smell, even taste. He left touch for last. Jamal remained perfectly still, but the tension melted off his body, the fine lines of pain around his eyes and mouth smoothed. "On a scale of one to ten, where is your touch at?"

"A three."

Rum raised an eyebrow, not buying that answer.

"A one."

"Let's work—"

"No."

JAMAL HEARD his own words echo back, overlaying his voice as he spoke. A one-, maybe two-second delay. It didn't sound like him, but rarely did a recording sound as you heard it in your head. He tuned it out and ignored the Vargr's voice double, like a short echo or a translator that repeated everything you did.

He listened instead for the enemy. Those who would take away the Vargr. In the enemy's room there were four heartbeats, but he heard the echoes of hundreds, thousands that caused a thrumming beat without pause.

His internal voice shouted regulations and procedure at him. *Stand down. Submit to your Vargr.* But he'd wanted a Vargr he could control so he would have at least some freedom. Nothing about this wolf suggested he'd allow Jamal to take the lead.

Extra strength and heightened senses didn't require a collar or a babysitter. He could be his own man, a soldier for his country, not a freak show needing constant supervision. That was why having a malleable woman for a Vargr would be better. The recognized power boost, both in position and in the control of his senses that such a bonding gave, would make him a better soldier. But that didn't require him to submit to another's sexual needs. *Hell. No.* At least with a woman, she'd probably settle for cuddling and kisses, and allow Jamal some say.

Since waking minutes ago, he had warred with the dividing factions in his head: follow the rules, turn his own way, or keep the Vargr. Currently the keep-the-Vargr force was winning. The Vargr had pulled him from the void, and Jamal's senses were flexible, pliable under the Vargr's presence, adjusting with ease as Rum spoke.

He answered Rum's question absently, "A one."

"Let's work—"

What is this? Hamra Indoc? "No." He couldn't open to this man. He was grateful for the assist, but now that he was back on his feet, he planned to walk, run, *sprint* back to his training. Innocent people caught in the path of extremist groups were dying at the rate of one every forty minutes. Four months meant over forty-three hundred people had died while he was lying on his ass. At least that was the rate before his activation. Who the hell knew how many genocides or holocausts or crusades had started in the last four months.

"There will be plenty of times when we'll disagree," Rum said.

The accent was thick enough that Jamal had to decipher it. He watched the lips, the hands as they gestured, the whole package. He'd underestimated the smaller man. He saw the very solid muscles now that he was coherent enough to look. Rum was built like a wrestler: power in his arms and legs, his stomach flat.

"Oh, I'm right sure there will be."

Jamal smiled. That Southern twang didn't fit the man's accomplished reputation Jamal had heard about in training.

"But to avoid testosterone chest-pounding, a little more than 'no' will be required."

Jamal laughed. Testosterone chest-pounding? Jamal felt unfamiliar warmth saturate his limbs, rolling toward his guts—unlike desire, which always rippled outward. Bonding heat. His instructors had been right; you recognized it when you felt it. He tried to concentrate on the situation.

Jamal looked down at his palms and saw each individual pore. He jerked back on his level of sight and sighed. "I feel... filthy. Hot, scratchy, oily. So I'm keeping touch down."

"Oh. Well, there's the bathroom." Rum flushed. "You can get cleaned up. Just no razor until your touch is normal."

Jamal hesitated, considering an idea that was forming in his head when Rum cleared his throat and rephrased his words. "Smudge. I mean you should consider waiting to use a razor."

Smudge? And what was different in his second statement? Jamal silently considered his idea, watching Rum watch him. He took a half step toward the Vargr, listening for a change in heartbeat, smelling the air for pheromones, and watched—he took another step—as the Vargr's eyes dilated, the smell of arousal pulsing from his skin. *Hell yeah.* Rum was feeling the bonding heat too.

Okay, so maybe they would allow him to walk away and be paired with a Vargr of his choice. Might even find another that he felt bonding heat with. *Sure, and the USHP is a bunch of progressive pacifists.* "Come help me. Scrub my back? Maybe shave me?"

Rum swallowed, which drew Jamal's eyes to his neck. "Sure."

Jamal grasped Rum's forearms, anchoring himself on the wolf's skin before he extended his hearing as far as he dared and listened to Major Sanderson, the head of Medical, and General Khan argue. Khan was holding his own, and security wasn't coming to separate them yet. Rum might be worried about a potential court-martial, but Jamal's own fate would be redrugged and strapped down. Already he would fight to stay by Rum's side.

"Sugar?" Rum called.

The loud noise pounded at Jamal's eardrums. Rum had stepped forward and wrapped his arms around him. Jamal adjusted his hearing back to normal and stared at the man pressed against his chest. The cadre had talked about Lieutenant Walker as if the man had seen hell and walked away carrying a litter of puppies. Awe, respect, but also bewilderment.

"Thought you were about to collapse," Rum said.

There really was no other choice to make. Jamal couldn't go back to sleep, but he didn't want to be a danger to others. Rum had figured out how the hell to get him out of the fury state. He'd be a strong enough Vargr to keep Jamal out of the destructive rage.

Jamal turned them toward the bathroom and left the door open at an angle. He turned the shower on, his hands slipping over the controls twice before he focused enough to turn it on.

Standing in view of the open door as well as the security camera, he started to strip. He kept his eyes on his Vargr—*Yes, okay. My Vargr.* Crossing his arms, he grabbed his shirt and pulled it over his head.

Rum liked what he saw. Jamal could see that without his heightened abilities. Rum frowned and pantomimed from behind the door to indicate there was a video camera.

Jamal smirked and caressed down his chest to his pants and slid them off in one motion. Might have been a little less than graceful as he stepped out of them. Tiny tremors still cycled his body as his unused muscles tried to keep him upright.

He turned to enter the shower stall, and Rum grabbed his hips from behind. Even with touch turned down, he felt it in the base of his balls.

"Let me check the water." Rum pressed up behind him, one hand sliding across his waist, the other angling upward over a pec. Rum wasn't wearing a shirt. Oh sweet Lord, that felt incredibly good. "Make sure it ain't too hot."

Rum felt the water, then adjusted the temperature. He kissed Jamal's shoulder and nudged Jamal's head to the side so he could place a sucking kiss where the neck and shoulder connected. It was hot and moist and way too brief. Rum smelled edible, delicious.

There was a *click* behind them, and Rum immediately stepped back, having closed the door with his foot.

The new shivers at the sudden lack of heat blended just fine with his already-trembling body. No one need know how hot Rum made him.

"Can they hear us?" Rum's voice was breathy and deep.

Jamal looked at him over his shoulder. He no longer heard the delayed repeat of his own voice in his head. "The water creates an effective white-noise barrier."

Rum dropped the toilet seat and sat to unlace his shoes. The breathy voice was gone, and so were all indications that Rum had been very aroused moments before. "You want them to think we're bonding, right? Thanks. Sorta." He nodded to the shower. "Hurry. It's cold out here."

Heat fused Jamal's cheeks. Didn't Rum realize this was their best option? As he showered, he listened to Rum rummage through the cabinets. As Jamal rinsed the last of the soap out of his hair, the shower curtain slid open. Rum held up a razor and cream. He used his eyebrows to ask and Jamal nodded, stepping forward out of the stream.

A touch that could have been so sexy was medicinal and distant. Quick lather, then down strokes to take most of the long beard, slowing only around his mouth. Then, spreading more of the scent-free shaving gel, Rum did the closer, upward strokes. Rum stood in nothing but his tighty-whities—this tightly built older officer—and shaved Jamal. Jamal didn't bother hiding his interest. Rum had lovely skin and was several inches shorter, which would make it easy to pull him close and tuck him under Jamal's chin.

Rum talked—how long he'd been in the USHP, that his parents were a Hamra Pair who worked at one of the New York airports. Jamal listened for intruders and to his Vargr, and mapped Rum's flesh in his mind.

"So, how do you want to do this?"

Jamal turned his face into the spray and slid his hand up his now-smooth cheek. "Do what?" He turned back to find that Rum had stepped out of his underwear. His dick was straight and broad, and Jamal just about bashed his head against the side of the shower trying to get a better look at it.

"Scoot up there." Rum pushed Jamal out of the spray, tipped his head into the water's path, and used the bar of soap over his body in quick, efficient motions. Turning, he swiped the bar across his face and rinsed it at the same time.

Jamal realized Rum had spoken again only when the silence registered. "What?"

Rum soaped his head with the "unscented" shampoo that really smelled of marshmallows. A huge foamy mass of suds slid down Rum's throat, pooled for a moment at his collarbone, and then slid down his pec, snagging on Rum's small brown nipple. *Whoa.*

Rum squirted more shampoo in his palm and started to stroke his half-hard dick.

Holy shit! Heat no longer rippled but crashed and swelled so quickly that Jamal could no longer tell if it was coming or going. Jamal clamped his eyes shut and braced against the shower wall.

"Listen to me! I'm not going to do this while you check out."

Jamal opened his eyes and looked at Rum. Was his sight up or was Rum closer? Closer, he realized, as Rum's hand bumped Jamal's thigh.

"They'll send a Hamask to check. Do you understand? We have to smell like sex."

Jamal could only nod. His ability to talk was…. Wherever it was, he couldn't find it.

Rum laughed. "Get to work on yours." He nodded at Jamal's fully erect cock and then closed his eyes and leaned back against the shower wall. Jamal watched, and the water fell between them as if Rum stood under a waterfall. Rum tilted his head farther, exposing his long, graceful, corded neck.

Jamal reached down to his own painful erection and stroked, but he was too caught up in the show to give it his full attention.

Rum shuddered. And it was so fucking hot, that shudder. Jamal bit down on his lip to keep himself from moaning and jerked his fist up and down his wet cock.

Rum, eyes still closed, reached for the water control and shut it off. He arched forward and moaned. The tight ripple of muscles across his chest was beautiful and so damn sexy. "Oh God, yes." And Rum was coming, spurting cum over Jamal's fist and hip.

"Oh holy *fuck*." Jamal's body clenched, and all the heat inside bunched and shot out the end of his dick. He shivered as Rum's hand, slick with his own juices, spread across Jamal's chest. Efficient swipes, distant, and Jamal felt his dick go completely flaccid. He opened his eyes in time to see Rum smoothing Jamal's come over his own belly. Rum was breathing heavily, but his eyes were emotionally flat.

In a sexy tone, Rum said, "Let's get you cleaned up, sugar." And he turned his back and restarted the shower. Within a minute he'd rinsed his hair and run the soap across his body and then stepped out of the shower, leaving the now-cold spray.

Jamal groaned. *Fucked* that *up, Zumati. How the hell do I fix something like this?*

Training said you fought side by side. Even first-day Hamrammr knew you could only reach your full potential as a bonded pair. Vargr might be the ones that led, but Hamask protected, watched. So why would Rum not be glad to be chosen? Was it because Jamal was classified unfit? His training incomplete? That was bullshit. Rum wouldn't have stepped into his room if he didn't want the chance to work with Jamal.

Damn right Rum should want to be paired with him. Jamal was going to make a difference in this world by serving with honor. He knew, other than gender, Rum was everything he'd been looking for in a wolf. He would prove himself to his new commanding officer and lover, and then Rum would lead him into a proper Hamra Pairing.

Chapter 4

RUM JOGGED across the compound. Jamal, beside him, face completely red, wasn't going to last much longer. His muscles had atrophied, and it would take a while to rebuild his stamina. "They'll have us on our own rotation to finish training before they assign us an MOS."

Jamal nodded.

Rum kept talking. "Which is good." *Thank you, Captain Obvious.* They needed the time to adjust, to find a place of acceptance. It didn't help that they were constantly watched; even now a pair of cadre were keeping pace behind them. They'd spent the last three days jumping through hoops and filling out paperwork. Jamal, still confined to the med ward, seemed obsessed with reading everything he could about Dios Provee and other military threats in the last four months.

"That's enough for today." Rum touched and released Jamal's arm, and though Jamal slowed to a walk, he hunched his shoulders and dropped his head to his chest. "Lean your head back. Raise your arms. It opens your chest so it's easier to breathe."

"I know," Jamal snapped.

Regulations told Rum that as the senior officer and the Vargr, Jamal not addressing him with proper respect was grounds for reprimand.

Rum eyed the smirking cadre over his shoulder. He was going to get heat over not reminding Jamal of his place. So far he'd managed to keep that away from Jamal. Rum's continued debriefing took place in soundproof rooms so that Jamal couldn't hear him battle with the brass to do things his way. Didn't hear the snide "Too strong for you? Or are you too weak?" Or the threatening "If you can't control him, we'll find somebody who will." Khan was backing him, and the doctors said that Jamal was struggling with the lingering chemicals in his body from the long medical coma.

After each debrief, Rum would go to Jamal's room, where he would be immediately grabbed and pushed back into a corner while Jamal once again shielded him and blew short, hot breaths onto Rum's neck.

"Sorry, sorry." The moist air curved around Rum's head like a caress.

Rum would stroke Jamal's arms or neck, and accent back in place, would say, "It's tight."

And that's why Rum couldn't pull rank and wouldn't, even at gunpoint, bridle his mustang. The protector was the real Jamal, and Rum would guard that at all cost. Jamal wasn't violent or hurting anyone. Jamal's instincts told him to defend his wolf, and the bear would do exactly that.

They questioned Rum alone, but so far he'd managed to always be present when they were questioning or testing Jamal.

Earlier that day, they had tested Jamal to establish his sense abilities. Softly, in his thick accent, Rum said, "Before you start, let's identify the excess sounds and eliminate them. Do you hear Vargr Chakosky taking notes? His heartbeat? You don't need those sounds. Turn—"

Jamal touched him and he immediately stopped talking. "Why do you do that?"

Jamal initiated touch so rarely and not at all outside his med room, so Rum had trouble forming the next word. "What?"

"The accent." Jamal moved his thumb, a one-direction caress, and Rum felt his dick harden.

Down, boy.

"Sugar, it's real."

Jamal lifted his hand. "It's just...." Jamal looked across the room at Chakosky, and Rum desperately wished it was one of the green, wet-behind-the-ears trainers so that he could order him out of the room. He was about to anyway—to hell with the fallout—when Jamal said, "Save it. When it's needed."

For when his senses were acting up, that's what he meant. Using his military voice, Rum continued—the whole time thinking *what the fuck*, and the whole time wishing for time. Time alone so they could talk.

Rum could tell that Chakosky set Jamal's nerves on edge, and though he'd told the general he wouldn't manipulate the cadre, if the captain oversaw any more testing sessions, Rum would stick a knife in a few choice places. The asswipe would be breathing with a new pair of gills.

Rum walked Jamal back to the med ward, dictating a brief report into his watch as they headed across the compound. He chose his words carefully, emphasizing Jamal's determination and focus. He left out the attitude. The cadre would report on that in triplicate.

Jamal was exhausted. That caused an echoing ache inside of Rum. He rubbed at his gut and blinked back the water in his eyes. He needed to be patient. Jamal was recovering better than anyone thought possible. Soon Sanderson would let him resume normal duties, and they would be housed as a pair.

Yet now it was even harder to sleep. Rum's mind ran constant scenarios, real and improbable. Was Jamal safe? What did the general really want? Each movie reel unfurled to a gruesome scene. Or worse, a pathetic scene of him desperate and pleading, and them all walking away. No use for a dried-up old hack of a Vargr. He felt the need to knock his head against the nearest surface until unconsciousness took him. Instead he watched his old collection of Blu-rays until he was lulled to sleep.

They'd reached the med ward, and Khan was there waiting. He returned both Jamal's and Rum's salute and then, without saying a word, left. Maybe he too could see the ashen features and the tremors of exhaustion. So much for Rum's scripted report.

Jamal turned to address Rum, maybe salute him as well. *No, not today.* Rum knocked his hand out of the way and stepped in *way* close. He hooked his elbow behind Jamal's neck, pressed his forehead into Jamal's shoulder, and took a deep breath.

Centering himself, Rum hoped Jamal had time to do the same. "See you in the morning."

RUM HAD finally slipped into sleep when his smartwatch vibrated with an incoming call. He blinked the sleep away, promised himself a whole bottle of vodka tomorrow night and a Dianna Fogel movie marathon, and then answered the video call—one of the hospital corpsmen, looking agitated. "Your Boo Boo is triggering all the alarms. I'd give him a sedative and let you deal with it in the morning, but General Khan has special orders on this."

Rum didn't understand the reference, but he knew from the corpsman's tone it was a derisive one. "Good thing you didn't give him a sedative, since he's allergic to all kinds of medications." *Idiot.*

"Yeah, Yogi, whatever. Are you coming?"

"Already en route."

People had to have such pissant attitudes about Hamra Pairs. *We're a couple of guys trying to develop a relationship. Big deal.* They were trained for advanced military designations, but that wasn't all that different from the corpsman. The guy was trained in weapons and safety, and…. It bothered Rum that he could detail, week by week, the type of training the corpsman had received. He could tell from the guy's accent where he'd grown up and his—82 percent likely—preference for salt over sugar.

Rum rolled out of bed and snagged a T-shirt as he slid his feet into a pair of sandals. *We're like any other couple.* Except for the constant chaperones. He groaned.

Civilians were even worse to his parents. People assumed his father was the submissive bear to his mother's overbearing wolf. It wasn't anything like that. Even beyond having the wrong roles assigned, theirs was a partnership. His mom was the Hamask, his dad the Vargr. They cooked together and did the grocery shopping every Sunday and held hands in public. Strangers would stare at them while they were working, make bitch jokes while Mom searched for drugs among the luggage, laugh as dad quietly guided Mom through the process so she didn't white out on smell. Usually Mom would get her revenge by marking those idiots for cavity searches.

The walk back to the med ward would give Rum a chance to plan the appropriate revenge on the corpsman. It wouldn't be particularly hard to convince the man that his salt intake was slowly killing him.

JAMAL KNEW things weren't going well. He was supposed to be past the territorial, possessive bullshit by now. And maybe he would be if they ever bonded. All the training manuals and vids said that the Vargr was supposed to lead, sexually as well as in training. Yet they were both officers, the same fucking rank, even. Yes, Rum did have way more experience than him and a bonded pair followed their own ranking system, but he was struggling with it and it didn't help that Rum wouldn't step up and take charge.

Jamal knew how to handle rank, how to work as a team. That was ROTC freshman basic shit. Day one of Reserve Officer Training Corps you learned the pecking order or you made life harder on yourself and your college classmates.

Half the time Jamal was trying to take the lead, the other half he spent, dick hard, jonesing for a simple command from his Vargr. And Rum? He seemed determined to be pals.

The cadre said that the bonding heat would indicate how often they needed to have sex to renew their bond, but either he had blown it all to shit before or it wasn't that sort of heat that he had felt or—fuck, he didn't know.

All Jamal knew right now was pain.

Way back, when he was fifteen, he had wanted to take Gladys to homecoming. She was openly bisexual, unapologetically on birth control, and they both liked to dance. A fifteen-year-old's holy grail of girlfriends. Dating wasn't a simple thing when you didn't have parents, let alone an allowance. Jamal had talked three neighbors into letting him do odd jobs. A full day in the sun, mowing, cleaning out garages, and mending a fence. That evening was the first time he'd ever had a migraine. Now, years later, this migraine felt like an upgraded über version of that pain.

Hamask senses—all that extra information to process—made headaches common issues, but most had a Vargr they were living with. The Vargr would work their mojo and *bam*, mental energies aligned and the pain would cease. He had definitely not felt that way when Rum breezed through PT. Did the man ever get winded?

Two weeks and they hadn't released him officially from the med ward.

Rum had told Jamal that Colonel Browning was protesting Khan's covert move by preventing the housing requisition from going through. They weren't willing to assign bonded housing without greater proof that their newest Hamra Pair were in fact bonded. Which they weren't going to accomplish without Rum showing him the ropes.

Saliva gathered in his mouth and his stomach pinched and flexed with nausea. With each note of sound from the rooms around him— ventilation machines, the nurse walking the ward, the guard outside his room texting on his watch—thunder struck across his head, leaving flares of pain. He'd muffled sound and light by clamping his left arm over his left ear and both eyes. He'd pulled up his knees and rolled to his right to further dampen the input. When the migraines set in, time went blurry. It felt like hours, but he knew from experience it had been less than two or he would have started to vomit by now. Earlier he had tried to meditate with yoga. Wasn't he supposed to be all fit and polished now?

"We've got to stop meeting like this," Rum said.

And bless him, he knew to speak softly rather than whisper.

"I just have a headache."

Rum chuckled and stepped toward him. "That is awesome."

Jamal didn't muster up a response, focused on letting the pain pulse through him. Fighting it before the vomit state never worked.

"Sorry," Rum said, "movie joke. The room's sensors detected extra activity in your nociceptors. The floor nurse called me."

It seemed counterintuitive to tell the man to go away when he'd been lying here bitching about their messed-up bond dynamic. But if Rum continued to spout medical crap, adding to the pain, Jamal might struggle out of bed to kick his ass. Or puke on him. Rum, as an active Vargr, might have faster reflexes than Jamal, but Jamal was stronger. He'd pound at the guy's head until the room registered the same pain activity in both of them.

"Whoa, some pain? My heinie." Rum must have been reading Jamal's vitals on his watch. He edged closer and placed a hand next to Jamal's head. "I'm sorry, Jamal. They can't give you anything. They're still running your blood work through the system to figure what else you're allergic to. Beside the standard trank."

"I know. Just need quiet."

"You need a sight more than that."

Jamal listened to Rum breathe for several minutes. The jagged pain still stormed through his head, intent on making him whimper or groan in front of his man.

"Can I touch you?" Rum asked.

"You're not required to ask. You're supposed—"

"We choose—"

Jamal flinched away from Rum's loud outburst. "Get a bullhorn, why don't you? Fuck, man."

"Sorry. I'm sorry." Rum brushed his fingers across the top of Jamal's head. "I've turned down the lights. Please roll onto your back."

Jamal rolled onto his back and focused on Rum's voice, pushing out the other sounds. Rum started to massage Jamal's temples. Jamal felt as if each flare of pain were met with pinching fingers, like putting out the flame of a candle. Snuff. Snuff. His smell came back online and he could tell that Rum had showered. He smelled like the deodorant he wore, a sandalwood soap he used on his body and hair, and like paper. It was calming.

"Do you know what triggered this?"

Jamal started describing the memory of that Saturday, years ago, the pain in his lower back that he hadn't realized was his kidneys bitching about dehydration. "It was the first time I ever drank. I snuck a beer from the guy's garage fridge. Don't even remember their names now. I remember the land field that was their backyard. They had a corgi."

"So, you're dehydrated? I can get you water."

"I do need to drink more. But I smelled beer and felt this pinch in my kidneys—"

"From the self-defense falls we practiced."

"And my senses seemed to be stuck there. I'm even yammering like I'm drunk for the first time."

"Heightened sense memory is rare in Hamask." Rum slid his hands into Jamal's hair, then lifted them back to the hairline to repeat the motion. Always with the grain. "But you've already proven to be unique."

"Feels good." Jamal's voice sounded surprisingly husky.

"I'm glad," Rum murmured, hot against his ear. "So, we've got a couple of options. I called in a favor in the labs for them to do basic testing for the major analgesics, painkillers. We can use heat or acupuncture in the meantime."

"Heat. I don't want someone else coming in here while I'm down."

"Tight. I'll get a compress. It'll be really hot. That's the point, to get your body to reroute endorphins and adrenaline."

"I can take it."

Rum pressed his lips briefly to Jamal's forehead, and Jamal made the stupid decision to open his eyes. He whimpered and swallowed back the bile that rose in his throat. Desperately he tried to sink into sleep to escape the horrendous pain. Instead it became his complete awareness, consumed all thought and time.

Searing wet towels were placed on his forehead and chest. They were hot enough that they'd leave red marks on his skin for several minutes after they were removed.

"How you doing, sugar?"

He felt his muscles release and calm seep into his blood. "Better."

"Let me know if they get too cold. We'll switch 'em."

"Why does this even work? Not the rerouting heat thing but...."

Thankfully, Rum didn't need him to be any more eloquent. Jamal didn't have it in him.

"Not buyin' the vague explanation the cadre teach?" Rum sighed. "A man, a doctor actually, did a lot of research and figured out that pheromones change with activation. We both release them, like normal, but our Hamra side is missing components that we get from each other.

It's one of the ways we get the missing pieces. We both emit chemicals the other one needs to stay healthy. Like Blue Kryptonite."

Jamal smiled. Superman was the shit. "Sir, can you tell me more about sense memory?"

Rum encouraged him to take several sips from a straw while he described in a soft drawl his mother's fear of thunderstorms. Plenty of people with normal senses had phobia triggers, but with the Hamask-heightened senses, the brain sometimes had a hard time processing the extra data without associating it with memories, with pain.

"So my body is recreating my first migraine?"

"Pretty much. But we'll change the memory."

"Yeah, now it'll involve this fucking med ward and wet heat."

"No." Rum removed the chest cloth, and Jamal's skin quickly dried. "We'll get you ripping drunk and then—" He leaned close to Jamal, and Jamal could feel his heat at the fringes of his own body's presence. When he spoke, it was so soft that Jamal knew no one outside the room heard. "—then I'll suck you off. Deep-throat you. Another beer, another blow job. Until you can't smell hops without getting hard."

The pain was still present, but he finally felt more. The bonding heat was seeping through his body in slow, mist-like waves. Rum removed Jamal's head cloth, and Jamal opened his eyes without pain.

"It might not work," Rum added, "but it'll be fun trying. We're going to make it through this."

And Jamal knew he meant more than the shitty testing and the migraine.

Jamal reached for Rum's hips and pulled him close, stretching his neck forward to capture the other man's mouth. Rum had a hot, wet mouth, and the association made him feel as if his forehead, chest, and dick were all surrounded by perfect heat. Once invited, Rum had no problems kissing the hell out of Jamal. Tongue and teeth and soft breaths of shared lust. Jamal pulled back to look at Rum, at this man he was kissing. He was honestly waiting for a bit of panic to set in or worse, disgust. He didn't even feel awkward; it just felt good. It tasted delicious too, he finally realized, licking his own lips. All these subtle tastes and textures burst like fizzy soda across his mouth.

"Ya good, sugar?" Rum asked as he started to pull back.

"It's tight," Jamal said as he pulled him back.

The second kiss built intensity until he was urging Rum to climb up on the bed with him.

Instead, Rum pulled back and carefully pressed his forehead to Jamal's. "Feel free to do that. Anytime." He kissed Jamal's forehead. "Get some sleep. Hydrate in the morning."

"Yes, sir." Jamal closed his eyes and listened to Rum talk to himself as he walked down the hall. He sounded happy, his energy elevated but not manic. The taste of his Vargr coated Jamal's senses, and he drifted to sleep, believing things were going to go sideways any second.

Because this happy was a little too good to be true.

Bur, Brad S., 572092-Longwei.
Page 6

IT WOULD be great if I could leave a detailed recounting of what happened once Longwei was unconscious. Some of it is a chaotic mess in my head; the rest is hard to believe. Not hard to imagine me in the middle of such crazy-ass shit. Just hard to picture anyone would go along with my wild rants.

I'd seen what happened to a Hamask in a fury state, at least once the government got ahold of them. A Hamask can last up to thirteen months on the suppression drugs and mechanical support systems. This man had saved my life, and I didn't want that slow fade to death for him.

Step one to claiming your unconscious, recently raging Hamask? Handcuff yourself to him. This prevents dickwads and idiots—like Longwei's FBI partner, Agent Bazzini—from trying to separate you. You can identify these morons by their cocked guns and shaking boots. It didn't help that the bloody arm was only lying inches away. It's scary to think that any man is capable of the act and even more unsettling not knowing what he could do once he woke up.

I get that. But the man was unconscious, and I was unarmed.

Though I'm sure I was more tactful than to proclaim "I'm unarmed."

Okay, so I totally said that.

It has been thirty years since a Hamask did large-scale damage in Cairo. Yet, anytime it's mentioned in the media—fury, berserker, raging—they pull the footage out and reshow it to the frightened, uninformed masses. A newly activated Hamask ravaged Cairo, killing forty-five people before the local military was able to take him down. It's the reason Egypt no longer has a Hamrammr program and diplomatic relations between the

US and Egypt are still strained. There are several strong factions that want the Hamrammr programs decommissioned. Like the nuclear arms race, those who have it don't want others to have more than them.

Military brass want you to believe that Hamask are primal bears controlled by base instincts to mate, protect, and fight, and that Vargr are their circus trainers. That's not the case. Not only had I been paired to an amazing, easygoing, kind Hamask, but no one led Daire Viano around by the balls. The man had been my dominant in every way.

I am decidedly of the opinion that the digital-lock bracelets I used, which don't have a standardized key, are what swayed the medics and the FBI Agent in Charge to allow me to stay attached. They'll probably quote my manic state and verbal threats to sue anyone who stupidly decided to separate me and Longwei, but my money is on the cuffs.

They need to get me medical attention. Oh yeah, I'd been shot. And they wanted to contain Longwei through sedatives, so they load us up into an ambulance. They place him on the stretcher, the big lug.

Perhaps this is a good time to explain my theory. Hamask, when angry, are more like a kid having a tantrum. No, you don't want them destroying things because it means more to clean up later, but you also recognize that the fastest way out is down. Let them release all the steam. They exhaust themselves, and then their adult brain or what-the-hell-ever kicks in, and you've got an intelligent, logical human to work with rather than the raging bear. You want the technical jargon? Read my research.

So they have him on a gurney and me sitting next to the EMT, whose hands are shaking while she's trying to get an IV in. Me, not Longwei. Never a fun thing to do when I'm dehydrated, let alone with the potential raving lunatic unconscious right there. I did some fast-talking to make sure no one strapped him down—he'd bust out even more pissed and we'd have more bloody stumps to clean up. I may have actually worded it that way. Yeah, I'm not some delicate fucking Vargr who wants to talk feelings all day.

The ambulance pulls away from the crowd. I stretch my right arm out and clench my fist to help the EMT do her thing. My left wrist is still attached to Longwei's left so my arm lies across his stomach.

Turns out Longwei has a good recovery time, even with sedatives pumping into his arm—his IV was much easier. Which bodes well for the future of our sex lives. She'd managed to attach some medical electrodes, and I notice a change in heartbeat and blood pressure. He's waking up.

Now remember, this is a raging bear in a tin box on wheels, siren blaring and engines full tilt as they race us to the nearest hospital. A Vargr—me—bleeding from a gunshot wound. Talk about sensory hell for a Hamask. Even touch might be a mess because of the blood on his hands and the stiff clothes he's wearing. Only taste is left; hopefully it isn't as haywire as the rest of him.

"He's waking up," she says but doesn't go screaming for the driver. She's still trying for a vein. I brush her off. "Don't jostle your arm. The compression unit won't hold."

But I'm only focused on him. I put one knee up on the gurney and lean over him as his eyes open and stare directly into mine. He is pissed off, face flushed, and he takes a breath to scream or something, and I just go for it. I plant the messiest kiss—definitely coloring outside those lines, you know? My lips don't even try to stay on his. He tastes good and he is way sexy. Pissed-off brutes have always been my eye candy of choice. I've unintentionally trained my dick to like such images, and I wasn't having any issue engaging with the feels on this. I'm slicking up his chin and nose, partly because of the jostling of the ambulance, and I think, *Wow, it's working.* He hasn't kissed me back yet, but he seems startled, seems to be melting.

Nope.

I've been thinking about it since—I didn't think about it before I acted. I might have groaned. Leaned on my arm wrong or the compression unit gave up the ghost and I'm gushing blood. Something that he registered as me being in danger.

The EMT described me being thrown against the opposite wall, but that's not how it goes down. He lifts me off him, eyes flashing hatred, the ambulance takes a tight corner, and the momentum gets out of control. The ambulance has all these cabinets with supplies and gear and shit, and what I don't destroy does its best to destroy me. I slide to the floor of the ambulance and I can see over the gurney that our arms are still attached by the metal cuffs. He picks her up one-armed and yells. I think he would have thrown her toward the back door next, except two things happen.

The driver hears the commotion and turns off the siren, and I say, "Please. Please don't hurt her."

He pauses and scrutinizes me, tilts his head to the side, his narrowed eyes looking down to our joined wrists, up to my gunshot wound, then back to my eyes. He pins her against the side of the ambulance wall and tells her to stay. That's when I realize I don't know his name.

"I'm Brad. Bur." I try to stand, but my knees are wobbly. "That's my name."

He gives another warning glare to the EMT and rolls over the gurney to crouch down beside me, which thankfully relieves the tension in my arm.

"What's your name?"

He feels my forehead and takes my wrist to check my pulse.

"Maybe we could get me some help. Would you like that?"

He doesn't say anything.

The EMT begins to cry and Longwei flinches from the sound. I mean, full-body reaction. His eyes tighten to small slits and he raises his shoulders and ducks his head.

"Miss, please shut the fuck up," I tell her.

He finds a new compression unit among the debris, then starts an IV like he's done a million and knows right where to find my best vein. I talk to him. I don't know why, maybe more of my own instincts kicking in. "I grew up in Idaho. A place called Gardena. In the summer I stand outside on the front deck and listen to the wind run through the trees. You've ever seen them do the wave at a professional meet? And you can see where the wave started and where it is going next. It even has its own sound. The wind is like that at home. This roar, like ocean waves but it doesn't ebb, just rolls past you."

I lick my lips and squint at the IV. "Don't you dare give me drugs. I need to stay awake for this."

"I won't." It's the first time he hasn't yelled. He starts using different things to first wash his own hands and then my face and hands as well.

I keep talking. "You see it in the little leaves of the aspens first. The wind. Like pom-poms, shaking, creating their own noise, and then the evergreens start to move."

Longwei looks over at the lady and then nods for her to leave out the front. The driver is long gone, and though I haven't heard anything of significance from outside—cops or anyone yelling for us to come out—I know they are probably there. Even if we've made it all the way to the hospital, that doesn't mean we're in the clear.

"Where'd you learn first aid?"

He looks back at me and reaches to cup the side of my face.

My heart does this stupid thing. It melts. I feel a bit like I'm standing on that front porch, listening to the wind, waiting for the sound of crickets to kick on as evening falls, letting all the worries puddle at my feet. I've only ever felt that way at home.

"I'm sorry about what happened." He brushes a thumb across my eyebrow. "Your car windows were down, and I could smell you when we came on site, could hear you from outside." So if there had been a bonding heat, he might have felt it before I was shot.

I practically live in that car so the fact that it reeks of me doesn't surprise me. I nod, hoping he will continue.

"I couldn't let him kill you, and then when I smelled your blood…. Did I…?" His face loses all color and his eyes mist up. "I didn't know I could still use my senses like this, let alone…."

"You saved me. Thanks for that. Maybe after we figure out this clusterfuck, we could…." I distinctly remember blushing at this point. Hey, I can admit to being nervous. That's human. "Maybe we could go to dinner. Get to know each other."

"No." He shakes his head, and he looks so sad. Like we are long-time lovers and he is saying good-bye. I know that face. After Daire, I saw that look in the mirror every goddamn morning.

"Why?"

"They're outside, and they're waiting for me to turn myself in."

"Okay, we'll go together. We'll talk it out."

He sighs, runs that gentle thumb across my eyebrow again. "I'm not letting them take me."

Chapter 5

RUM HAD been briefed on their training mission. He was supposed to spend the next twenty minutes briefing Jamal on the same information. Jamal, who had probably listened to the whole meeting. Hell, the tactical room where he found Jamal wasn't even two rooms down from the conference room. Further proof was the fact that Jamal had already packed their gear and was just finishing loading his HK45. Rum wouldn't pretend that Jamal hadn't heard every word of the intelligence-training mission. The man had tested exceptionally well on hearing.

But they had *twenty minutes*.

It had been three weeks since the migraine and their kiss. Rum had known, as Jamal kissed him back, that it was his first time kissing another man. It wasn't so much a lack of skill or hesitancy—the man was a talented kisser—but he gathered data with wide eyes, processing the new experience, looking awed instead of returning to the familiar. Rum wanted to give him time to accept his new sexual orientation, if that were even the case. Rum still didn't know a whole lot about him besides the fact he could bench-press an insane amount and was quickly proving to be an excellent marksman.

USHP had offered them the Military Occupational Specialty of Intelligence 35HV, which was a broad MOS that allowed Joint Operations to lend out Hamra Pairs as needed. It was a good fit for their skill set, and they'd accepted. Today's training would be part of that new MOS skill training.

Jamal was still housed in the medical ward each night so they could monitor him and run additional scans. Major Sanderson, in charge of HAVOC Medical, was sure Jamal would slip back into a fury state at any moment. Colonel Browning was sure the bond was a fake attempt to further manipulate Rum's position in the USHP.

So they were still generally screwed. Nineteen minutes.

God, could this be any more awkward? I'd rather be teaching Indoc sessions to candidates.

Jamal slid multiple clips into his vest and then looked at Rum with his hands on his hips. The clips were orange and had rubber bullets in them.

Jamal looked good. His coloring was healthy and there was no trembling in his limbs. His strong healing factor was doing its job to get him back to normal. *Hamask* normal. Jamal kept staring.

What? Have I missed a button on my fly? Nope, all fastened. Rum looked back up and realized he hadn't said anything since entering the room. "Do you have any questions?"

Jamal laid the tactical vest on the counter and asked, "You hungry?"

Rum nodded.

Jamal crossed his arms. "Let's get something from the mess hall before we gear up."

Jamal held the door for him. Their bodies brushed but neither reacted. Rum kept his own desires in check, and if Jamal felt any attraction, he was good at hiding it. There were other tells Rum didn't have any problems identifying: Jamal would rub his fingers together when he was focusing his sight and he held superstill when he was sorting out smells.

"What do we need to worry about on this op? Besides the standard corporate line they fed you in there."

Rum smiled and blew out a short breath. Training had given them at least this much; being able to talk as coworkers. Understanding at least on a surface level what the other man thought about their situation. "Most recon teams rely too much on the Hamask's senses. You won't have any issues finding the asset and knowing how many people are guarding him. But that's where the trap lies."

"Because it doesn't paint the full picture."

"Right. Are there other environmental hazards? What kind of weapons and communications do they have? If it could be done remotely, they'd send in drones. This type of work is done in deeper. We will go places the drones can't go or don't work. Out in the real world, we'd be working as trackers for an FBI or SEAL team."

If things went the way Rum thought, they'd be playing backup for the Bur-Longwei pair until they had enough experience to lead their own team of WREAC.

"Good." Jamal nodded and pulled open the door to the mess and let Rum precede him. "That's why I'm here. Doing work that will make a difference."

"Heck yeah!" Rum snagged a PB&J sandwich and a box of raisins. Jamal went for an apple and a bag of cheese puffs. "Any other questions?"

Jamal grabbed canisters of water for them both and led the way to a quiet corner. "Why don't you cuss?"

Rum blushed and fumbled his sandwich as he laughed. "My mom is Hamask. She always knew." He laughed and shook his head again. "I know better now, that you aren't always tuned in to sound, that other things can take your focus. But as a kid I was sure she had a sixth sense when it came to me and misbehaving. Like she literally knew everything. The first time I masturbated was at summer camp because—" Rum's head caught up with his mouth and heat flooded his cheeks. He shook his head and knew the blush deepened. "—for obvious... privacy reasons." *Good save there.*

"I had a foster mom like that. When I was seven, I think. We'd be playing in the back yard, and someone would pick up a dirt clod or start whispering about girls, and she'd bellow from the house, 'Don't you even dare!' She probably yelled that out every half an hour to keep us on our toes."

Jamal opened his bag of chips and shook the opening at Rum to offer him some. Rum pulled one out and munched on it while pulling his sandwich in half and passing the bigger piece to Jamal. It was nice that Jamal hadn't made fun of Rum's awkward confession. "How come you were in foster care?"

Jamal quirked an eyebrow. "You didn't read my file?"

"No. Have you read mine?"

Jamal shook his head. They took a moment to eat, and then Jamal said, "Don't have parents. As near as they can tell, I was left at a hospital when I was three or so. My prints didn't generate any kind of match, so no records. I grew up in the system."

"What about your family? You asked when I... when you came out of the fury, about—"

"I've created my own family. Mostly kids I grew up with and stayed close to. A foster mom. I call her a few times a year, like a grandma."

This was incredibly comfortable. It felt like a good-looking man had asked him out to coffee, and for once Rum didn't feel the pressure to overanalyze each response. He didn't need to make sure it went a certain direction or steer Jamal's opinion any particular way. "And they know you're awake?"

Jamal nodded, but then he looked at Rum, the corner of his eyes tightening, a small shift of his head. *Really* looked. Whatever Jamal was about to tell him crossed a point of no return. Jamal was laying down a level of trust that Rum prayed he was worthy of.

"My Grandma Karen, she was Special Operations, Cultural Support Team in Russia."

"The female Green Berets." Rum nodded his understanding.

"She has all these incredible stories. Anyway, I'd been in her house—" He pursed his lips, looking briefly over Rum's shoulder. "—four days when I broke my arm. Jaxx, another kid at the house, was trying to teach me how to ride a bike." Jamal rubbed the back of his neck. "Long story. She shows me the medical bills and I just shrug it off. I've got full medical from the feds. She nods and asks if I know how much she gets each month for me."

Rum felt himself lean closer to Jamal. What did Jamal look like as a kid? Chubby or all long, awkward angles? It would be nice to see pictures of little Jamal struggling to find himself, looking up to the foster mom.

"Which I'd heard like a hundred times before. Foster parents bitching about not getting enough to put up with our bullshit." He smiled for the first time that day. His eyes softened. "So I'm thinking, 'Here we go again. Thank God I didn't unpack.' Instead she tells me about taxes. About her neighbors, a pair of teachers, and how much they pay each year. About her sister who lives on a fixed income, and how she pays to fix my arm and pays for my schooling and…. And it wasn't about the medical bills so much, or that we'd stolen the bike, but the way I just didn't give a damn. I didn't think people cared, and yet all these strangers were helping me. Man, she gives the *toughest* lectures."

"And you're good at math."

Jamal's eyes focused back on Rum. He nodded. "At one point I figured it out to exactly how much I'd cost."

Since it had no negative associations and because he'd probably relived the memory several times before activating, Rum wasn't worried that Jamal would get caught in a sense memory. But just in case, he touched Jamal's forearm. *Yeah, to prevent sense memory.* He pursed his lips to hide his grin.

"It no longer felt—" Jamal took a deep breath and squared his shoulders. "—disconnected, like something that just happened. I can pay taxes the rest of my life, and it still won't cover what I was given."

"You've got a red ledger." Rum let his smile show. It didn't matter that Jamal didn't get the reference. Most of the time Rum was funny for himself. He very much liked the idea that Jamal would have some grand, noble motivation behind joining the military. Best of all it wasn't anything he'd imagine as to why Jamal would join. It eased something in Rum to see this side of him.

"Basically."

What Jamal was really saying was that he needed to make it mean something. He wanted to matter, to make a difference, but deeper than that he wanted to prove he was worth it, worthy of it. The tightness in Rum's chest and shoulders eased.

JAMAL FELT taller, more focused in tactical gear. Like he was a doctor putting on his white coat. Like rising up to the next level on an escalator, your torso seeming to elongate as you reached the end. Which, okay, was totally silly, but he couldn't help feeling excited. He'd had no problem with these types of obstacle courses before activation, and he had the advantage of working with one of the best and most experienced Vargr ever. Okay, "best ever" was stretching it a bit, but still. He was going into this feeling pretty damn confident.

Rum led him to the starting point.

It made sense now why Rum would be pissed about the whole fake bonding in the shower. Rum had chosen Jamal to work with, but Rum didn't think they needed to posture for anyone.

Jamal heard the brass dressing Rum down every time they thought he was out of earshot. Some of the slander he didn't get, which meant there were still gaps in his knowledge, but as a Hamask he knew from training he would be required to submit physically and mentally to all things for his Vargr to fully lead him. Rum was his senior officer, knew a hell of a lot more than Jamal, and treated him with respect. He had no issues letting his wolf lead.

At least in situations like today's training.

Rum wanted something deeper. He knew firsthand how long a Hamra Pair could last, how integrated they became. No longer a pair, but a couple. Rum avoided orders but instead addressed Jamal as if they were… friends, who worked together.

The cadre ignored them, and Rum didn't engage either. Instead he turned toward Jamal. They were dressed the same except for their hands and forearms. Rum wore fingerless gloves and had his sleeves rolled up.

Easy skin access for Jamal's bare hands if he needed to anchor his touch so that he could increase one of his senses.

Rum pulled a map of the base up on his smartwatch and nodded for Jamal to do the same. "Let's make this a bit more fun."

"How?" Jamal stifled a grin.

"I'm going to mark on my map where I think they've got the asset. You do the same. If I'm right, you have to shine my boots tonight."

"That better not be a euphemism."

Rum snorted. "And if you're right?"

Jamal remembered watching the shower cascade across Rum's body, but his new fantasy included Rum looking at him with heated eyes and licking his lips while porn music played in the background. He cleared his throat. "You teach me how to throw knives."

Rum looked up from his map and smiled. "Heard about that, did you? Deal."

"What if we're both wrong?"

"Not going to happen. They're using Chakosky for the asset."

Rum watched him as he said the name of the Vargr who had been present during Jamal's activation. Jamal looked toward the cadre, both writing notes on a tablet for a Hamra Pair processing before them. They were at least partially listening.

When Jamal looked back at Rum, the man gave a brief nod. "Predictable, high maintenance, thinks he can elude Hamask by using natural barriers."

Was Rum baiting the cadre? "That's because his Hamask barely registers as active."

Rum's smile was both proud and evil. "So take a moment and then mark your map." Jamal wrapped his fingers around Rum's forearm and let his hearing and sense of smell expand like echoing waves. In his mind he could see the pathways across the base. Chakosky still felt gross to him somehow. Like the memory of eating sauerkraut for the first time. Plus, he had a voice like a rubber band, tight and high strung, as if he'd snap if you didn't calm the fuck down.

In a building with classrooms and base-wide maintenance vehicles, he found Chakosky. If it had been a bit farther, maybe he wouldn't have heard the man. As it was, at this distance he couldn't make out specific words. But it was him. He confirmed the building by distinguishing the smells of cleaning chemicals and the noise of the motor crew working on an engine. Hard to filter through if your Vargr wasn't as good as Rum. As Jamal pulled back to his immediate surroundings he could hear Rum telling him in a quiet, accent-heavy voice about his dad teaching him to drive in the back roads of Tennessee. Innocuous, simple story, accent in place, to cover the fact he was helping Jamal find his way back with his voice.

"Do the faster reflexes make you a better driver?" Jamal asked to show he was listening and to let Rum know he was present. He tapped on his watch face and marked the motor pool building, and slid the screen around to scope out different pathways there.

"I had horrible eyesight until I activated. Almost kept me out of the program, it was so bad. And then it flipped everyone's mental lid when it got better. Thought maybe I was activating as a bear instead of a wolf."

"I've seen your reflex tests. If that was all I knew, I'd know you were Vargr. Thought it was a typo."

"You and me both."

The senior cadre was notified via earpiece that the previous team was finished. Jamal nudged Rum forward and tapped a finger against his own ear to indicate he knew it was their turn.

Rum turned on his earpiece. They listened to the cadre's last-minute instructions, and then Rum walked forward. Once they were past the first building, out of the cadre's immediate sight—though they'd be watched with drones and security cameras—Rum paused and turned to look at Jamal.

He used hand signals to indicate that Jamal should lead, to turn down sight and to turn up his hearing. *No one sees us.* Jamal nodded and took up lead. He kept track of the drones and any possible training groups in the area. They were two buildings away from the garage when Rum touched his waist to stop him.

Slow, careful.

Jamal nodded and then stepped back behind some parked jeeps when his awareness shifted. He felt Rum brush fingers along his nape, just under his helmet. But it was distant, almost outside his consciousness. They were moving Chakosky. Someone had gotten him to shut up, but his heart and breathing had accelerated. It was hard to narrow down how many guys were with the asset, but he was guessing seven. Very typical small unit size. He took Rum's wrist and flipped to a drawing app while he gave the gesture for target and moving.

"Where?" Rum asked.

Jamal marked inside the building where they were and in which direction they seemed to be heading. Rum zoomed out on his watch and tapped for a street view. He traced a line toward one of the barracks then drew a line from where they were currently to intercept.

Jamal nodded and then indicated it was safe to move forward. It was getting easier to work together, to read with little to no words what Rum wanted, to tell what Jamal needed from him. Yet, he didn't know who Rum was trying to prove something to—him or the cadre. He didn't know why Rum was so sure they would go that specific direction. He focused on getting there, and they had to duck and cover a few times more than before as they moved into a busier section of the training field.

The cadre and Chakosky had the advantage of moving quickly, not trying to avoid detection. Jamal knew Rum was trying to show off by avoiding the drones at the same time as pursuing, but which was more important?

They'd reached the back of the mess hall and Jamal had to switch off scent to navigate through the trash bins behind the kitchens. He signaled a stop and pulled Rum to lean against the wall. Jamal focused on breathing for a moment and then signaled all clear. Though he hadn't double-checked.

"Sir, we're not going to make it to the intercept point in time."

Rum pulled up the map on his smartwatch. "Do you think we can get to their destination before—"

"Sir—"

"Rum, dammit. Or Walker. Just call me—"

They didn't have time for this shit now. Jamal touched Rum's forearm and used his senses to scan their perimeter. "Why would they move him?"

"Because they knew we were coming."

"The mission is to gather intel. I know how many there are. That they're lugging explosives with them. And beef jerky. That Chakosky is aiding in his own capture."

Rum sighed and started moving hands over his own weapons, like braille, confirming their placing.

"You know their training, the weapons they are most likely to be carrying, and where they're going."

"Single officer housing," Rum said.

"Makes sense. Outside of the mission parameters and off-limits to me until my restrictions are lifted."

Rum pulled a knuckle blade out from some secret pocket and let it spin on one of his fingers. "We've got two choices. Double-time it to the destination, fully exposed and monitored, or keep our cover and arrive after them," Jamal said.

Rum looked at him and Jamal watched as he slid his bottom lip to the side and tucked it beneath his upper teeth. He tapped the surface of his watch and then looked down the alleyway. Thinking mode.

"There is a third option."

Jamal wasn't going to play his mental games. "Tell me why we're going against mission, and I'll follow your lead."

"This is a real mission." Rum waved away Jamal's startled response. "Not Chakosky, of course. They're using us to run scenarios on an actual rescue. I'll give you the long version later, but there is a missing Vargr named Wickham Ieti. I want us on that mission. The sooner they think we're ready, the sooner they'll leave us the *hell alone*."

Rum had this expressive face that Jamal had quickly realized he used to his own advantage. Rum showed you exactly what you expected, exactly what he wanted you to see. But on occasion, the real Rum broke through, and that guy was scary—because he wasn't nice, and he wasn't respectful. That guy would easily bury the knife, the one he casually hid in his vest, in your throat without hesitation. Remorse would never even occur to him.

Jamal nodded and followed Rum into the sewers.

Chapter 6

RUM KNEW he was asking a lot by coming down here. Hamask struggled to handle the lack of light, horrible smell, and sound dampening of tunnels and sewer systems. For weeks after, they would complain about the stench their scratch-and-sniff memory was happy to conjure up hourly. Their skin felt oily and filthy for even longer. Rum wouldn't let Jamal suffer those side effects, even with the sense memory. He had a plan. He palmed his mini flashlight and resisted the urge to twirl it between his fingers.

"If you start overloading on any one sense, let me know."

Instead of answering, Jamal reached forward and pulled Rum's shirt out of the way and touched his neck. Jamal's skin was slightly rough, hot compared to the cool sweat on Rum's body.

"We don't need to keep quiet down here. The base has motion and heat sensors that will go off. Maintenance and base security will be sent down, which gives us ten minutes, but we aren't going far and the cadre won't be notified until much later."

Rum glanced back once they got to a junction. It was tough going, running crouched over, avoiding the rivulets and more noxious debris, hearing the occasional press and suck of muck as they stepped. Jamal wasn't giving him any visual cues and continued to follow him in silence, probably concentrating on keeping his smell turned off.

"I sent them a bit of our earlier conversation. I'm supposed to send them audio clips as check-ins. Really, I needed them not to go to the officers' quarters. So I leaked that information. When we marked our maps for the bet, I knew they'd move Chakosky. I thought they'd stick to the mission area, but... well, this will work too."

They got to a smaller side tunnel. "Last section," Rum said.

They began crawling, the Maglite clinking against the thankfully dry metal tube with each move forward. Jamal passed Rum a small battery-operated power drill, and they opened the floor grate into the base of the Chem Disposal building.

"Why here?" Jamal asked. Out of all the buildings, how did Rum know they were headed to this one?

"Chakosky. He doesn't question himself or his methods. He is 100 percent confident. Makes him predictable. Now, me? I second-guess myself all the time. I can't sleep at night for all the questions."

Jamal signaled he would go first, silently, and to be ready. Rum nodded.

It would be easy for Jamal to carry the heavy Chakosky, wouldn't even elevate his breathing. In the real world they'd be working with backup, operational support, and with a cooperative target.

Fifteen minutes later they returned to the sewer with an unconscious Chakosky, appendages duct-taped to make it easier to pull him along the first section. Maintenance had already cleared the sewer and reset the sensors. Two buildings over was the med ward, right before a drain point. Neither man was surprised when Colonel Browning and the MPs met them at the outflow. Browning's bald pate was flushed red, and he sputtered for a minute before he turned on his heel and stomped away. For a short guy, he had a long stride.

They handed Chakosky over to his pissed-off but silent Hamask, Dim Knox, and followed Browning and the MPs toward the main training building for debrief. Knox, a short Korean man, carrying his massive-in-comparison Vargr, was quite the sight.

"Question?" Rum said.

"Sure." Jamal walked beside him, wisely keeping his body language noncombative.

"How'd you get your name? Did you come with a note?" He could imagine this chubby little boy, eyes huge and hair supercurly. Would he have known his own name, his parents' names, at the age of three? He could have been even younger.

"Random name generator," Jamal said. He didn't sound anything but matter-of-fact. No pity. No embarrassment.

"Jamal is Arabic for beauty."

Jamal cocked an eyebrow at Rum and then rolled his eyes.

"It's true. I speak Arabic. Can't write it worth a damn, though."

Jamal snorted and smiled, "That's because it looks like chicken scratches. Artistic chicken scratches." Jamal shoved at his shoulder and preceded him into the building. He'd smirked once in the mess hall, but the rest of the time he'd played the part of stoic soldier. Rum liked this smiling, playful Jamal best.

Through the training scenario, Rum made strategic decisions to help Jamal. He had kept his accent heavy through the sewer. He would continue to reinforce this camaraderie later by bringing the meaning of Jamal's name up again—like a running joke—and the whole time Jamal knew a dressing-down was possible. Those things kept his Hamask present, no slips back into protective mode. No fury nor even anger. Yeah, he'd showed off a bit for the cadre, but more importantly he and Jamal were learning to work together.

General Khan was waiting for them at the training building. He looked at Rum until their eyes met, and then he frowned.

In that brief moment it took Khan's brows to drop, Rum scanned the whole man. *Drat the rising crick.* The back of Rum's throat tightened as if he had tossed back a finger of sake. He felt strain along his shoulders from carrying all the extra gear. This did not bode well.

Rum tried to redirect. "I'm shocked, I tell you. Shenanigans? Here?" No one reacted to Rum's words. If a *Casablanca* reference couldn't ease the tension, little would.

RUM'S BRIEFING was different for three reasons; they'd made extra efforts to keep it private, General Khan was in actual attendance rather than via video, and Browning was smiling like the conceited, smug bastard he was.

The privacy worried him. After seeing Jamal in the field and knowing exactly how strong his hearing was, Rum wondered if the previous lectures had been even more embarrassingly public. It would explain why Jamal had initially struggled with the threat of them being separated—the brass continued to threaten.

Yet, Rum couldn't take this whole thing seriously when they messed up the basic stuff. The staging was all wrong for this interrogation scene. The investigators needed to stand or sit at a point of higher authority. Or they could have Rum restrained some way that showed the audience the stakes were high. Even the windows to the holo room had been left open—a missed opportunity to make this more uncomfortable. At least Khan and Browning had avoided the unrealistic pristine uniforms. Rum never bought that in the movies. If it was Rum's interrogation he'd pay attention to the details.

Rum needed to stop thinking about movies and focus on their questions. Khan didn't look happy. Rum knew Khan was on Jamal's side and wanted them to be a success story, proof that a fury didn't mark the end of a Hamask's usefulness. For the first time since waking Jamal, Rum doubted the general had his back too.

That Browning was smiling was bad. Rum was tired from the op and two-plus hours of debriefing. It had been a long day, and he wanted to eat a decent meal and sleep. He'd gone longer and had far, far harder days. But he was frayed. And Browning knew it.

Browning thought he'd gotten past every diversion, trap, and move Rum had with his handful of questions so far. Of course Rum could always pull off the kid gloves and twist the colonel up. Expose the colonel's abuse at the hands of a child molester, his struggles to learn to read, and his difficulty with money. But Rum had not yet been pressed to that extreme. Just because he could read those things off the cocky, short man's skin like a book, didn't mean he should use them as a weapon. Tempting, though, so he turned his back to the colonel.

"You and Zumati haven't renewed your bond." Browning was so old-school with the physical side of bonding that he probably waxed poetic in his reports about male maidenheads and scent-marking.

Read some erotica, why don't you, and leave my sex life to my own hands.

Which was exactly Browning's complaint. "Neither of you have even mentioned bonding heat in your training reports."

Jamal could write whatever the hell he wanted, but Rum wouldn't be discussing a fictional characteristic to play along with their misguided fairy tale of what a Hamra Pair was really like. Bonding wouldn't save Browning the possibility of future pain. There were no guarantees. Your Hamrammr mate could still hurt you. It made sense that Browning would cling to ideals from the twentieth century.

He sat facing Browning again. "We're bonded because we trust each other. Because chemically we're compatible." Yes, that could lead to sex. But it wasn't some silly urge that *had* to be fulfilled.

Rum looked at Khan to gauge his reaction. Didn't look like any help was coming from that quarter.

"Walker." First time the colonel had addressed him so informally. Browning placed a fatherly hand on Rum's knee. "Zumati's Hamask abilities are very strong. He needs a strong mentor that will guide him—"

Didn't the idiot realize how creepy that felt? Rum pulled his knee away and stood to walk around the small group of folding chairs.

Hopefully the move hid his revulsion to Browning's touch. "It's not exactly private in the med ward, and he isn't allowed in my quarters."

"So you're saying that having your own quarters would allow you to renew your bond?" General Khan asked.

In Rum's head he heard his father misquoting that old movie—"So you're saying I have a chance?"—with a sarcastic glint in his eye. *Gawd, how tired am I?*

He didn't want to force Jamal into a situation that he wasn't ready for. Since the kiss, Rum hadn't seen any indications that Jamal wanted to pursue him. Their teamwork should stand on its own. "Sir, you've seen us work together—"

"Actually, no. Very little of the operation was recorded," Khan said.

"My report—"

"Is what you want us to hear." Browning's smile was back.

Shit. He'd done this to them. Confident that an impressive training mission would show how perfectly he and Jamal worked together, they would finally get some privacy. Maybe the brass would lift Jamal's restrictions so he could leave that stupid lab where they continued to poke him and run tests. Instead Rum had just convinced them that Jamal and he had something to hide.

Rum wasn't going to sit here and rehash how epically he'd messed this up. His temper would make matters worse. He needed out of this room *now*. He stood at attention. "Do you have any further questions for me?"

Bur, Brad S., 572092-Longwei.
Page 14

WHEN YOU'RE a Vargr, your brain runs scenarios. It's just how it works after activation. So Longwei—though I still don't know his name—has announced he was about to commit suicide by SWAT team by not letting them take him in, and my supercomputer starts to run hot like I've overclocked it. Neither of us have guns, but both of us have enough military training to make do with the items inside the ambulance. I can tell he's ex-military the same way I know which chemicals go boom. It was part of my training. Hell, the oxygen tank alone has a lot of potential.

They haven't rushed the ambulance, so they don't have a Hamask among them. A Hamask would have alerted them to the threat of Longwei taking option B: death by shoot-out. With high probability, we were at the Mercy Medical Center. The closest military base with Hamask would be Fort McCoy, Wisconsin, which is a three-hour drive or a thirty-five-minute helicopter ride. Which gives us at least ten minutes. I need surgery. We could leverage that against his release. I won't use the word "negotiate," since we all know how that will turn out.

If we can get to a point that has video cameras, we might have a chance. I haven't turned off my smartwatch since entering the burger joint, so all his responses and mine will be 3-D mappable. They'll see he isn't in a fury state, that he's calmly listening to me, trying to keep us both safe. But that requires a holo room or a computer to sync with. If I'd had tech training, I would know how to send the feed live to my director's personal teltom phone. The hospital won't have a holo room, but if they have surveillance and we can make it before they start shooting—

"I've got a plan."

He's already shaking his head, and then scenario seventeen comes to a screeching halt as I factor in another variable. "Wait. Are you running away from me? I'm not going to judge because I wasn't always good at sticking around, but come on. If you don't want to be my Hamask, just say. We'll get this sorted and go our separate ways." Scenario twenty-six pushes to the surface of my thoughts. "Oh fuck, you're already paired. Dude, I am sorry. Will your Vargr be jealous?"

"Never had a Vargr. That's why I went dormant and ended up as a medic in WREAC." He says the words, but he isn't focusing on me. He's got us untangled and sits me on the gurney.

To save time I continue to spew ideas as they come to me. "So, not a delayed activation?"

"No."

He takes a deep breath like he's about to jump into the deep end, and I grab his wrists and hold on with all my strength. "I was paired before. He died."

"Look—" He shakes his head, and I get the feeling he's about to let me down easy. "Kid—"

I snort and shake my head. "Not a kid." I turn my touch into a caress and try for my smoldering eyes. I've been told my poor communication skills are another reason I rotate through partners so often. I still think it's because I keep landing them in danger.

I could always leverage my injury against this big lummox. "My partner, she isn't here. Don't know any of the local agents. Who's going to make sure I make it through surgery? Fill out my paperwork?" I take three short, fast breaths, like little kids do right before they cry, and let my eyes water.

He isn't buying it. Just rolls his eyes.

"Okay, let's go for honest, then, okay?" His eyes meet mine and I feel a shift in the air around us. Subtle, yet so deep that when I speak next, my voice is breathy with passion. Fuck off; it's not funny. It scared me a bit, feeling so quickly and deeply for this man. "You saved my life. I can't let you die. What's your name?"

"Longwei."

"Brad Bur."

"You said that already."

He's still talking to me, which gives me hope. I smile. "Tell me what I need to know to convince you."

He looks down at my watch, places his hands on my thighs, and leans forward so he's standing between my knees. Daire always said he could tell when our watches were recording. Said the sound was like the old tape recorders of the 1970s, this spiraling series of clicks. I believed he was imagining things until that day. Because Longwei knew. He brings up the right app and pauses the recording and then shuts the watch off completely. Then he pulls my key out of my front pocket and unhooks first my wrist and then his own. He folds the bracelets down and puts them and the key back in my pocket. I'm watching him at this point because he's nice to watch. Handsome, lithe, built.

I guess trust starts here.

"If we weren't Hamask and Vargr. If we were two guys looking to fuck"—he says the word filthily, like I didn't even know that was a thing outside of porn. And I'm not laughing, then or now, because it was incredibly hot—"I would top." He presses down on my thighs and leans even closer, and with each inch, the danger ramps up my arousal exponentially. I'm about to come in my slacks. "And when we were done, I'd untie you."

He looks at my right eye and then my left, and I'm just sitting there panting shallowly.

"Yes, please." I lean forward and kiss him. It feels like our first kiss. The attack on the gurney was more a tactic, a battle strategy to get my hormones linked to his. A desperate plan to short-circuit his fury state.

So this kiss is way different. It's sweet. He starts out a bit stiff and then tilts his head and softens his mouth, and I'm reeling from the power. I don't think. For several minutes and for the first time in years, maybe even in a decade, I don't analyze or categorize. I just feel. If you don't know what that's like, the relief overwhelming your senses, then you're lucky.

"Rope, chains, whatever you need. Just keep me," I say.

His eyes are full of all these swirling wet emotions, and he opens his mouth to reply.

From outside the ambulance we hear, "Special Agent Hamask Longwei, you are in violation of military regulation. You will stand down or we will put you down."

Turns out I misjudged how long since his initial fury. "Fort McCoy?" I ask Longwei.

"Four local cops, three hospital security guards, FBI SWAT, Hamra Pair from McCoy and a WREAC team." His hands are still on me, one on my thigh, the other cupping my cheek. He closes his eyes and focuses his hearing. "A couple of reporters, armored vehicles—based on the smell—and one helicopter, but I can't tell if they're a vid channel or military."

"Man, you're good."

"*We're* good." He picks me up and I link my arms around his neck. Then he yells, "We're coming out. Stand back."

"Shit, did they hear the part about the chains?"

Chapter 7

IT WAS another full week before Jamal and Rum were given their own quarters. Jamal's personal effects were in boxes, stacked three-high along the south wall. Rum had a single duffel that he dropped near the bathroom door.

Jamal decided this was what it would feel like to be released from prison. Relief, obviously, but also apprehension. *What now?*

Yesterday they had finished the fitness exam with passing marks. That left a single week of classroom training before Jamal would be certified for search and rescue like Rum.

Their new quarters were a two-bedroom, single-bath-and-living-room Hamra Family Housing unit. The kitchenette was enough for an occasional simple meal with a single burner and hydroslot. He'd been in a foster home with one other kid that was smaller than this, but it had looked better than this place, on the surface, with bright yellow walls and artwork on the fridge. He'd take this place over that one any day.

Small and drab, but it would be heaven if there were no electrical bugs. Jamal signaled that he was going to take a look and listen, and Rum quietly ran dialogue as he found linens in a cupboard and made up a bed on the west side. As Jamal stood completely still in the living room, he kept an eye on Rum's movements. He slid his thumb along his index finger, using the tactile sensation and the smell of Rum nearby to extend his hearing. No electrical feedback from a recording device and no alert Hamask in the area. The other housing units were full of general domestic chaos.

"We're clear," Jamal said.

Rum sagged, boneless, facedown onto the bed. "Thank God."

"Where are the sheets for the other bed?" Jamal asked. He tried not to look at Rum but failed miserably. Especially his well-defined and tight butt. *Shouldn't look there. Haven't looked every day as we went running. Each day in the weight room. Nope. Haven't looked.*

When Rum rolled over, Jamal went from ogling the man's ass to his crotch. Jamal looked away, leaned against the doorjamb, and lifted his leg to press his foot against the door frame to hide his arousal.

Jamal knew Rum had taken way more heat over their last training op with the sewer than he had. Instead of less observation, they'd spent the week without a moment alone.

In the last week, each time he'd reached to touch Rum—even innocent touches—the guards had started snickering or whispering reports back to Sanderson and Browning. Jamal had thought his first week of being awake had been hell, but this was much harder. Because now he knew how amazing Rum tasted. Rum's nerves were overextended. His eyes were bloodshot and puffy, his shoulders always rigid.

"The other bed? Is that what you want? Separate rooms?" Rum quickly added, "I'm okay with that. But we haven't discussed that… us."

Jamal didn't say anything. Or move. Or look at Rum.

"This didn't go as planned." Rum's voice was heavy with the tension. No trace of accent. A serious conversation was long overdue, but leave it to Rum to launch in like the last six weeks were just a pause. Sounded like it didn't matter if no one was watching, they'd continue to awkwardly jockey around their attraction and the bonding heat.

"So what was the mission objective?" Jamal crossed his arms and turned his head to look at Rum.

"Draw you out. Then let you choose. I didn't know if you… had a preference."

A sexual preference. Like Jamal couldn't speak his mind. He knew that either pairing was possible. If it had truly been a deal breaker, he wouldn't have gone through activation. There were always the WREAC teams that provided essential support to Hamra Pairs. But he needed to be honest with Rum. "I wanted a girl."

Rum had been lying back on his elbows, but at Jamal's words he stood and continued making the bed. His nice round ass shorted Jamal's brain. He forgot what he was going to say.

"You should request a reassignment," Rum said.

Jamal watched the muscles appear and disappear as Rum clenched his fists. Bands of tight skin, veins, and tendons. The little man was built like a brick. Solid. Sexy. In better shape than Jamal had ever been. The muscles appeared again. Arm porn. Jamal could lick a path around Rum's body and map all the contours. The bonding heat and attraction became his full focus. He didn't need to ignore or staunch it. Not anymore.

Rum's powers of observation weren't working or he was ignoring the lust Jamal was sure he was radiating.

Jamal stared right into Rum's eyes. "And when they split us up?" He lowered his bent leg, walked a step into the room, and fixed his gaze on a patch of light that moved with the setting sun. He'd taken the lead in the med ward and the botched hand job, as he now thought of it. He was sure to screw this up too. Rum was more experienced, his senior officer and his Vargr. He needed Rum to steer this.

"You were my last chance," Rum said.

Jamal was better than nothing. Only nothing else was available. *What the hell?*

Rum gave the tightly made bed a pat and scooped up the other linen. "The USHP won't officially assign me to a Hamask. Not after—"

Jamal spoke over him. "Not after Chicago. That's where you were stationed last, right?"

Rum looked at him with surprise.

"I hear them whisper about it."

"Well, that's a great way to get to know me." Rum scrubbed at his forehead in frustration. "Listen to gossip."

"Well, at least it's something. You don't talk to me. Not about personal stuff."

"Yes I *do*," Rum seethed.

Jamal rolled his eyes. God, this was going so far sideways, they'd end up on the floor in a minute. "You talk about safe things. Not real things."

Rum seemed to know what he meant without him clarifying. As his Vargr, Rum talked all the time. "We were being monitored. I'm not discussin' private—"

Jamal talked over him again. "What the hell is with the accent?"

"It's real."

Jamal wanted more than a two-word explanation. The Southern twang had tremendous power over him. And a single "Sugar," said just right, had him chomping at the bit to pin Rum down with his teeth, or mouth, or hands—preferably while sucking hickeys on Rum's neck. It scared Jamal a little. He'd rather do raid drills complete with flash bangs and tear gas than lose control.

Though the mental image wasn't purely sexual, it still turned him into one massive, aching dick, which left no room for cognitive thought or patience. "You turn it off and on," Jamal enunciated each word.

"I'd hoped to distinguish my voice—"

"Hamask are trained to verify voice comparisons. Even as evidence in court cases."

"It seems to work to pull you—"

"It manipulates me, you mean."

"Lieutenant. I am your Vargr and senior officer. You will address me with respect and stop interrupting me, or I'll kick your puny ass." Rum smiled, making the intended mockery of his words.

Still Jamal snapped to attention, his eyes focusing on a point over Rum's shoulder. *Yes, this. Give me some kind of direction.* He knew Rum didn't want to be reassigned. He knew Rum used the accent to help him. What he didn't know was how to get them to the next point.

Rum groaned. "I hate that." He sighed and it rattled across his chest and his shoulders dropped. "At least you didn't say 'Sir, yes sir.'" Rum touched Jamal's arm, then stepped away. "I want this to be based on trust." When Jamal remained at attention, Rum gave him a shove and laughed. "Come on, I'll help you with the other bed."

I don't want the other goddamn bed. Jamal lost it.

Sometimes people describe anger as seeing red. It wasn't like that. Not really. And this was nothing like the blinding hate of the fury he had felt in the activation shack. He didn't go berserk. Yet a primal side of him shredded his humanity and instinct drove all else away.

Jamal came out of the state with Rum caressing his bare back under his shirt.

"Sugar, I'm trying my best to think unsexy thoughts. But it's obvious I'm not managing it."

Jamal blinked, tried to jerk his sight back to normal, but realized he could see the wall's texture over Rum's shoulder because he was so close to it.

"This is hot." Rum's voice. Breathy, slow, Southern sweet.

Hot? Like the tight body pressed between him and the wall. Like the burning, hard erection pressed into Jamal's thigh. He leaned, pressed, pushed in tighter, ran his bristled chin across Rum's head, felt the shiver so thoroughly he couldn't decide if it was his or Rum's.

"Please say you're coming out of it."

Rum's drawl shot heat down Jamal's spine. Jamal shifted his hips and pressed his own erection into Rum's, had to bend his knees a bit and pull Rum up to his toes to manage it.

Rum groaned and tilted his head back. "Or... you know... stay zoned. I'm good here."

Jamal chuckled and Rum stilled. Jamal scraped his teeth along Rum's neck. "I love your neck." He nipped one sharp little bite and groaned when he registered the smell of pheromones bursting from Rum's skin.

Jamal eased back a bit, giving Rum room to breathe. He didn't know what to say, so he said nothing.

"Which sense did you zone on?" Rum finally asked.

Jamal took another step back, felt every shift of fabric along his body as they separated. He leaned his forehead on top of Rum's head and breathed a moment with his eyes closed. He could hear their hearts jackhammering. Air wheezed out of him. He needed to even it back out. Not only did he not want to scare Rum, but he wanted to remember each moment of pleasure. Holy shit, being pressed against each other had felt spectacular.

"Or was it... protection? Did you feel some type of threat?"

He should have known that Rum would fall back on analyzing the situation to regain control. "Sixth sense."

"Huh?"

Jamal opened his eyes to look into Rum's. "I've read your research, that paper on Hamasks' sixth sense—sensing danger, the need to protect. It was good."

"When have you had time to—?"

"Six weeks of going to bed alone. Though some of your stuff I read before the whole...." Jamal shrugged, not wanting to say "psychotic episode." "Your reputation precedes you."

Rum paled. "Oh." Jamal could track the retreat of heat and there were no new pheromones. "So you've... you know my history?"

"Only the research and general stories. Except for this Chicago thing. I've heard base gossip on that."

"Oh," Rum said again.

Rum tried to step around Jamal. *Did I say something wrong?*

Jamal stopped him and lifted Rum's chin to make the smaller man look at him. Maybe mutual attraction wasn't enough to keep Rum by his side. "Maybe *you* need to ask for a new assignment. For your own safety."

"I can't." Rum shook his head. "I don't want to."

"I could have hurt you." Jamal made sure each word was stern. No, it wasn't what he wanted either, but Rum deserved someone better. "The threat? Is me. You aren't giving me anything to go by here. All I've got left is to respond to instinct."

"You wouldn't hurt me." Jamal felt Rum tighten his jaw, saw the little lines around his eyes as he narrowed them.

"I manhandle you into corners." Jamal stroked his thumb across Rum's chin.

"It's instinctual—"

"I could hurt you."

Rum hit Jamal's wrist hard with his fist. At the same time he planted his right foot behind Jamal's left leg, shoved him, and rode his body down with an elbow to his stomach and a knee between his legs. Jamal gasped at the pain, and before he could even gather his defenses, Rum had flipped him and yanked his elbow up tight behind his back, pinning him to the ground with his knee to Jamal's lower back. Jamal's left leg was pinned with Rum's boot.

"Shit." He twitched to test Rum's hold. He'd be able to get loose with sheer force, but not before Rum buried a knife between his ribs or into his spine.

Luckily he wasn't so inclined.

"You can hurt me. But I know you won't. I let you protect me. I trust you. Do you get that?" Rum jumped to his feet, all fluid grace and speed, and walked past Jamal, who snagged his ankle. With a powerful yank, he pulled Rum off his feet. Rum caught himself in a push-up, then quietly rolled to his back. A wolf exposing his belly.

Jamal realized that Rum was waiting for Jamal's next move. He didn't know whether to laugh or cuss the arrogant ass out. Jamal crawled up Rum's body, feeling his desire pound outward and the bonding heat flare inward. This wasn't how it was supposed to work… him stalking his wolf. But it felt right. It felt natural for him to lean over Rum. He wanted to be buried in Rum's heat and feel Rum quiver with need below him, around him.

Rum had closed his eyes and was whispering soft enough that only a Hamask would hear, "He thinks it's bonding heat."

Once Jamal was over Rum, he lowered his body until they barely touched, then slid back and forth. "It's not *just* the bonding heat."

Rum shook his head, kept his eyes closed. "You want a female Vargr."

"I didn't want someone who would control me."

"You wanted someone to control?" Rum opened his eyes, searching Jamal's face.

"I wanted to have a say."

Rum kept his hands passively to his sides. He swallowed and shook his head. "And I didn't give you a choice."

"Yes, you did." Jamal leaned the rest of the way down, keeping most of his weight on one forearm and the knee between Rum's legs. It felt like sinking into bliss. Heat mounted, all those perfect angles lining up to maximize the delight surging through him. *Oh, holy shit. This. Yes.* "When my touch was so low, you suggested I wait to shave."

"And that was code for…?"

"It meant you realized I could and would make my own decisions." He was proud of his ability to continue talking. "You continue to give me choices." He smiled at Rum, then frowned. *Oh yeah*, he reminded himself, *there's a point to make.* "I'm the one who didn't let you choose. With the whole show for the camera."

"Yep. I'm remembering that part just fine."

"Are you angry about it?"

"What indicated my anger? The tone of voice? The back-off-asshole body language?" Rum finally moved, rolling his hips up once, groaning.

"More the pissy attitude."

Rum socked him in the side. Jamal coughed and rolled off Rum, but since they were in the doorway to the second room, he didn't get far. Jamal stared up at the ceiling and used his close proximity to his Vargr to anchor himself as he scanned the area again, looking for a monitoring device or another Hamask listening. *Nothing.*

He leaned up on an elbow, looked down at Rum, and took a deep breath, better able to focus. "Rum, I want you to be my Vargr." He brushed the back of his knuckles across Rum's cheek.

"You're my Hamask." Rum lifted his head and captured Jamal's lips in a kiss.

The heady flavor was intense and the press of lips—so simple, so chaste—was unbearably erotic.

Rum mistook Jamal's stillness and pulled away. "Sorry. Not ready, understood. If you decide to act on this attraction—"

"Act on?" *What? Practically dry-humping you into the floor and the raging hard-on isn't an indication?*

Rum ignored the interruption. "We can keep it physical. No kissing. Whatever you're comfortable with—"

"Fuck no." Jamal had seen him work a room, remembered how he'd tricked the cadre into moving the target when they did that intel training op. Rum was always thinking about the angles, had plans in place to get them to their own rooms, to their first assignment. Yet, all of that seemed to break down with Jamal. Either he was too complicated for Rum to read—which Jamal knew was a very naive thought—or Rum was being honest with him. No bullshit, no tricks.

Rum tried to pull out from beneath Jamal. "Right. No. Exactly. Got that."

Jamal shook his head. "So, you want to fuck?"

"Sugar, I want to do a whole lot more than that. I'm good at it. Or so I've been told. And I ain't comfortable hiding who I am. All about being me."

"And here I was thinking you were the reserved type," Jamal whispered with a smirk.

"Ha, funny. But I'm trying to do right by you so when we're in separate relationships later—"

This time the slide into primal was palpable. Jamal felt it fold over him. He pinned Rum's legs down with one of his, captured Rum's wrists and held them above his head, and pulled them a bit to stretch over him. Jamal watched, almost detached from his actions, as he pushed into Rum's neck with his teeth. Not biting. Not really.

Rum's whole body bucked into Jamal's. "Oh smudge. Yes. Want that."

He forced himself to relax his grip on Rum's wrists so he wasn't hurting his Vargr. "Let's establish some rules. First, no talking about other relationships until I've fucked you good and plenty and convinced you I'm the best and last you'll ever have. Second, that kiss was amazing, and you better not be stingy in the sharing."

Rum made some noise as if to speak, and Jamal cut him off. "Shut up." Rum got very still. Jamal sighed. "Please be quiet so I can get this out without fucking us up even more." Rum bent his fingers and rubbed Jamal's hands that were holding him in position, to encourage Jamal to continue.

"Third. The accent is very"—he couldn't have controlled the shiver if he'd been made of granite—"hot. And—" He looked at Rum's ear, chin, and eyebrow. "I'm…. I don't want others to hear it. It's private. Okay?" When Rum used it in front of the cadre, it felt like his boyfriend was walking around in only a towel. This man was his, and nobody else deserved to see that.

"Okay."

"Okay." Jamal felt there should be a hell of a lot more, but his vocal cords had definitely reached their limit. Besides, he was way better with his hands. With his free hand, he tugged Rum's shirt free from the waistband and stroked his hand up Rum's warm, muscular chest, stretched taut with his arms above his head. Jamal spread his fingers, feeling the prickles of chest hair until he almost reached a nipple. With fingers together he slid them back down and squeezed Rum's hip, then, fingers spread again, back up. Then retreat. With the third pass, Rum was straining to push his nipple into contact with Jamal's hand, but Jamal avoided touching him again.

"Bully," Rum whispered, then kissed Jamal.

When he slid his tongue into Jamal's mouth, Jamal forgot what he was doing. He brushed roughly over Rum's pebble-hard nipple, and Rum shook and pressed up into Jamal's body. In that moment he forgot about strategy or plan of attack, forgot about teasing Rum to the point of quivering need. They'd passed quivering need. It had fallen off the tank as they busted into the gates of all-out-mindless bonding heat.

Their kisses were almost brutal: teeth and tongue and scrape of whisker. Jamal let go of Rum's wrists and they started fumbling with each other's belts and buttons—a race, bare skin the prize.

"I win," Jamal whispered as he firmly clasped Rum's cock.

Rum's hands stilled on Jamal's pants and he moaned, arching into the touch, exposing that beautiful neck. In Jamal's mind, the image of himself, buried to the nut inside Rum, flashed into existence. He was leaning over Rum's back and keeping the smaller man from moving by biting into his shoulder as he pounded his ass.

In breathy, stuttered words, Jamal whispered this to his Vargr as he fisted Rum's dick and tweaked sharply one of Rum's nipples.

"Smudge." Rum shoved Jamal away and squeezed the base of his cock to stop himself from coming.

"Hey, I was busy there."

"Who knew the silent one would be so chatty during sex?"

"Who knew soldier boy had a kink for talking dirty?" Of course Jamal wasn't normally so recalcitrant, and Rum was proving to be the soldier boy only when it suited his purposes.

Rum chuckled and pressed into Jamal. Jamal cupped his ass and pulled him into his body and inhaled the scent of his Vargr.

"How's about we take this to a bed?"

"Race you." And before he finished speaking, Jamal was up and running to the first bedroom, shucking his shirt and stepping out of his shoes.

Rum tackled him to the bed. "No fair. I had these pants down around my thighs."

They rolled a bit, trying to stay close and yet strip off the rest of the clothes. Jamal licked and nibbled and kissed Rum's mouth.

"Wait." Rum pressed into Jamal's chest.

Jamal groaned. "No."

Rum just kept talking, knowing Jamal would listen—which he did. "We need lube and… and maybe we should talk about this."

"No." Jamal said again, though he slowed his current activity of devouring Rum's chest.

"Are you avoiding—?"

"Yes."

"*Jamal.*"

And since it was the first time Rum had said his name in that breathy way, Jamal stopped. Okay, not completely. He still stroked, everywhere, across Rum's skin, and he still gave little random, rolling thrusts into Rum's body as they lay facing each other. But he did listen.

THERE WOULD never be a good time for this discussion, but if he waited, there might be a better time. Rum had listened to that bit of logic as they kissed and stripped clothes off each other. But he'd never been one to procrastinate scary things—that just made it worse. "We need to talk about positions," he said.

"My favorite is against the wall in the shower. Nothing better than quivering legs from shower sex," Jamal joked, but Rum knew he was listening. That he was trying to be patient.

"Policy says…." Rum felt Jamal's hands still on his bare hips. This gorgeous, naked, beautiful man was inches from him and he was talking. What was up with that? But Rum's earlier realization was correct. Jamal wasn't comfortable with the idea of being the bottom. "Well, actually the policy is pretty vague because of the whole don't-discuss-sex mind-set. But they expect the Vargr to be in charge—"

"To top. What do you expect?"

"I expect them to stay the *fuck* out of our sex life." Jamal lifted his eyebrows in surprise at Rum's cussing. "But you have a physical tomorrow."

Jamal's eyebrows drew together in confusion and unconsciously stroked Rum's hip. "Yeah?"

"A full exam." Rum let that sink in. "I actually like it best when I can do both. Top and bottom."

"In your past relationships?" Rum pinched Jamal's nipple with a sharp snap of his fingers. "Ow! Hey."

"No diversionary tactics, sugar. *We* decide what we want. But I don't want them messing this up because of some perceived notion of how a Hamra Pair should work."

"What if they're right, though?" Jamal closed his eyes and pulled his hand completely away.

"They're not." Rum threaded his fingers through Jamal's short hair and tugged. "Chicago? I was monitoring a recently bonded Hamra Pair. And I do mean recent. A pair of guys and the Hamask topped each time. Even had to—" Rum felt himself blush and couldn't continue.

Jamal totally pulled completely away. "You listened to them having *sex*?" He spit the last word out with disgust.

"As if. I made sure they weren't recorded any longer. Went so far as to file complaints and make sure my equipment 'failed.'" The demotion had been worth it. "But the Vargr working before I got there, Colonel Browning? He recorded their first time. I had a direct order to listen. I've never felt so…." Rum struggled to reveal how petty and small his actions were. "Jealous. I was jealous because they have this totally beautiful and trusting relationship. Well, okay. They were still working on the trust. The Hamask was…." He couldn't tell Jamal what had happened to Longwei when Longwei had still been with the USHP. It felt like one more violation of Bur and Longwei's privacy.

Instead he explained the potential fallout for them. "I know from the report that Browning tried to break them up the very next morning. Would have if either had been part of USHP. Just because their relationship didn't fit the standard roles."

"It was a civilian pair?"

"They are both ex-military, and the Citizen Safety Act allows you to be redrafted. Gives the military access to monitoring." Rum breathed out the tension that had gathered across his chest and swallowed down the discomfort. "I don't want them—not their policy, not their messed-up ideas—in our bed. And if we can convince them we've done this 'right'...."

"They're not monitoring us." Jamal placed his hand back on the slight curve of Rum's hip. "But with the physical...."

At Jamal's returned touch, Rum's tension and worry eased even further and his dick snapped to attention. He continued to run his fingers through Jamal's coarse hair. Jamal needed time to decide, perhaps come to terms with his decision.

Jamal's brown eyes showed his warmth and intelligence. He'd need a cut soon, but for now the tight curls added a bit of flair to his chiseled features. All that mocha skin stretched firm across the wide chest, dipping and contouring around his beautiful stomach. He had a lovely large cock, curved and uncut.

Images like this moment were what filled that echo in Rum's chest. Sleep was still a judgmental, flighty bastard, but the worry about his own mental splintering was gone.

"You're right," Jamal whispered. He pulled away and turned his back to Rum and lay on his side.

What the heck? Rum was confused until he realized Jamal had pulled one leg up to give Rum access to his ass.

"Okay."

That single word sounded so sacrificial lamb that Rum had to bite his lip from snapping back in anger. He'd show Jamal what kind of lover he really was.

Rum pulled Jamal's shoulder until he was lying on his back again, and he cupped Jamal's face. "*Sugar.*" He added a bit extra to the nickname as he pressed his body into Jamal's. "I'm goin' make this *so* good. Whatcha say? Good and plenty. And you'll know I'm your best and last. It's going to be wonderful. Trust me."

Rum kept things light for a while. Easing them both back into hot kisses and clever touches as he waited for Jamal to relax. He qualified for sainthood, he was so patient. But really, it felt right to be in Jamal's arms, to feel Jamal flex into his touch. Very right.

"Sugar," Rum breathed against a wet nipple, "goin' to make this good."

Rum pressed hot, openmouthed kisses down Jamal's belly, following the happy trail to right below his navel, then spent some time tonguing the twists of Jamal's belly button. Jamal jerked and laughed and then moaned. Rum ignored the pretty, glistening cock that bobbed a come-hither. Instead he left marks along the inner curve of each hipbone, alternating between bites and sucks. The doctors would have plenty of "bonding evidence" to include in their reports. Plus, bonus, Jamal liked it.

Jamal fisted the sheets and spread his legs open. He jerked up when Rum reached the sensitive skin that was half inner thigh and half asscheek.

"Rum," Jamal moaned. "Fucking suck me already."

Rum dropped his head to rest against Jamal's hip and groaned as a shiver ran across his shoulders. "Hush, sugar, or this'll be over too soon."

Jamal laughed. "Come on, Rum. You know you want to place—" Rum tried to stop him with a finger over his lips. "—that hot, wet mouth—" Rum tried to kiss him, but Jamal just talked against his mouth. "—over my huge cock." Rum shuddered and closed his eyes to try and concentrate. But that made it easier to imagine what Jamal was describing. "Draw me deep—"

"*Enough.*" Rum snapped Jamal's nipple again. "We can have a race to see who can get the other off by talking them to orgasm next time." Rum smiled, then shifted back down to kneel between Jamal's legs. "Now, where was I?"

"You were about to—"

Rum smacked Jamal's hip, and then he gripped Jamal's dick at the base and slid his mouth down in a single motion, almost to the hilt.

Jamal rolled his hips forward. "Holy fuck."

Rum licked and sucked and nibbled as he fisted Jamal's dick. He kept switching his actions. Never quite enough friction, never quite long enough of a stroke to allow Jamal to come.

"Rum. Come *on* already," Jamal yelled.

With a final lick across the slit, Rum laid his head on Jamal's thigh and continued to gently stroke him. "I've got an idea. Trust me?"

Chapter 8

So sexy. Jamal's Vargr was so sexy. And a complete sadist. Jamal had never ached so bad with the need to come. "Trust you," he said.

Rum climbed off the bed and went to turn on the lights—at some point evening had arrived—and to get lube, as he described what he wanted to do. Jamal knelt as he waited for Rum to lie on the bed. With gentle hands on Jamal's hips, Rum positioned Jamal so he was straddling Rum's lower stomach, facing his feet.

Rum leaned up on his elbows and kissed Jamal's back, handing him the lube. Jamal dribbled a bit on their cocks and smirked when Rum hissed as the cold liquid hit his sensitive skin. Jamal spread the lube over both cocks; then, with a slick palm he rolled Rum's balls a bit. Rum clutched Jamal's hips and his knees came up, legs spread. Jamal continued fondling his lover's balls, then slid a slick finger over Rum's perineum.

Rum gasped, and Jamal could smell all the lust Rum was leaking.

"God, that was close."

"How close?" Jamal said and slid the slicked finger down across the sensitive skin again.

Rum groaned and smacked Jamal's hip.

Rum had a nice dick. It was different from Jamal's but seemed to like the same things. There was this really great vein that ran down the side of his shaft. It reminded Jamal of Rum's forearms after they had finished PT. The veins would be raised to the surface, all sinewy strength.

Rum lifted Jamal up and slid him down Rum's hips a bit so that their cocks lined up next to each other. "This is all about making it feel good."

"I think we've got that part managed."

Rum scraped nails up Jamal's sides, which sent trembling heat through his body. Jamal moved forward a bit. Their cocks brushed against each other—*very good*—but when he leaned forward, tilting his pelvis down, adding friction and lifting his ass in the air? *Great.* And when Rum stroked his ass and massaged his pucker with slicked fingers? *Amazing.*

"Come if you can." Rum's words were more a challenge than permission. Jamal kept it slow at first as Rum massaged his perineum, but he stilled when Rum slid the first finger in.

"Oh, sugar, you are so tight." Rum turned the finger pressing outward in a circle, filling Jamal, stretching him.

Jamal placed his elbows against the bottom of Rum's raised thighs and let his body lean forward, his shoulders almost resting on the bed by Rum's feet. Rum's finger touched his prostate. Words could never convey how incredible it felt.

Keeping his finger pressed forward into Jamal's happy button, Rum encouraged him to continue his thrusts across Rum's pelvis.

Jamal leaned further down, gripped one of Rum's ankles for support and focused on the build of his own orgasm. The sweet, hot, intense pleasure of it all. As he came, he thrashed forward, realizing in a distant, surprised way that he was biting the back of Rum's calf. Then, with a sweet numbness, he collapsed forward, draped over Rum's legs.

Rum slid a second finger in, scissored his fingers, and rubbed Jamal's prostate. Jamal could do nothing more than twitch. "Oh, tight. That was so hot. You're so beautiful." Rum was still hard beneath him. "Sugar, oh sweet."

The man must have steel balls not to have come yet. Jamal kissed and licked the abused calf, then kissed gently up Rum's leg, over the knee, and back down the other leg.

Rum added a third finger. "Are you okay? Is this too much?"

"Feels good." Weird, really, this dormant part of him that had awakened, and each time Rum touched his prostate, it nickered with pleasure. Jamal slid back into Rum's stroke and was surprised as his cock twitched with interest. He wasn't likely to come again, though, not in the next little while. But it drew out the afterglow, sent little tremors through his body. "Want me on my back or stomach?"

"Neither."

Jamal looked over his shoulder at Rum. Rum's eyes were heavy with desire, his skin flushed with passion, and he rubbed in soothing circles while he slowly thrust, tapping that prostate like a homing beacon.

The view was spectacular—Jamal hadn't felt the need to use so many adjectives since college English.

"Turn around." Rum slid his fingers free and lay back, chest heaving with need.

Jamal quickly restraddled his lover's hips, and Rum clutched Jamal's knees as he tilted his head back with a groan.

"This way." Rum breathed, quivered. "You're in control."

Holy fucking incredible. Jamal knew instantly he was falling for his Vargr. He turned down touch, added a bit more lube to Rum's cock, and then raised and lowered himself onto Rum's dick. For a split second, he worried it wouldn't work—Rum was bigger than three fingers—but then, with a small *pop*, Rum slid past that first set of muscles.

Jamal stilled, overwhelmed at the beauty spread below him. Rum thrashed and moaned, and as Jamal started to lower himself the rest of the way, he sobbed. "Oh God. Please, sugar. Please."

That beautiful neck, rivulets of sweat, the defined muscles and gorgeous blue-green eyes. "So beautiful, Rum."

"I need to…. I can't." Rum jerked up off the bed and buried himself to the hilt. His body jackknifed as he came and came and came. He laid his head back on the pillow, only to arch his back as a second orgasm took him. "Oh God, yes."

Jamal carefully eased down, placing his weight on his forearms. Rum mumbled something but didn't move otherwise. Jamal felt a hollow ache as Rum slipped out of his body; then, easing to a hip, he draped himself over his Vargr's chest and closed his eyes. He sent all six senses out to scan the area, analyzing a thousand details and discarding them.

They were safe.

Jamal followed Rum into sleep.

Bur, Brad S., 572092-Longwei.
Page 20

THEY LET us go home. At least they did once they'd cleaned and stitched my arm. It was deep, so they had to do some fancy work on the triceps or biceps in question. I refused general anesthesia and opted for the localized equivalent. Longwei held me still and talked to me. They even had him gown up. He told me about growing up north of Chicago, his first name, even a bit about his time in the FBI.

Nephi Kimball, FBI Director of the Chicago office, had a bunch of questions for us. Nephi is Longwei's boss, a total sap who is convinced he's been gifted a superteam with us hooking up. He practically skipped out of the room when he was done.

We were under guard from the WREAC team, who staunchly refused to interact with us. They even flew in a Vargr toward the end of the six-plus hours of question monotony. He was this short, squinty-eyed, unpaired pinhead. I think USHP thought bringing him in would allow Longwei to bond and avoid another fury. I watched him case the room, and I knew he had everyone's measure. I may have growled at him and been a bit of a jerk in general. He set my teeth on edge.

It would have been nice if Longwei had ignored him, but instead, as soon as the guy is out of the room, he starts whispering to me about the guy's service record. You want to know what it is? Go look up Vargr Captain Ryan Walker. The only part that made any damn difference to me, at least then, was the knife story.

Longwei got one of the nurses to bring us sandwiches. You can burn through a crazy amount of calories bleeding all over an ambulance. Longwei is eating all the fruit off my plate when he tells me about Walker. "He was working tactical support on a rescue of a Hamra Pair. This was in New Tokyo. They hadn't been paired all that long, had activated together, and finished Advanced Field Training. But that's about it. New Tokyo was the pair's first assignment. They got captured by the local Chinese Triad." He has a nice voice, and listening to this silly story means I can stare at his mouth without it seeming too weird.

I continue to eat and listen.

He says, "A Pair taken? That hasn't happened, not in recent memory. While everyone had their thumbs up their ass, trying to figure out what to do, Walker decides to go in.

"Those Mafia guys were using a sound-distortion machine to screw with the Hamask. The right frequency, and our brains slam around like dumplings in rice soup."

He pops a grape into his mouth and then passes me a napkin while pointing at his chin. I wipe the mustard off my own chin. "They're in there, sawing on the Vargr, while the Hamask goes nuts trying to get loose."

"Physical and psychological torture."

It's what I'd do if I needed information desperately enough. Did do. You want to quibble about the Geneva convention, do it with the people who give the orders instead of the guy made to carry them out.

I am quiet for a while and then Longwei bumps me and I raise my eyes to meet his. "Then what?" I push my plate toward him. I'm not hungry anymore.

"Walker slips under the perimeter guards, kills the interrogators, frees the Hamask, and then leads the way while the Hamask carries the Vargr."

He nudges my water glass closer so I'll drink some more. I can't decide at this point if he's a mother hen normally or just when people are hurt. I hope it means he likes me well enough to put up with the politics of keeping me. "It's all classified, but they say he was in and out in under twenty minutes, not a single alarm raised."

I'm not buying this Chuck Norris story. "Killed them with what?"

"Knives. WREAC team comes in behind him to clean up and they find four men, all with daggers sticking skyward. You ever hear of Clive Cooper?"

"The man could teach SEALs how to war."

Longwei nods in agreement. "He collects all the knives, gives them back to Walker. And *poof*, they disappear."

I laugh and Longwei smiles. "Bullshit."

He shrugs. "Clive told me it was a blur, how quickly the man tucked them away."

I know that the enhanced flexibility and speed can vary between Vargr. For me the improvement to my reflexes mean I'm not a total klutz. Pop says I'd stop tripping over my own feet if I looked where I was going. To which I always reply, "I'd stop tripping if I'd just lay off the drugs." He knows I don't do drugs.

"Still, single Vargr in a Triad compound? I don't buy it. Who were the Hamra Pair?"

He scrunches his nose up in this over-the-top smirk, raises his eyebrows, and says, "Minophen and Jones."

I laugh my head off. Man, I need a release after my shitty day. And I'm thinking that's why he told me that story. Not to impress me—I couldn't give a fuck—but he's sharing: stories, food, space. Total mother hen.

Walker comes back at that point, tells the WREAC guard to take a break while he keeps watch, all polite, and then he closes the door with just the three of us in there. Yeah, total Chuck Norris tale. This small man isn't capable of killing.

He walks toward the bed they've got me propped up in, and Longwei stands and steps between us. Walker ducks his head, blushes and stammers a bit. He takes a solid step back and sits in a chair, his hands on each armrest. I guess to show he isn't a threat. Then he sighs and lifts his head. I can see strain in his eyes, like the clerk that has to work with the public for sixty hours a week and desperately wants to make it through the next *two minutes* without someone bitching.

Normally I poke that sore until it bleeds. I'm a total dick; don't let anyone tell you otherwise. It works for me. Keeps people where I want them—the hell away from me. This time the target is too easy. No challenge there. Doesn't mean I'm going to be polite.

We might exchange a greeting, I don't remember. Walker says, "I'm heading back to base. I'm sure they'll have me back in a few days." He looks toward the door and then lowers his voice to a whisper. "They're letting you go home." He looks specifically to Longwei, who has his arms crossed and is leaning back against the bed. "You'll be monitored. They'll be looking to see if you've bonded."

"Why would the FBI give a fuck about our personal lives?"

Walker keeps his eyes on Longwei for another minute before turning and addressing me. "No, USHP. The Citizen Safety Act would allow them to pull him back in."

Longwei pales and unwraps his arms so he can place a hand on mine. He's got really great hands. "I'm not going back."

Like Walker said, he would go back to prison or solitary. It is obvious that Longwei is even more scared than he'd been in the ambulance. Whatever the USHP means to the man, it's bad.

Walker stands and clears his face, narrows his eyes, and he tilts his head to the side. At this point I'm thinking the Vargr patches on his uniform are fake. He's reading Longwei like a Hamask. Which is ridiculous; he's way too small to be a bear.

"I'm sorry you don't have more time." He looks back to me. "Looks like you've proven your dissertation, Dr. Bur. You can still make this work."

Then he pivots and leaves the room.

"Good fucking riddance." I'm not quiet when I speak. Vargr or Hamask, he must hear me.

I thread my fingers through Longwei's, use it to pull him close. "The mouse is right. If we want to make this a permanent pairing, we need to bond before the Army gets a chance to meddle."

"We both want that." Longwei starts unhooking me from the monitors. If we leave against doctor orders, I'm giving my man serious brownie points. He gets a bandage and removes my IV. Super gentle. Gives me my shoes.

"Not worried we won't work out later? I mean, like if I'm a slob or snore or whatever?"

He slides his big hands around my neck and back to cradle my head. "I think you're a good man. Deep down."

"Deep, deep down."

He snorts and his eyes get all soft like I've said this really adorable thing. "You'll let me lead."

I baa like a sheep. Which, being a wolf, super ironic. He smiles for real, but I can see hesitation. I'm actually looking, actually trying to fully see. Maybe this is something I shouldn't rush for once. "I'm good with you leading."

"The rest—" He takes a deep breath. "—we can figure out. It'll be like having sex on a first date."

I've never done that. *What?* Don't judge. It's hard to convince strangers to see past the mouthy git to the sexy potential with just one date.

"So, we'd be dating? Try and see if it works?"

"Civilian pairs aren't required to bond, but with my fury, the military could use that to pull me back in. So we'll give them what they expect."

"Meanwhile, getting what we want. I like the way you think."

When he kisses me, I can taste him. I like his unique flavor. It reminds me of the clean taste of fresh mint picked from the garden back home; warm, good. I like how he tips my head to get the angle he wants, caresses my cheek and neck at the same time. Like my whole head is being assaulted with sensation. He slows his roll, pulls back to soft presses to the edge of my mouth.

"You're a good kisser."

Which is a sweet thing for him to say. A good response would be "you too" or "easy to be good when you're with a talented partner."

Have I mentioned I'm an asshole?

"Well, you could use a few lessons." I open my eyes as he drops his hands to his sides. With his warmth gone, I'm light-headed from the drop in temperature. Like that feeling you get when you lift your long hair off your sweaty neck? Don't know that feeling? Ask your mother.

He must be pissed. My heart even kicks up, and I reach out and grasp his shirt to keep him from storming off. Oh, shit. I fucked it up already.

He laughs. "I can tell you like it, but feel free to give me lessons."

"How about now? Now good?" I swing my legs off the edge of the bed and pull him between my thighs. I want him to feel how much I like his kisses, not rely on the smell of my desire, the sound of my elevated pulse, the visual cues of my pupils. I swipe my tongue into his mouth and just go for it. Showing him what I like, figuring out what he likes, finding new things to like.

Longwei pulls back suddenly and pulls the blanket to cover my lap as the door swings open. "Dr. Bur, we'll be sending you home."

I nod at the nurse as she hands me a clipboard with papers to sign. She starts grousing about my IV being out. We both ignore her.

I say to Longwei, "Do you live close?"

Chapter 9

GENERAL KHAN watched Walker and Zumati enter the testing room.

They knew they had an audience—that was a given with this specific room. Yet, he wouldn't be surprised if they communicated telepathically and knew the head of Joint Operations, South American Theater, was sitting next to Khan.

Major General Amalie Franke had used the excuse of important intelligence that needed to be given in person to come and observe their main attraction. He scanned the room of cadre, medical experts, Sanderson from Medical, and the Chakosky-Knox pair. The room might have been even fuller if not for the recording device that would allow others to observe later.

Khan knew the notoriety was only partially due to the miraculous recovery of Zumati from his berserker state. The stunt with Chakosky had become base legend and was making the rounds through Special Operations. He'd received requests from two black ops groups within the military to send them complete records on the Walker-Zumati Hamra Pair, and they were up for it. Walker alone, now that he had his head out of his ass, was an excellent candidate for covert missions. Add the powerhouse that Zumati was under Walker's guidance and Khan was surprised he hadn't gotten more requests.

He'd already told Special Operations Command that he wanted the pair for his Valhalla program. Perhaps that was why Franke was in attendance; she wanted to take back her own opinion of the pair to SOCOM.

He still felt that Valhalla would be a better fit, at least for Walker. That overeager, enthusiastic advocate for Hamrammr rights that Khan had met his first day, that man would make Valhalla possible. The program would be Khan's crowning achievement. He could retire in a few years knowing he left behind a powerful legacy.

Zumati was a different puzzle. Khan wasn't seeing the same passion on that end. He doubted they'd want to be reassigned to different Hamras now, so if he wanted Walker, he would need to convince Zumati.

If Walker accepted one of the black offers, Khan would have to start looking all over again. Which was why Khan might have agreed to throwing a wrench in today's testing. Plausible deniability was a prerequisite of much of his job.

Both Walker and Zumati wore the required Army combat uniform, and Khan would put good money on both being recently ironed. He was glad to see them not only on their best behavior but not exhausted or trying to sneak a senior officer out of the sewers.

They stood shoulder to shoulder inside the room, and both glanced at the mirror. Then Walker took Zumati's wrist to gain his attention and whispered, "I just remembered, I borrowed a book from Lisa." The microphone picked up his every word.

Zumati simply shook his head. "Not one, ten."

"Seriously?"

Was there something between Lisa Naylor and Walker? The female Vargr was technically paired with Travers, but both were adamant they were not bonded. She hadn't been active as long as Walker, but perhaps she was starting to have similar issues with paranoia. Khan would assign a detail to keep an eye on her and require a weekly report on her progress with Travers.

"At least. Plus you have two of her video files," Zumati said.

"Huh." Walker turned toward Zumati, leaning a hip against the nearest wall. "Well, before anyone else gets here, let's talk strategy."

Zumati laughed, a short burst of mirth, and then his mouth settled into a smirk. "I'm not fussed. It'll be tight."

Walker narrowed his eyes and let go of Zumati's wrist. "I got a case of beer back home."

So much for best behavior. General Khan felt Franke turn toward him. He ignored her.

Zumati, still smirking, raised his eyebrows. "How'd you get beer on a dry base?"

"Technically, alcohol isn't prohibited or even illegal. They just don't sell it on base. Army regulations six hundred dash eight five addendum."

"Sure. And the beer?"

"Knox traded it for a bottle of my sake."

Behind the general, both Knox and Chakosky scraped their chairs back and left. Khan ignored them. Every partnership had issues, and if they needed to talk theirs out, they damn well better do it outside of Franke's view.

Walker checked his watch and then tapped against Zumati's chest. A double tap of fingers, not exactly what Khan would call affectionate, though Walker looked with warm eyes at Zumati. Neither seemed particularly interested in the obvious one-way glass wall.

"You were right about Sanderson's personal aide."

"Just base gossip." Zumati rolled his shoulders back.

"Yes, but foreign vid calls would cut seriously into Med's already tight budget." When Sanderson shot to his feet, Khan groaned. They were being played. He waited for Sanderson to leave the room and then pulled up the observation room's control on his smartwatch.

"Walker and Zumati, Major Browning will be in shortly to conduct the testing." Both men snapped a proper salute to their reflections. "As you were."

Walker nudged Zumati as Browning entered the room. "Head of training himself instead of a testing cadre. Told you."

"Only partially right. Seven, and Khan isn't the most senior."

They saluted Browning as he entered the room and then sat as indicated next to each other on one side of a conference table. While they got situated, Khan scanned the room. Counting himself, there were seven people. *Shit. Naw, they didn't know. They were guessing.* The testing room had sound-dampening walls.

Browning was enjoying being the Officer in Charge. The man had been right about the Chakosky training plan, that Walker-Zumati would easily complete the task. Being good at his job didn't mean Khan had to like him. Khan still felt he needed to take a pumice stone to his nerves to smooth out the rough edges each time he met with Browning.

"You've both met all physical fitness requirements. Yesterday's written was acceptable as well. Today will be the practical portion of the exam."

Walker addressed Zumati. "Lieutenant Zumati, I believe what Major Browning means is that the perfect score on the written was impressive."

Though they sat with proper posture, Walker seemed to radiate smug defiance.

"Lieutenant Walker," Browning warned.

"Sir, yes sir."

Browning sighed. He placed a kit on the table as well as his field tablet. "You'll need to identify each item in the case as well as the sounds on the files I'll play for you. Any questions?"

Walker opened his mouth, and Zumati grabbed his wrist, touching him for the first time.

Zumati said, "No."

Which reassured Khan. It reminded him that for a Hamask to reach past the type of sound dampeners in the testing room, they would need extensive skin-to-skin contact—both hands, maybe on the Vargr's neck—and complete silence. Zumati hadn't touched Walker at all until then, and Walker had yakked the whole time.

"Let's begin."

The digital wall displayed each item to be identified as Zumati picked each piece out of the container. They could still see the testing room, but the wall also displayed stats, background information on Zumati's record, and details of the item he was currently evaluating. It was for ease in later study but made the whole event look and feel like a sports match. Only the numbered jerseys and electrolyte stations were missing. Besides identifying the eighteen specimens, he also found a strand of hair, two separate prints—one of which he said was Browning's—and the type of packaging of each specimen.

Throughout all of this, Walker sat separate and still in his chair. Occasionally he'd make inane small talk with Zumati. Khan had seen a few tests processed, both live and as later case studies. Usually the pair underwent simultaneous tests. The Hamask would reach out and touch the Vargr whenever the Hamask needed to extend a sense. Occasionally they would discuss the answer before giving it to the testing cadre. Zumati only spoke to identify each item and had yet to touch Walker again.

Once the container was empty, Zumati ran his hands around the inside of the box. Walker spoke now, but softer. "I'm not worried about that. You're passing with flying colors. Let's just do the testing."

Khan glanced at Franke for the first time. She sat with her legs tucked demurely beneath her seat. He'd felt her shift a few times, but she was keeping her expression neutral.

Zumati glanced briefly at Walker, then closed the container and set it aside. He pulled Browning's tablet toward him and pressed the screen to play the first audio clip. Khan couldn't hear a thing, but Zumati immediately shook his head and shoved the tablet back toward Browning.

"Woodpecker, walnut trees, park in New York. Training files? Where's the challenge in that?"

Walker placed his clasped hands on top of the table and glared at Browning. "What's going on, sir?"

Browning didn't respond to either man but instead touched the screen a few times to supposedly bring up an additional file.

"Sir, you're lying. You didn't start a file, you were only acting like you did," Zumati said.

"Perhaps it's too low for—"

"No."

Browning rolled his eyes. "Whatever. Try this one."

"Again, I'll ask, what's going on?" Walker spoke through clenched teeth.

"What, we're supposed to believe the test results when you used to facilitate these exams? With your eidetic memory, how do we know Zumati isn't parroting what you've trained him to say?"

"Don't piss on my leg and tell me it's rainin'. Y'all coulda done a field test."

Walker hadn't started yelling yet, but it was a near thing. Instead of reminding Walker of the chain of command, Browning continued to slouch insolently in his chair, one hand tapping the screen on the field tablet to bring up a new file.

Walker wasn't done with his suggestions. "Take us into the city, pick random stuff off the ground, or ask him to listen to diners in a restaurant."

Browning shifted in his seat. When he lifted his eyes to look Zumati straight in the eye, it was with a burning glare that startled Khan. Shit, what was going on? Did Browning mean to push Zumati into another rage?

Khan reached for his smartwatch but paused when he saw movement from the room. Zumati stood and pushed Walker and his chair back a foot. Before Browning could question his actions, Zumati picked the container back up, flipped it over and smashed its corner against the exam table. It was a ballistic-grade field box and it came apart like a piñata. The corner of the desk crumpled like tinfoil.

Khan and the soldiers around him were immediately on their feet. He used his watch to order Med and MPs on site. Franke had pulled out a gun and headed to the door.

"Wait, wait!"

This was from Walker, who stepped toward the one-way wall with his hands raised.

Zumati pulled something from the field box and held it up for Browning and the video recorders to see. It was a soundboard to a white noise machine. Khan had seen them out in the field, and Intel said they sold like hotcakes on the black market. Anti-Hamask gear. Khan brought up the comms with the incoming guards. "Hold at the doors."

Walker turned toward Zumati. "Are they holding?"

Zumati kept his eyes on Browning. "Is this standard testing? To use a noise device to mess with my head?"

"What do you think?"

Walker stepped behind Zumati and placed his bare hand on Zumati's neck. "It doesn't matter." He rubbed across the Hamask's head. It should have been patronizing or a bit like patting the head of a dog, yet Walker's eyes and Zumati's shift in shoulders made it look flirtatious or sexy. Way more intimate than Khan felt comfortable looking at.

Walker crossed his arms and glared at Browning. "Lieutenant Zumati, to complete your sensory testing, please identify the seven people in the viewing room."

"It's eight now. I think Sanderson came back in. There are also four guards and two medics outside the door."

"Can you tell Colonel Browning how you deciphered the number and specialty of the men outside the door?"

"Six heartbeats, and the medics smell different than the MPs. One of them is named Rogers."

Khan had never even heard of a Hamask who could smell through a closed door, let alone distinguish the number of heartbeats. Their heartbeats would be elevated from the hustle to get to the testing room, adrenaline running high, knowing they were about to face a fully powered Hamask with rage issues.

Franke holstered her gun, and the room went from being filled with silent observers to them having too much to say.

Walker tilted his head and looked at Zumati. "Khan isn't the senior officer?"

"No. I don't have a name. Female. I heard her heels, and she's armed. They were whispering about Dios Provee before we came into the room."

Holy fuck. Khan rubbed across his forehead and down over his eyes, trying to suppress the groan he felt. The wrench meant to derail the

Hamra Pair had made them shine like the fucking Maltese Falcon. How the hell was he supposed to diminish something like this?

"I want them," Franke said.

Of course she did.

Chapter 10

Three months later

JAMAL WOKE as Rum pressed his cool body back into Jamal's heat.

Rum must have gotten up to use the bathroom. Three months ago, when they'd started living together, Jamal woke with each shift of Rum's body. His eyes would pop open when someone walked past outside. It took a while to develop a trust of his perimeter. Thankfully they didn't have to switch bases when they were assigned to Franke's detail. It would have meant a whole new base rhythm to adjust to. It was comforting to open their front door to their home and only smell the two of them, know no one had been there except the cleaning crew each time they were out on assignment. Out in the field, he could sleep if Rum was awake watching over him. But here it was different.

Jamal squeezed Rum's hip to pull the man further against his front. He pressed his nose into Rum's shoulder and imagined all the pale skin beneath his dark hand. The sight was quite hypnotizing. Rum gave a pleased sigh, shifted to a deeper relaxation, and went back to sleep. Jamal let himself drowse too. It was their morning off, and they needed plenty of rest for the mission later.

He rolled his shoulder to bring the sheet higher. The sheets were this earthy yellow color and smelled like Rum—the man, not the liquor. They were building a home together, which was both awesome and disconcerting at the same time. Like they had skipped forward over too many important steps.

Rum had bought the 1600-thread-count sheets last month in Spain. Jamal's foster brother Jaxx had shipped the quilt from Grandma Karen as a gift for completing his HAVOC training. It was a summer weight in blue and green interlocking rings. They had unpacked, and with the morning light shining around the dark curtains, Jamal could see the outline of Rum's vids. They were in two tall bookcases but also left around the house: on top of the television, the desk by their bed, even the kitchen counter. Jamal had never owned a physical vid, always stored them online.

As he put the last one on the shelf, Rum had explained. "Some of these are collector's editions, but mostly movies go out of fashion. They take them off the streaming sites, and I want to be able to watch them. Plus, the Blu-ray quality is better than streaming over the military's limited bandwidth."

Their relationship felt a bit like those vids—scattered.

"Aren't you going to go back to sleep?" In the morning, Rum's voice sounded like smoked molasses.

"Just thinking." Jamal pressed a kiss into Rum's shoulder. "Need to get up and do my yoga and go for a run, or I'll be sore later."

Rum snorted. "Whatever, Hamask. You'll be as right as rain with your superhealing."

"That last parachute jump still has my shoulder twinging."

Rum rolled over to face Jamal and started to massage his shoulder, a sleepy half caress. Jamal was glad Rum had left the hall light on. Other housing had premium units that gave you the option to use voice commands to turn on lights and appliances. You could get the shower warmed up before stepping in. Hamra Pairs could request it, but it wasn't standard. The electronic noise bothered most Hamask, and Rum didn't want the extra chance to be monitored.

"You did smack into that tree pretty hard. Might have broken your arm if you weren't all souped-up." Rum slid his hand down the front of Jamal's chest, his whole hand brushing down Jamal's pec, over his nipple. Then Rum turned the hand as he slid it over Jamal's stomach and stopped at his waist. Jamal's lover was fully awake and focused on him. It had been a few days, what with travel, tactical training with WREAC Team 7, and verbal reports to Franke. Last night they'd stripped out of their clothes and fallen into bed, exhausted. In two hours they needed to head toward Command.

"Instead of yoga and a run…." Rum slid even lower to grip Jamal's half-hard dick. He leaned forward to kiss Jamal.

Jamal slid his hands over each pert cheek of Rum's ass and gripped and pulled Rum into his body, loving the way Rum twitched and gasped. He trailed kisses down the side of Rum's face and sucked the blood rushing beneath his skin to the surface of his neck, liking this warm and lazy thrust to get them there. It always made Jamal feel like they had all the time in the world. He got to touch so much of Rum's responsive skin. The bed and blankets around them isolated them, created a cocoon, a place that belonged to only them. Plus that slow-building burn in his balls, easily among the top five best things in life.

Jamal slid his fingertips down Rum's crack to get him thrashing. Then Rum was flinging back the covers and reaching for the bottle of lube.

"Come back. This was working just fine."

"Let me get myself ready."

Rum liked being watched. If Jamal wanted to get his lust really flowing, he'd walk into the bathroom while Rum was in the shower, which seemed like a contradiction to the rest of his vigilant, let's-not-be-watched mind-set. Perhaps it was just Jamal watching that got Rum excited. Hell, Jamal was the one with the waterfall fantasy, so no complaints that it turned them both on.

Rum slicked up his fingers and lay on his side, one leg pulled up to reach behind himself. Jamal made sure to stroke his knee and say, "You are so sexy, Rum."

Jamal pulled him to the center of the bed and climbed over Rum so they were both on their sides. Jamal stroked Rum's chest, and when Rum said, "Okay, ready," Jamal lined himself up and pushed in to Rum's tight heat.

"Good?" Rum asked.

"Yes, very." Jamal reached for Rum's dick, but Rum was already fisting himself, so Jamal's hand changed course to play with Rum's nipples.

Sometimes, when Jamal's orgasm was particularly explosive, his senses would blink off. Tingles would build down his spine, there would be a churning heat at the base of his dick, all his muscles would clench, and then… off. He continued to move, or perhaps at least shudder, but his consciousness of such things vanished.

Rum bucked against him and shouted his name. It felt good, easing out of Rum's body, becoming aware again of the sweat that clung to their bodies, the intoxicating scent of semen, watching Rum's shoulders heave with each breath, seeing him with such a satisfied grin on his face. *Damn good.* Yet….

He couldn't vocalize the idea, what steps were missing, especially not after having his brains blown out his dick with that orgasm.

"We have time for a shower," Jamal said, "before we have to get ready."

"We're ready." Rum's mind was clearly someplace other than the sticky sheets.

"But?" Jamal sat up against the headboard and reached for the tissues to pass them to Rum.

"Huh?" Rum said.

"We're ready *but*? Sounded like you had something to say. Nervous?"

"Of course. A bit." Jamal waited for Rum to continue. "We're working with two other pairs." Usually a Hamra Pair was sent out with a support team of WREAC troops or did patrols on their own. Two weeks ago they'd worked an even bigger training mission with two squads of Army Rangers.

They hadn't been given particulars yet, but if they had three pairs, it had to be important. "It's a big operation," Jamal said.

"It's tight. The three sets are needed."

"But?"

Rum sighed. "I want to get in, accomplish our mission and get back. I don't want to be scrutinized."

With Rum's colorful record and Jamal being the only known Hamask to recover from a fury, they were still getting more than their share of attention. Jamal's family—his Grandma Karen and two foster brothers—had released his miraculous recovery to the press. For once, people's talk about Hamrammr didn't involve the Cairo massacre. There was sure to be a rise in recruitment. A major news feed had done an extensive report on all the USHP's positive work against terrorist groups like Dios Provee and the Liberation Force. The networks and web channels had picked up the story. Maybe foreign relations with Egypt and countries that disliked the US Hamrammr Program would improve. Pictures hadn't circulated, due to a very determined General Franke squashing it.

Jamal figured scrutiny would continue to be part of their life. People whispered about them—about Chakosky and the sewer, and the testing fiasco—but thankfully Rum didn't ask Jamal what the gossip was. If people didn't want them to know, they could have waited until Jamal and Rum were off the base. Ultimately people would think what they wanted.

Jamal swung his legs off the bed. "We've got this." He smacked Rum's ass and walked naked to the shower.

Rum was quick to follow.

RUM KNEW Jamal was listening. If he was close enough, the white-noise generators wouldn't deter him. Rum also knew that Jamal trusted him to fill him in with all the information. Procedure be damned. They were a team.

A team that was about to go on a major covert operation. They'd worked hard for the last several months on training missions with Franke's Black Ops group—so black it didn't have a code name. Two of the ops had been in Europe, one in South America. They were ready for this. It didn't matter that Sanderson had convinced Franke that Jamal still needed monitoring by a medical professional to prevent further fury issues. It just meant that each time they returned to America, they were based out of HAVOC. For once Rum had decided not to dig deeper on Sanderson's agenda. It was nice being able to keep the same housing.

Rum sat around an oval conference table, at the place dictated by his rank and Vargr status, and listened to the mission briefing which included a HoloPoint presentation.

"You will have your Hamask prepped and geared at 0200," Lieutenant Colonel Gelbrit said.

Like they were a piece of equipment. Under his breath, Rum whispered, "*I'll* have you ready? Idiots." Jamal would hear, and it gave Rum comfort that Jamal would know he didn't support this bull.

"Was there something you wanted to ask, *Lieutenant* Walker?"

General Franke was fond of emphasizing his rank. They were all aware that Rum had once been a captain.

"No, ma'am," Rum said.

The office door opened, and Jamal led the other two Hamask into the room. Rum leaned back in his chair and slowed the world down enough to enjoy his man's entrance. Just looking at Jamal raised Rum's heartbeat and body temperature. His blood rushed through his veins. Even now, surrounded by fellow officers, his body reacted as if he had plenty of time to suck in the desire and hoard it like a dragon's treasure. He could even imagine pulling Jamal across the table, stripping him of each piece of clothing to reveal more and more of his rich, deep brown skin. Then Rum would wrap himself around Jamal, curving against his hip bone, pressing his hard, hot cock into Jamal's flesh, inhaling the scent of his mate.

To rein in his sudden slide into day-porning, Rum assessed the other two Hamask. He noted the differences in their body language and rankings. Made mental snapshots that, if asked, he could use to identify them from files or a crowded room. Then he turned to evaluate the team leader doing the field prep.

"You were ordered to remain outside until we finished with the briefing," Captain Clive Cooper said.

Rum liked him. He'd originally met Cooper back in New Tokyo. The man had a good history with Special Operations. After a couple of years with the Rangers, he'd processed through HAVOC and joined a WREAC team. Yet, Rum didn't read that off the surface of the man. Cooper knew how to keep his tells quiet.

"Right. And you're finished," Jamal said. He picked up the white-noise generator off the middle of the table and shut it off. With a derisive snort, he passed it to its owner, probably able to tell who it belonged to from the smell. Then Jamal sat at the table across from Rum.

The other two Hamask, unsure of their reception, stood behind their Vargr's chairs.

Six months of training and Rum was proud of the difference in Jamal. Jamal was more confident, had a deeper knowledge of HAVOC history, and had mellowed about regulations.

Jamal and Rum were one pair. Tony Travers, the Iowa farm boy, and his female Vargr, Lisa Naylor, were the second pair. The last pair was one of the most senior pairs still active in the field: Milo Otis and his Vargr, Sai "Scott" Karmine.

Before Major General Franke or Captain Cooper could order them from the room, Jamal pulled a purple box out of his jumpsuit's chest pocket and tossed it across the table. "Got you something."

It slid across the table and stopped in front of Rum. Rum looked up from the box of candy at Jamal. Jamal smirked, sexy and devilish.

Rum felt the heat rush to his cheeks and tightened his jaw. His blood thundered south again, and he felt his whole body flush with desire. The 3-D, Technicolor image of Jamal and him in the shower that morning focused in his head: Rum had pressed chest forward into the tile as Jamal bit into his neck while sliding hilt-deep into Rum. He couldn't quite contain the shudder and instead of picking up the candy, reached up and rubbed his neck where the love bite was. "Thanks, sugar." Rum knew the single word would have Jamal jonesing, but turnabout was fair play.

Jamal nodded, then turned his attention to the map still displayed on the screen, and Rum realized what Jamal had just done. Rum must be pumping out enough pheromones to turn on the whole USHP. The other Hamask would not miss it. Jamal was staking his claim. Yes, but more than that, there had been no more invasive physicals or probing into their bond. It didn't hurt to emphasize that they were officially bonded, a Hamra Pair. Jamal was letting them know what kind of a relationship they had. That they were bonded.

A surge of pride settled in Rum's chest. Looked like he'd taught Jamal more than just how to handle knives.

The Hamask present would get it and would pass it on to their Vargr, but in case they didn't, Rum would do some of his own maneuvering. He might have resolved to play by the rules after Chakosky, but that didn't mean he was their puppet.

Franke was working into quite the rant, but Rum stopped her. "General, I think Naylor and Travers would be better suited to take the electronics building. Naylor is excellent with computers."

Though Rum's statement was true, Travers was more concerned about Lisa's ability to keep up. She was physically fit but not very advanced, and Travers was overly protective of her. He needed his head in the game if he was going through that front gate.

Travers shifted and crossed his arms, and Rum got the distinct impression that he said something. Jamal nodded. Whatever it was, Travers didn't want his Vargr, Lisa, to hear. Most likely it was a good thing if no one was protesting, so Rum continued.

"I would, however, leave Scott and Milo on the sentry position coming up the rear. They are both excellent marksmen, and Milo can make the run." Rum knew the second pair better and felt comfortable using their first names.

Gelbrit snorted. "Oh, and of course we'll have to put you and Zumati at point? Is that what this is all about?" Gelbrit was in charge of Cooper's WREAC team, which would provide support for the operation.

"Walker and I can do anything you send us to do." Jamal leaned back, resting his arms on the sides of the chair, his body language open, dismissive.

"But we don't want point," Rum said.

"Send the WREAC unit in that way. The tunnels would be a better idea for us," Jamal said.

Rum watched Cooper's expression and was pleased to see a smug agreement there. The WREAC team leader had probably suggested it to Gelbrit himself.

Jamal stood and picked up a set of tunnel plans from a side table, rolled it out on the conference table. "Good thing I can see in the dark."

While he worked to tack the corners, Rum finally picked up the box of candy. He gave it a shake. "Anyone want some Good & Plenty?"

Chapter 11

THE HOUSE had been built during the first Russian Prohibition by the local jihadists to smuggle information and people into the area. If the captors did know of the tunnels, they weren't guarding them. Intelligence had decided that they didn't know, which gave Jamal and Rum a perfect way in.

The operation required a HALO jump and extraction in a UH-90 Ghost Chinook, which they'd pick up in New Tokyo. They had been given mission parameters but not their target—that would happen in New Tokyo too.

Rum should have spent the eight-hour flight sleeping. Sleep had gotten easier. Jamal would pin him to the bed and practically purr in Rum's ear. Rum would fall asleep, quickly and easily, but there was no place to pin him among the WREAC team and cargo.

All Rum could do was think. He'd sorted through all the details he did have and narrowed their target down to one. Eight months ago, Vargr Wickham Ekewaka Ieti was classified as a prisoner of war. Rum had gone through HAVOC activation with Wick.

There were two reasons it might not be Wick; first, he was a highly trained and experienced assassin with Vargr reflexes. Wick wouldn't let just anyone hold him. Yet Gelbrit's intel—location, number of guards, not knowing about the tunnels—all added up to amateur mercenaries. Second, Intel was unsure if there was a leak or a Hamask on the inside. The Hamask in question would need to be Wick's bondmate, otherwise Wick would have slipped that noose long ago. They could be holding something over Wick's head, though Rum couldn't think of anything that would motivate the Vargr into trusting his captors.

Since the botched training mission, Rum was working on trusting his team, working as a pair; Old Rum would have formed his own plan and asked for forgiveness afterward. But any punishment would now affect Jamal as well, and he was back on track to promote through the armed forces. New Rum would keep his nose clean and work his ass off to make this partnership good for Jamal. They could monitor them in the field all they wanted if it meant they left them alone otherwise.

So Rum told Jamal about the possible Hamask on the inside. Jamal nodded. He was practicing palming knives while they sat in the belly of the very large metal can that was their air transport.

"We'll look for one. I think we can sense each other." By "we" Jamal meant he and the other two Hamask assigned to this op. "Let's talk about the tunnels."

"Trying to distract me?"

"You're pretty keyed up."

They both knew why. This was important.

"I took a tour of the Cu Chi, the tunnels the Vietcong used during the Vietnam War. There's sections they've converted for tourists." Jamal slid the knife away while he pulled out another. "Cleaner than the sewers back at the base, but smaller. I don't have any issues with small places. Do we know if the hostage does? Can we extract from that point?"

"As a plan B? Depends on how small. Wick is not a small man. Bigger than Cooper." Rum nodded toward the WREAC team leader.

Jamal turned to look at Rum. "Wick?"

There was a lot of meaning in that simple question. How did he know the target's name, let alone know him on a personal level. "We're from the same activation group."

"You can't know it's him," Lisa Naylor said.

"Yet I do."

"Why do you believe the target is Vargr Wickham Ieti?" Milo had worked with Rum enough to know how to ask good questions. His Vargr, Scott Karmine, was sound asleep with his head on Milo's shoulder.

Sometimes it was hard for Rum to explain how his mind worked, even to other Vargr. They at least understood the T1 speed on terabit steroids that his brain processed at, but he had focused on personnel rather than the chemicals needed to blow up a building or the best ways to kill based on human anatomy lessons. Other Vargr had specialized in chemical warfare and assassination. Rum had specialized in sociology, human communication, even anthropology. Besides the two other Hamra Pairs, they were flying with WREAC Team 6. He could tell the stats, status, and preferred sexual positions of everyone on this flight. Okay, that was a ridiculously dramatic exaggeration—only half of the people here. The rest he could guess about at a high accuracy.

To answer Milo's question, Rum ticked his points off on his fingers. "They refused to let Wick go at the end of his tour, citing the Citizen Safety Act. He was then stationed at Kamadel Outpost as a hospital corpsman, temporarily paired with Hamask Jordan."

"May God watch over him," Tony said, his voice hushed with reverence. One of the WREAC team members crossed himself, as if warding off the dead.

"Ieti was placed on the missing-in-action list. His family contacted me about four months ago when they were once again blown off by the HAVOC staffing department." Rum placed his hand on Jamal's thigh, and once Jamal looked him in the eyes, he said, "Right before the Chakosky training op."

Rum had finally explained to Jamal what Rum had meant all those months ago about Chakosky being a real mission. Jamal placed his arm across Rum's shoulders and pulled him into his body for a brief squeeze. It felt nice to have Jamal show such open affection.

Jamal stood and slid his knife out to practice his grip and spin with his nondominant left hand.

Lisa leaned forward to better see Rum. "Tony and I were sent on a recovery mission about the same time, but the target was moved."

Tony rubbed his right pectoral muscle. "They'd left a small unit behind, and they got me with ketamine."

"Horse tranquilizer?" Milo asked.

Rum said, "Common tactic of Dios Provee, the same Christian extremists who are credited for the base attack. Same group that have kept Minophen and Jones busy all year."

Jamal asked, "So why not tell us the target? They've prepped us for the mission for months. And they'll wait until we're a go before they show us a picture and give us a name?"

Tony clarified. "They didn't wait until the last minute to tell us the target before."

"That was just an intel op, though, right?" Jamal asked.

Rum nodded at him, not waiting for Milo or Lisa to confirm. "They think there is a leak." He adjusted Jamal's grip on his knuckle blade; Jamal held it too tight.

"Well, great job blabbing, then." Milo looked at the soldiers sitting around them.

Two of the WREAC slept in the corner by the cockpit, legs stretched out, arms crossed. Another pair played games on their teltom phones; their thumbs tapping and swiping in rapid succession. Cooper, their team lead, was reading on his field tablet. Their sixth member was up with the pilot. They'd been a team for a while, and none of them were anxious. Hell, Cooper laughed about every fourth page.

Until Jamal stood to practice.

Then Cooper stopped flipping pages. It might be that he was listening. Except it would be hard for Cooper to do so clear across the plane, with the engines rumbling below them. Rum had seen Cooper check Jamal out as they boarded the plane. A head-tilted-to-the-side scan with a long linger at his ass. Cooper had good taste, but if he was looking at Jamal now, he was being subtle. Rum decided to see that as a show of respect.

No one commented on Milo's outburst.

Rum said, "A Hamask among them would be more likely. Expat or merc from the Israeli or German military. Both have excellent Hamrammr programs…."

"But?" Jamal asked, and then quickly, before Rum got a chance, he teased. "*You're* a butt."

Rum smiled. Jamal knew him pretty well. He was keyed up, and yes, it was partly the importance of this mission. Things were working out with Jamal. He had amazing Hamask abilities, was able to thrive with Rum's help, and Rum himself? He was sleeping. He could focus solely on Jamal and know the rest would fall away. His mind would quietly meander through childhood memories that he could share with his friend. He still felt the need to tuck away little moments of Jamal—the taste of his skin, how full and complete he felt with Jamal buried inside him, the sound of his laughter, how he liked his eggs in the morning.

But Jamal knew those things about Rum, too. And for once, someone else being able to read him and anticipate his thoughts and needs didn't scare the holy shit out of Rum. He recognized that he was falling in love. That *did* scare him.

Feeling secure and confident, he said, "I think I'm wrong. Not about it being Wick. It's him. Why hasn't he escaped? They moved Wick twice when recovery teams got too close. Transfers would have been the best time for Wick to escape."

Rum rolled his shoulders, trying to relieve a bit of the ache. "An active Hamask he's maybe bonded with doesn't fit. There's a piece we're missing."

JAMAL REALIZED Rum's comment earlier about Wick's size wasn't a short man's perspective on what big was. To a five-foot-six guy, surely everyone was tall, bigger than him. Yet no one would mistake Vargr Wick Ieti for small. He had been carved out of the side of a volcano; his skin was as dark as Jamal's, but it had a rust undertone that must come from his island background. His nose was wide and flat, as if he'd slept on his face his whole life. Each of his thighs was bigger around than Rum's waist.

They had a small viewing window from the wall grate they'd climbed to. The grate led to the single tunnel out of the complex. It was actually a bit of a disappointment. Sure, there was debris from the wind and the smell of cats and the mice they hunted. But Jamal had built up the idea that there would be a mazelike cavern with dripping sludge and stalactites. Even Rum had muttered his disappointment at "set dressing" when they'd turned the single corner.

From this distance, and without a point of reference, Wick looked at least six and a half feet tall, but Jamal bet he was taller. He wasn't fat. Even from across the large room, Jamal could see the veins popped out on his forearms, indicating a ripped physique.

This massive man was draped in a tent-sized lab coat and was using a hologram interface to mix chemicals in an adjoining lab. Jamal smelled lavender and the starch of rice water. Purer than the cleaning solution the activation team had used. Why would Ieti be building a cleaning solution?

"Sugar?" Rum stroked the back of Jamal's neck, centering him, keeping him from whiting out on the smell of chemicals.

"*This* guy's a Vargr?"

Rum pulled his hand away, and Jamal blinked to refocus his sight back to normal.

Rum put his finger to his ear, listening to the progress of the rest of the team. T6 had created a diversion to pull guards to the front of the house where they could pick off combatants. Everyone had expected a response down in the lab. Guards rushing in to defend the Vargr, but so far, all they could tell was that they'd radioed the guards at the back door to hold their position.

No radio in this room. No response to any chime or alarm to indicate Wick was equipped with a communicator.

"How are your senses?"

Jamal wasn't offended; it was a good question while they were waiting. Since it was his commanding officer and his Vargr, he took a brief moment to survey himself. "Five by five."

Rum looked at him and then at his smartwatch. "Scan indicates your pain receptors are active."

"Check, but verify?" Jamal bit his tongue. They needed to be focused on their mission, not on Jamal's headache. "Head hurts."

"Taste?"

Really? They were going to do this now? Jamal wanted to blow the question off, but Rum was his Vargr and... and Rum didn't want their relationship to be about regulations and what was *expected*, so Jamal could speak his mind. "I'm fine. Tongue feels a little fuzzy. Got that turned down."

Rum nodded, and Jamal quietly removed the grate and set it out of their way. They kept low, and Jamal looked for any kind of response from Wick. He could hear the hum from the hologram interface, like busy insects or a large electrical box. It was louder than he thought it would be, and the smell of lavender was stronger as they got closer.

Wick noticed them. His hands paused in the orange and green lights at midlevel, and he lifted his head to look around. Jamal moved the strap of his assault rifle; it was rubbing his collarbone raw.

Rum spoke with his best military tone. "Lieutenant Commander Ieti. We are from the US military. We need your cooperation as we extract you from the building."

Wouldn't it have been easier to say "we've come to rescue you"? Jamal swallowed the sudden fit of nausea and purposely pressed out with his hearing to check the perimeter for activity. He could also hear the operational chatter on Rum's earpiece.

"They're letting a captain do a black run?" Wick asked.

That quickly he had recognized his fellow Vargr, processed the situation, and asked a relevant question. No floundering. Any surprise was registered and moved past between two heartbeats. Wick then started shutting down the interface, his eyes scanning both Rum and Jamal.

Rum sighed and lifted his shoulders. "What's going on here, Wick?"

Jamal pulled his hearing back so that it didn't sound like the other occupants of the room were hollering at each other. Damn, this strap was going in the incinerator when they got back to base. He could feel the abraded skin on his chest tear as he shifted his body between Rum and the entry point. Like a really bad case of leg chafe, each brush of fabric caught and pulled his flesh.

When Wick didn't respond, just started to stack odd bits of paper and file drives into a bag, Rum pressed his smartwatch to give a sitrep. "Target acquired. Either extraction point is an option."

"I'm not going with you, Ryan." Wick stepped to a door that led to the mixing chamber.

Rum followed him. "The hell you aren't."

Why hasn't anyone been guarding the prisoner? Jamal remembered Chakosky during that first training op at the HAVOC base. Chakosky had worked with the cadre, aiding his own capture. Jamal had thought Chakosky, the asshole, had talked the cadre into screwing with Rum. Maybe it was part of their extended intel. Wick was not a prisoner but a compromised asset. That would turn this rescue into a kidnapping. Wick was no longer a damsel in distress but an enemy combatant.

Wick pressed his thumb on a control pad and the smell of blood— of Vargr blood—flashed through the room like an invisible tsunami. Jamal grabbed the counter to brace himself, expecting the wave to hit and knock him on the floor. The panel was a security device like the old-fashioned retinal scans; a biometric lock to allow only authorized DNA into highly secure areas. All Jamal knew was this Vargr was not his.

Gross. Wrong.

Rum was his Vargr. Rum was stepping toward Wick—he needed to stay back. Jamal couldn't let him get too close. *Didn't he realize Wick was dangerous?* Jamal lunged forward and pushed Wick aside, pulling Rum out of the way. The door of the bio room swung open and Jamal's mouth was swamped with the pungent stench of rice starch.

Wick snarled, his eyes wide, nostrils flaring. "I said I'm not going with you."

THE WORLD slowed and the air thickened as even resistance decelerated. It allowed Rum to analyze this cluster unfolding in front of him. His Hamask was going into a fury without an obvious trigger. Jamal was allergic to the tranquilizer Rum had loaded in his spare sidearm. If he used the trank on Wick, Rum wouldn't be able to carry the big man by himself. Those three facts were looping through Rum's head in a useless feedback from his Vargr instincts to keep Wick away from Jamal.

He knew the shit had just hit the fan and all the ways to step out of the falling fecal matter, but he didn't know why it was happening. *Why* always influenced *what*.

"What the hell is wrong with you?" Wick said, and then, before anyone could further speculate, "Hamask."

As soon as Jamal pulled one of his new knives out, Rum had his out as well. "Lieutenant Zumati. Stand down."

"No, it's fine," Jamal said quietly. "Just give me a minute." But instead of having an open, back-off stance, he'd crouched, tucking the knife along his forearm to use the blade as another barrier.

Jamal's stance and the tone of his voice reminded Rum of the vid he'd seen of Jamal's activation. Jamal had, with little effort, snapped bones and torn flesh. Now, with clear intention behind his actions, the damage would be severe. Would he kill Wick to keep him away from Rum?

Rum needed to pull Jamal back from whatever precipice he stood at. They could not afford to have him going berserk on this mission—on any mission.

Rum tried to step between Jamal and Wick. Jamal lunged forward and Wick roared like a bear. Wick didn't see Jamal reaching for Rum, trying to pull him to safety, and all Jamal could then see was the threat Wick presented. Bigger than both Jamal and Rum combined, with anger and aggression radiating off him.

No matter how brilliant Wick was, how strong a Vargr, he didn't recognize the nuance of Jamal protecting his wolf, guarding instinctively what was his. They weren't wearing obvious indicators, like a Hamrammr badge or HAVOC insignia to clue Wick in. But still he should have seen.

"Don't you hurt him," Wick said through bared teeth. His warrior mask had slipped into place, his eyes large and aggressive, his teeth on show like a true predator. "You're out of line, soldier. Stand down, Hamask, or I will put you down."

"Yes, *Hamask*. My Hamask. Wick, I've finally found mine." Rum spoke the next words before processing their full meaning. "I'll help you find your Hamask, Wick. I promise."

Wick shook his head, his warrior face tightening with each motion. He pulled the door to the lab open another inch. Rum didn't know what was in that room, but Wick's movement wound Jamal up even tighter. Jamal kicked out at Wick, who easily dodged his foot but not the fist with the knife handle forward, which smashed into Wick's jaw. With a second jab, blood and spit sprayed across Jamal's arm.

Wick hit Jamal in the gut, swinging his leg around to snap Jamal's knee.

With the trank gun, Rum shot Wick in the femoral artery of the swinging leg.

They were at a close enough range that it would do serious muscle damage and the major artery would quickly circulate the drug. Targeting his heart would have been faster, but aiming for his leg knocked the 300-pound man back and down before he could damage Jamal's knee. Wick slid against the lab door, closing it with his weight.

"Asset has been tranked," Rum relayed on his watch.

Jamal turned, keeping an eye on Wick but backing away from Rum and possibly the smell of trank solvent in Rum's gun.

"Zumati. At ease. Asset is neutralized." Rum holstered his weapon. Operations relayed that the building had been taken and Rum and Jamal were clear to bring the asset out to the waiting medics at the front of the estate. "Acknowledged."

Jamal had pulled his assault rifle off his shoulder; he dropped it to the ground with a clatter. His other hand still held his knife. Blood soaked through the cloth at his shoulder.

Shit, did Wick land another blow? "Hamask Zumati, what is your status?"

Jamal looked up at Rum; deep gouges bled openly across his neck. Rum pressed his watch and then froze. What was he doing? Procedure required that he report Jamal's state and then wait for backup to subdue the Hamask in fury. Procedure wasn't going to help Jamal. They'd subdue him, might even put him back into hibernation. All Jamal and Rum's efforts would be wasted.

"What the heck did I just say?" How could he speak in their military language? He didn't believe it, and yet, when it came down to an important moment, he had reverted to their brainwashing nonsense.

Rum couldn't get this wrong. He had tried to go solo, showed off for the brass with the Chakosky mission. He'd tried to prove that they didn't need anyone to get the job done. They had almost pulled him and Jamal apart. God, what would happen to Jamal if he weren't working with Rum? Would the next Vargr treat him with respect? Know how to get him through a migraine?

To get this right, he needed help. Jamal's help.

"Sugar, I'm so sorry." He took a moment to breathe out the military and with his next breath gather the *real* him. He surfaced out of a pool of wrong and breathed in the admiration he felt for his partner. "Listen to me, ya hear. I'm here."

He turned his watch on to record and pulled off his gloves as he stepped toward Jamal.

Jamal took a deep breath, raising his chest, and palmed another knife. Jamal knew how to kill with those knives, but Rum could disarm him if he needed. Like a fight sequence, each possible stage direction unfolded like echoes in front of him. He knew where he'd step, where his hands and feet would move. He could have Jamal's knives in his own hands or tossed across the room in less than three seconds. Several of those options would result in Jamal being injured and all of them might aggravate the fury state. None of them would he use.

"Sugar, ya need to help me. We need to skedaddle up out of here, and Wick is a mite big for me to heft." Rum pulled his hat and ballistic eyewear off so Jamal could see him clearly. "I need ya, Jamal."

When Jamal didn't move again, Rum placed his hand along Jamal's jaw and focused on his breathing while blowing hot breaths across Jamal's face. Jamal's knife slid across Rum's arm—not an attack, more just tucking the blade out of the way. But his depth perception had shorted out. Jamal straightened to a standing position, but his eyes were still black from his blown pupils.

"Not yet. Not safe."

"That be a sight better than a straight no. True. But for this to be tight, we need to get out of here."

Wick groaned behind them and Jamal twitched and crouched from the sound, hunkering, finding cover, trying to pull Rum away from the threat. Rum turned to face Wick while pulling and dismantling the trank gun. It was the fastest way to get to the ammo. He slammed a second trank into Wick's large chest. Wick's eyes widened, and he tried to stagger to his feet and face his enemy.

The trank didn't trigger, the fluid still sloshing around the chamber. "Dammit, Wick, stay down."

Jamal stepped forward and slugged Wick. Wick's head snapped back against the metal door. His body seeped to the ground, a boneless release of major muscles indicating he was out cold this time.

Rum began assembling his gun. A sharp ache radiated up his arm from where Jamal's knife had cut through his armor. The air felt heavy as it moved through his lungs, his shoulders trembling under the weight. He needed a moment to pull his own emotions back, to tuck away the fear. Gun holstered, he looked up at Jamal.

His Hamask had tucked away his knives, and he quivered, with a hand outstretched to Rum. Rum scanned Jamal's body, up over the gleam of partially hidden knives, body armor, and the bloody remains of his shirt. Jamal shook his head and heaved air in and out. His eyes wanted and Rum nodded, opening his arms to welcome Jamal.

Jamal pushed Rum against the nearest wall and breathed on his neck.

The rest of Rum's fear and tension washed away with Jamal's touch. It had been a damn long time since that hollow feeling had come visiting. When it did, Jamal sent it packing with a hug or a joke. "Hey, Wolfie, help me with touch, would ya? My skin's on fire."

Adrenaline washed acid into Rum's mouth. He swallowed and tried to relax. The smell of worry, danger, anger—Jamal didn't need any of that right now. Heat pricked at the corners of Rum's eyes and he pushed even that away. Tonight, in the true safety of Jamal's arms, he would pull these emotions out. For now he needed to focus on getting Jamal and Wick out of here.

Rum pulled Jamal's shirt off his shoulder so he could clean the wound. Jamal's skin had grown so sensitive that the strap of his assault rifle had grated his flesh into road rash. Rum pulled a small first-aid kit out of one of his pants pockets. He used a peroxide mixture pressurized in a pen aerosol to clean the skin. Jamal had shut touch down, so he didn't flinch. *Does he have any other senses turned off?*

Jamal radioed in their status and position. He sounded… on point. Like his sense memory hadn't nearly cost them this mission and each other. Like everything was fine.

Rum used a med stick to spray on a liquid bandage over the damaged skin. Jamal turned his head, his eyes watering from the noxious odor. "I'm sorry."

"I can take it." Their eyes met, and Rum felt this odd wave of heat flow into his body. Like Jamal was sending him comfort, but more intense than a warm blanket or hug. Jamal stepped back and focused his senses, rubbed his fingertips together probably to focus his hearing.

Jamal used his hearing to guide Naylor and Travers to their position. Rum took the time to gather Wick's gear and data sticks. He used his watch to scan the room for further analysis. Tony and Jamal ripped the door from its hinges and made a gurney, and the four of them carried the massive soldier to their transport.

Rum should have called for backup sooner or waited to engage the asset until Lisa and her partner were in place. He had known Wick was a threat and yet decided that he and Jamal could handle it. Even worse, he'd shrunk back from addressing Jamal's assumption about Wick's size predisposing him to Hamask. If Rum couldn't advocate for change in his own pairing, how would he ever change how the outside world looked at a bonded pair?

Chapter 12

THE SMELL from the chemicals and the proximity of the unknown Vargr had triggered Jamal like a veteran with PTSD. His body thought they were still in the activation shack, still in danger. If this was his response to every battle situation, how could he ever repay what he'd stolen? How could he protect Rum? Yes, this time he'd known who Rum was and hadn't hurt him, but next time it could be different.

Jamal was being debriefed in a separate building from Rum.

In other military units, soldiers wore smart mesh gear. Intricate electrical fibers sent biofeedback and physical mapping to Command during operations. Rum had compared it once to early moviemaking, using electrodes on a live actor to create special effects. They had yet to design gear that was soft enough for a Hamask's sensitive skin or silent enough to not distract their hearing. Vargr didn't wear it for the same reason.

Standard military also had the audio and visual from a drone guardian flying overhead or alongside the soldiers. You could analyze when their blood pressure went up, how exactly they would move to fire, or intercept, or disarm. In the holo rooms, they could project whole battle scenes and you could walk through and analyze what went right. Hamask and Vargr relied on the older technologies of the smartwatches or the PenTech bands around each forefinger. It was a bit like watching a dancing 3-D puzzle with pieces missing.

Jamal had watched himself enough to be past self-consciousness. It allowed you to analyze your form and decision-making and discuss it with a mentor. But unlike before, he knew this wasn't going to end with a pat on the back. The room was on the northeast corner of the building, shaded from the sun. A breeze blew through the open windows. It looked like an empty classroom; the vid plates looked a bit like acoustical ceiling tiles.

Jamal could hear the movement of the base personnel, like worker ants shuffling past with the purpose to follow, execute, achieve. He heard two different distinct genres of music. Wind pushed through the metal bins and across the trees in the eco area. He didn't hear Rum. He pushed the bile back into his stomach and clenched his fists. He knew Rum was in the med ward. He knew he was safe.

They wouldn't be able to do fieldwork because of Jamal's strong sense memory. He knew that now and was still working on acceptance. Instead they would probably turn him into an archive, a bloodhound observer to each activation or an envoy to diplomatic functions, a humanized recording device. How the hell did that help anyone? How did that make a difference in this life? What could he do that the tech couldn't? Maybe Rum would know how to work it to their advantage.

"Attention!"

Jamal flinched from the noise then rolled the imaginary dial between his fingers to turn down the sound. He stood and saluted.

Colonel Gelbrit preceded General Khan and Major General Franke into the room. Normally it would be just Gelbrit as the mission leader. What was the head of HAVOC doing here? And General Franke? Additionally, four MPs flanked the room.

Jamal had already dictated his written report. It was now three hours since they'd landed and over twelve since they left the compound. He was hungry and tired, and the lights were too bright. Jamal felt a wash of fear, like a cold wet tarp being draped over his shoulders as panic flooded his body. "Sir, I request my Vargr to be present."

At the corner of his vision, Jamal saw ghosts of hospital gurneys; he smelled the antiseptic of med sticks. *Shit.* His sense memory was kicking in again, and this memory would fuck his brain sideways. No. *No.* Not right now.

"All debriefs as part of an investigation to the conduct of a Vargr cannot include the Vargr in question. Obviously."

Colonel Gelbrit had a way of talking that made you want to punch him in the nose. His nose had been broken several times, evident by its curvature and shape. Jamal focused on that for a moment, allowing himself to feel satisfaction that the pompous holo jockey had learned his lesson the hard way.

"Is Lieutenant Walker being charged for a specific infraction, sir?" Jamal needed to keep it together. He couldn't fade out on that memory. Rum still needed him.

General Franke stepped forward and ordered Jamal to stand at ease. "Currently this is an informal inquiry to establish the events of the mission and to decide what the *fuck* we are going to do with two *goddamn* soldiers who can't hold their shit together."

As Franke spoke, she went from military precision to spitting foam out of her mouth on each syllable. Jamal recognized this was serious, but the general would need to hang out with drill sergeants for several years to make Jamal quake in his combat boots. Hell, the fact Franke was losing it in front of Khan just made Jamal want to laugh. He took a deep breath and guided his four-year-old self behind him, tucking the memory away.

He would focus on a different memory. The light had been this bright when he'd stepped out of his first movie theater into the blazing July sun. He could tell his brain that the smell was just cleaning solution and not medical waste.

Jamal took a second breath and continued to wait. Even though they had yet to ask him questions, he needed to listen to these people.

The colonel smelled like deodorant and his breath was strong and steady. Khan's heartbeat was slow enough to make Jamal think he was sleeping. Franke's heart rate was elevated, and Jamal could smell the sweat from here. They had already been in to see Rum. The colonel had touched him—Jamal could smell his Vargr on the man. Rum may have slugged the asshole. Maybe that was what this was about.

"Hamask Zumati, we have reviewed both your and Lieutenant Walker's reports and the mission footage." Gelbrit said.

Jamal nodded his understanding.

"Your Vargr and commanding officer needed medical aid and six stitches. Stitches!" Franke said.

Jamal blinked and shook his head. No, that wasn't right. First of all, no one had stitches when liquid bandages generated skin growth at two centimeters per second. It would have to be deep or… or… unattended to the point they worried about infection. He would have smelled the blood on Rum. Jamal would have realized he was injured by smelling the adrenaline, the pain. They'd been guarding Wick and attending Jamal's own injury; they…. Jamal had turned off his touch and smell to prevent the sense memory grabbing him again.

Why the fuck didn't Rum say something?

The stubborn ass had to do everything on his own. Hell, even in bed he refused to let Jamal lead. Rum insisted on controlling even their sex life. Jamal had thought Rum needed to lead in all things, but Rum continued to say they were partners until Jamal believed him. Then he pulled shit like this.

Without waiting for the men to engage him further, Jamal turned to the vid tech and told him to bring up the mission. He used the bar on his smartwatch interface to fast forward to the op team setting up a perimeter and him and Rum in the basement. The holo version of Rum stood a few feet in front of Jamal.

Jamal kept the sound off and raised his hands, perfectly happy to ignore the assholes who smugly stood around him as he searched for the right moment. The hologram's sensor tracked his movement like a symphony conductor which allowed him to manipulate the feed's timeframe. He could see from the vid that his sense memory had kicked in even before removing the grate, and he should have recognized it at the time. He paused the footage as both he and Rum stood at arm's length. The knife sliced across Rum's skin.

Franke crossed her arms and blew out a breath.

Jamal knew he'd had his knife out. He'd included the cut in his report but didn't think it had broken Rum's skin. His protective instincts should have kicked in.

But he hadn't smelled the blood, and even if he had, it wouldn't have sent him into a panic-induced fury. Rum was strong, brave, and totally kick-ass. Jamal wasn't so unstable that Rum being injured would reduce him to a helpless child. Did they honestly think Hamask were so insecure and dangerous? Rum was right: bonded pairs acted on instinct, even in this. Jamal had focused on protecting Rum, but his bear knew that the wolf could take care of both of them if needed.

They didn't think he and Rum were truly bonded, even with the evidence plain in front of him, because Jamal hadn't freaked out over Rum's injury.

Jamal brought his hands together with a booming clap to shut off the program. *Shit, this is bad.* If they believed the bond was fake or nonexistent, they could reassign them. Jamal was falling in love with the stubborn bastard. He trusted his wolf; they were friends.

These idiots thought they weren't bonded because a tripped-out Hamask hadn't recognized that his Vargr was injured. What a bunch of idiots.

"You're wrong." There was no way in hell that Jamal would let them separate him from Rum. They could take their black ink and shove it up their red ledger. No debt would require him to lose his heart. "You're wrong, and I'll prove it."

Chapter 13

RUM WAS desperately trying to turn off his brain. HAVOC hadn't taught the yoga meditation until after Rum finished his Hamrammr training and activation, but he knew Tai Chi from his days in Beijing. He stripped down to his boxer briefs and flowed through each movement, analyzed his form, and tensed his muscles in waves. He tightened and released his abs, flexed and held his shoulders and arms, and breathed out as he relaxed. If this didn't allow Rum to let go of his anger, he'd need to find a ballet barre or maybe even delve into porn. Except he didn't want Jamal coming back to their quarters with the place smelling like sex.

The techs had been through to clean the place while they were out. Even the bed was made and the lube put away. The idea was that a pair would need to return to their safe place and rebond after a grueling mission. Lisa and Tony and Milo and Scott would have had the same service. For once, it was an archaic policy that Rum didn't mind. Having someone else scrub his bathroom and change the bedding once in a while was a nice perk, but it had nothing to do with the health of the pair. His parents cooked together. That was how they relaxed after work, how they reconnected, quietly working together on something that was just theirs—not performing like a circus act for the public, not banging each other's brains out. Though, okay, they'd had sex at least once before. And to be fair, both his parents had been frank and blasé about sex.

Rum had stopped his movements and begun to pace. He was back to being angry about Jamal's stupid comment about Wick being the wrong size to be a Vargr and angry that Jamal would jeopardize their pairing by telling the brass that his injury wasn't a feral response to danger. Jamal should have known enough to tell them his protective instincts had taken over to protect their bond and Rum had stepped into his blade, and that Rum had forbade him from cleaning it. When, really, Rum had just forgotten. The tight body armor held the skin together and Rum only started bleeding when he took off his gear.

Knees bent, Rum moved his arms across his torso as he tightened his stomach muscles again. Jamal entered the room, looking guarded, guilty. No, that was just Rum's anger, he supposed, projecting what he thought of Jamal's actions.

"Rum," Jamal said, in way of welcome, perhaps.

"Why did you tell them you'd cut me? It made me look like I was lying." Rum stepped through the next movement, keeping his eyes on an imagined distant point over Jamal's shoulder. A rivulet of sweat slid down his arm.

"No, you lying made you look like you were lying." Jamal pulled off his watch and placed it on the docking plate to download and recharge. Rum's sat next to it in standby mode, with a green glow around it to indicate it was ready. "Rum, they're military reports. A lot of it they know from the watches. It doesn't do us any good to keep that from them."

Rum just shook his head and walked toward the bathroom to grab a towel. "They don't need to know every little thing. They've trained us and received our oath. There should be some trust there."

Rum walked out of the bathroom to find Jamal pulling things from the small fridge: eggs, cheese, and mushrooms. *Where did he find real mushrooms?*

"You know the intel is vital for statistics and analysis. Besides, how are they going to protect you from me if they don't realize I'm a threat? How can they decide to put me down like the dog I am if they don't know I'm sick?" Jamal leaned against the counter with his back to Rum, his head hung down. His shoulders lifted as he took a deep breath.

"I don't need their protection. Not from you. And if you make one more disparaging comment about yourself, I'm likely to kick your ass to prove just how much I can take care of myself. Again." Rum draped the towel over his shoulders and reached out a hand to touch Jamal's bowed head. Jamal kept his hair short, but Rum could still feel the kink of each curl as it twisted out of Jamal's dark skin. "It's my fault. We should have gotten our story straight on the way back."

Jamal pulled away and reached for a frying pan. He turned on the single burner. "Or, *novelty*, you could tell the truth and not try to manipulate one more outcome. You're not responsible for my actions—"

"Not responsible?" Rum pointed toward the front door. "They expect me to keep you in line. Like you're some circus bear and I'm your trainer."

Jamal gestured to the eggs and Rum handed the bottle over. He missed yolks fresh from the farm, but this substitute wasn't bad in a pinch.

Jamal shook the bottle, then poured the eggs into the hot pan. "You're the one who talks about not caring what they think. Not letting them decide how we navigate this pairing. We're boyfriends. That's separate from our jobs."

"No, it's not." Rum passed Jamal the bag of shredded cheese and then pulled a knife down from the magnetic strip across the wall that held all their kitchenware. He quickly chopped the mushrooms into tiny pieces. "If we weren't a Hamra Pair, we wouldn't even know each other."

Jamal sure wouldn't have chosen me, except in desperation.

"What kind of horseshit is that?" Jamal stepped to the side so that Rum could toss in the mushrooms.

"You wanted a girl."

"Come on, we've already worked through that." He set a lid over the eggs and opened a drawer to pull out plates and forks. "The bonding heat activated with you, Rum. You."

Rum pulled two canisters of lemon water from the fridge and set them on the counter. They didn't have a table but could eat standing at the high counter that separated the kitchen from the entry room. "Bonding heat?" He snorted to indicate his derision.

Jamal handed him one of the plates. "What does that mean?" His fork *ting*ed against the stoneware as he stabbed a bunch of egg.

"It's just like when you made that comment about Wick." Rum shoveled egg into his mouth, pausing just long enough to swallow and drink down some water.

Jamal raised his eyebrows and continued to eat.

"This is good." Rum took another bite, swallowed, and continued. "You said that you couldn't believe Wick was a Vargr. Like only women and small men are Vargr." Jamal rolled his eyes, and Rum poked him with his fork. "Maybe you can't help it. Having these programmed prejudice-based stereotypes wired into your brain. The propaganda around the Hamrammr program is insane."

Jamal scooped up the last of his eggs and then reached for his water. "Thanks," he said, lifting the canister to indicate why he was grateful. "Yes, I was taught certain things about Hamask and Vargr, but that has all been—" He seemed to search for the right word. "—put aside for actual experience. Rum, we've been bonded for six months. Me knowing you're my Vargr, feeling the bonding heat, has nothing to do with your size."

Rum gathered their empty plates and slid them into the hydroslot. The light on the cupboard turned red to indicate it was functioning. It would turn green once the plates and silverware were ready for use again. "But that's what I'm saying. There is no such thing as bonding heat."

Jamal added the pan and spatula to the slot, then leaned a hip against the counter, his head tilted to the side; maybe he was listening for Rum's heart to miss a beat or analyzing his eye dilation, looking for a lie. "You've never felt the bonding heat?"

"There is *no* such thing."

"I felt it. That first day in the med ward. Heat flowing in toward my heart. You've not felt that?" Jamal crossed his arms over his chest and narrowed his eyes. "I just spent two hours defending our bond, and you're telling me you've never felt that? Don't even believe we're supposed to be together?"

Rum remembered the flush of heat back on the compound but discounted it. "I desire you. You know that. I've got crazy lust swimming in my blood just looking at ya." He too crossed his arms; he wished he had more clothes on. "I don't need a mystical *bonding heat* to justify popping wood for you. It's called being gay, and there is nothing wrong with it."

"You're serious." Jamal looked at the ceiling, then rubbed across his mouth. "Shit. I can't believe you." He turned and headed for the bathroom. "I'm taking a shower. Alone."

Rum's brain decided to take that moment to engage fully. His skin vibrated with energy, the electrical currents raising the hair along his arms and at the back of his neck. He replayed the scene, analyzing what each of them had said. How should he have staged it better? What direction would have worked?

Rum was swiping a cloth across the counter when he realized they'd just cooked together. Jamal had come in and made enough food for them both without needing gratitude or permission or direction. Because this was their place and because they were friends and… and because they were a bonded pair. The heat from the mission, that warm inward sweep of comfort heated his skin like stepping out of an over-air-conditioned room into the dry heat of a summer porch. Cold, that he hadn't even realized was there, melted away.

Really, Rum was angry at himself. He had almost lost Jamal today. He rejected that terrifying thought. He was the one projecting, trying to hide this feeling of guilt behind anger and panic.

The heat made him need to move; it was not sexual, but passionate. He heard the shower turn off, pulled a fresh towel from the linen closet, and entered the bathroom as Jamal stepped out. His black skin shone, his hair was beaded with moisture, and his cock hung soft against his thigh. Beautiful. Rum stepped up and wrapped the warm soft towel around his lover's shoulders. "I *have* felt heat, a warmth different from lust."

Jamal shook his head and opened his mouth to protest.

Rum just kept talking. "I figured it was… affection. I'm—" He bit his lip and stared into Jamal's dark eyes. "—we *are* a bonded pair, Jamal. And not because we had sex the way they think we should, and not because…." He decided not to bring up the bonding heat again. "Because we can make dinner together like a couple. Because we're friends. Because I'm falling in love with you."

Jamal's eyes widened and then he smiled, this devilish little grin that turned his pretty face into a handsome temptation. Rum used the towel to dry Jamal's body, keeping the movement sensual and slow.

When Rum reached Jamal's hips, Jamal's arousal was evident in the full cock that bobbed against his tight stomach, and Jamal took the towel. "I'll finish. You rinse off."

Rum laughed. It was obvious his exercise had left him too ripe for his Hamask to handle. He made quick work of washing the sweat from his body. He used the same towel to dry off, smelling Jamal on the terry cloth. When he entered their room, Jamal had pulled the bedding down, lowered the lights, and had a bottle of lube at the ready. A quick kiss, and their bodies were humming back at the ready point.

Jamal picked Rum up, pulling Rum's legs around him, then pushed him into the hard surface of the wall, grinding a hip into Rum's erection. "Can I lick your ass?"

Rum let his head drop back and gasped, pulling Jamal even tighter to his body. "You want to?"

"Yeah. Have for a while."

Rum pushed back away from the wall and tried to steer them toward the bed, but Jamal wouldn't budge.

Jamal shook his head no. "I'll get us there."

Jamal had this way of kissing, superintense. It lit all of Rum's spotlights and he would think, *I'm going to come just from this*, or *We can't keep it this high for long*. And Jamal would just keep kissing him. Savage, aggressive, possessive, Jamal knew what Rum needed, even if Rum didn't or thought differently, and he would give it to him, pushing into his wet mouth, pressing Rum's teeth with his lip. Consuming him. If Jamal used the same moves on Rum's ass, Rum would die a very happy man.

His ass clenched. Yeah, he wanted that. "Please."

Jamal dropped him to the bed. "On your knees, ass up."

They didn't usually use this position. They both liked kissing, the press of the bottom's cock trapped between their stomachs. Or sometimes, when Jamal was bottoming, Jamal preferred them to lie on their sides, Rum up on his knees, coming in at the perfect angle to tease Jamal's prostate but not really pound at it like they both wanted, stretching out the moment until it grew too intense. Rum would come and then sink down to the bed and open his mouth to Jamal's dick, sucking the brief couple of strokes until Jamal came down his throat.

Rum leaned down on his elbows, his ass open and up, his balls and dick hanging heavy and tight between his spread thighs. Jamal worked a thumb around his entrance, and then with licks and nibbles first, Jamal opened him up. Rum could feel the waves of pleasure all the way to his toes. He keened and moaned. He tried to push back into Jamal's mouth but Jamal held him in place. His first lick over Rum's opening was cautiously short.

Rum turned his head to look back and up at Jamal, loving the view of Jamal's dark head disappearing between his lighter cheeks. *God, this feels amazing.* Jamal's tongue felt like the man's dick, wide and strong and demanding. He grew more confident with each of Rum's moans.

"More, Jamal. Please."

Jamal sucked on the puckered flesh and Rum felt his body detach and start to come, but Jamal was already backing off.

"Sugar? What?" Then Rum felt Jamal slide a slicked finger firmly into his tight channel.

He felt so exposed. He pushed up to his hands, wanting more of that feeling. Wanting to display for the world his wet cock dripping on the mattress. Let the world see how hard his heart pounded in his chest. He lifted his head and arched his back into the touch. "*Yes.* Do that."

"I'm getting you ready, Wolfie." Jamal slid another thick finger in with the first, twisted and scissored, just brushing his prostate. Jamal had not done that before, but somehow knew Rum liked to feel the stretch and burn across his perineum.

"So good. More."

"Don't boss me, Ryan. I'll get us there."

Rum kept his dick away from any friction. The pull of gravity and the press of air as he pushed his hips back onto Jamal's fingers, forward and back, was insanely intense. Jamal guided him farther up the bed and then pulled him back so that he was sitting on Jamal's thighs. Rum lifted up on his knees and slid down slow and easy onto Jamal's large, pulsing cock. Both of them sat back on their ankles. Rum tilted his head back onto Jamal's shoulder, his back fully pressed to Jamal's larger chest. Jamal wrapped his arms around Rum, his right hand going up over Rum's throat, and Rum turned his head so Jamal could kiss his mouth.

"Feel good?" Jamal asked.

"Yes, sugar. So good." In this position they couldn't get much of a thrust, but Rum loved being even further on display. His dick was purple with blood and hot to the touch. His ass felt stretched and slick and seared from Jamal's awesome cock. He swiveled his hips, rocking forward slightly, little movements.

Jamal sucked his bottom lip. "Look at me, Rum."

Rum opened his eyes.

"Fist yourself. Come for me." And then he grabbed Rum's hips and slammed him down, doing all the heavy lifting.

Rum liked the way his dick bounced against his stomach, liked the way Jamal huffed hot breaths along his neck. Rum slid a single finger and thumb around his base, a slow glide up, putting on a show for his lover, who watched easily over his shoulder.

Jamal groaned and stopped lifting Rum up. "Are you trying to torture me?"

"No, I'm thinking about bringing up horrible memories from your past and replacing them with watching me masturbate." Rum pressed his thumb against the slit at the tip of his dick, watching the sensitive head swell with each press.

"Oh, Ryan, you've got a gorgeous dick. Such a pretty cock."

Rum gathered a bit of precum and offered it on a finger for Jamal to taste. "Did you like preparing my ass? Like sliding your thick fingers into my clenching hole?"

Jamal groaned around the digit. With a satisfying suck, Jamal released it. "Yes. Liked even better that you let me. That we're in this together."

"Yeah." Rum squeezed his sphincter as tight as he could in its stretched state.

Jamal's hips nearly bucked him off. Jamal's blunt teeth pressed into the ridge of Rum's shoulder, and he felt radiant pressure shoot through his muscles to his balls.

He let out his own groan and said, "Be right back." He pulled free from Jamal and turned around before reseating himself on Jamal's dick. "We'll need to try this on a chair one time. I bet that will be crazy intense too." He braced his hands on Jamal's shoulders and got serious about thrusting, his thigh muscles quaking with strain. Jamal leaned him back enough to lick his nipple. The angle changed and Rum's world splintered apart.

Jamal helped him ride it out until his dick was so sensitive he pleaded for Jamal to stop. Jamal slid loose, laid him back on the bed, and then stroked his dick, with Rum egging him on until his own orgasm hit, pulsing semen onto Rum's thigh and stomach.

Rum smiled and arched to stretch out his sated body. "I'm feeling that was more than adequate to prove how much I like ya."

Jamal didn't tease back. "Yeah. We're in this together. You don't have to be in control, and you don't have to do it all yourself."

Rum nodded. His breath was still hitching through his chest and the waves of his orgasm still tightened his balls. "I'm starting to figure that out."

"Starting to?"

"Have figured that out. Just, I might need a few reminders until... well, until I'm used to letting someone else contribute."

Jamal dropped down beside him and reached for a tissue to clean them both up. Jamal's breath rattled his own shoulders. "We need to talk."

"Perfect line for a cutaway."

Jamal wouldn't let them spoon. Usually Jamal was the protective big spoon, always between Rum and the door. This time he guided Rum to his side so they lay facing each other. He stroked a hand down the side of Rum's face. "We might not have met if you didn't come wake me up. But having had the best Vargr in the world means I could never settle for anyone else. You're my wolf, Ryan, and that's why I need to tell you the truth."

Chapter 14

"I TOLD them I didn't know who I was. Really, I just didn't want to be that person anymore." Using the tactile presence of his wolf, Jamal stretched his bear senses back to the past. "I was four. I remember one of the other kids teaching me to raise up four fingers when people asked me that question. But they told me that I'd get sent back if they knew I belonged to someone. Unless I was an orphan, I'd turn right back up in that abandoned building. We slept under those tarps, ate what we could find in the trash. I'd be back to not knowing where my parents were, except when they got strung and came back to crash on the mattress next to me."

All the senses were parading past, but he knew he needed to exorcise this memory or it would rule him. It was safe with Rum here. So Jamal described the place he had been before and the vague memories of his parents, and how he'd almost relived his surrender during his debrief.

"Surrender?" Rum asked.

"I snuck on a delivery vehicle. The other kids stole bread off the back to distract the driver, and I climbed up front and hid behind a seat. I don't remember how far we went—probably a couple of towns over. The vehicle came to a stop, and I walked to the closest building that was well lit. It was a hospital, so I just pretended. Like an elaborate game of make-believe, surrendering to whatever they would do with me because it had to be better than the other."

"Your parents didn't come find you?"

"No. Why would they? But what about those other kids? Why did they send me to safety and not come with? I've always felt like lying cheated them out of being saved. Like I stole that from them. If I told the truth of who I was, maybe I would have saved the other kids. I don't even remember how many there were. That is a lot of lives to repay."

"They may have found another way out. You don't know. And you were just trying to survive."

"Yes." Jamal breathed deep and felt the warmth spread through his body. He curved his fingers around Rum's hip and breathed in the scent of their sweat, of the lube, and the softening agent used on the sheets. He liked that memory very much. He catalogued each sense and tied it to then, to that moment when he realized he was in love with Rum.

"You need my help." Jamal kissed Rum on the chin and slid his hand up his back to draw him closer.

"I'll gladly take a hand. Jus' give my dick a moment to catch up." Rum gestured with his eyebrows, trying to look seductive.

Jamal thought it was cute. "No. I mean, you need my help figuring out what we do next. We can't do field missions with my sense memory being so high. It puts everyone in danger."

"You want to pay back—"

"Wanted to. I'm an injured athlete past my prime. I don't need to prove I was worth the investment. I've already done that. I just need to work with my Vargr."

Rum moved the last inch to press his bare skin against Jamal's. "We'll figure it out."

As they lay there, Jamal debated telling Rum that he loved him. Would it change anything? "We" was a huge step for Rum. Not only talking about being a partnership but finally acting as a couple. Course they'd been doing that since they made the bed together, since they went shopping off base for supplies. If Jamal told Rum how he felt and Rum came back with rationing, explaining that Jamal didn't really feel that way, he would have to clock the guy. He rubbed his hands up and down Rum's sides. Yes, Rum had said he was falling in love, but that meant he still needed time, right? If Rum came back with an "I love you" too soon, Jamal would feel like Rum was just saying what Jamal wanted to hear.

Finally Rum asked, "What are you thinking about?"

"Stuff."

Up went the eyebrows.

"Feeling vulnerable." Jamal stroked a thumb over the ridge of one of Rum's eyes and took a deep breath. "Will you do something for me?"

Rum pursed his mouth and swallowed, his blue-green eyes huge and wet. "What?"

Jamal closed his eyes, pressed a sweet kiss to Rum's lips, and breathed out a sigh. Nope, it was too soon. "They'll have us in here for a while. Let's do a Joss Whedon marathon."

Bur, Brad S., 572092-Longwei.
Page 26

I DEBATED whether I should write this next part. Diary entry or not, this is superprivate. But here is what decided it. First, it'll be nice to have a sexy account of our first night. Second, I don't want their sterile version to be the only record of such a powerful moment.

Last, if we *are* being monitored, what will one more perspective hurt?

Longwei leads the way into his condo. It's in a decent area of town, two bedrooms, and has a lot of large-scale furniture. Nothing on spindly legs or delicate pedestals. It's stylish, even. I look back at him, standing just inside the door, waiting for me to take it all in. I realize he is stylish, too. We've both got shaggy mops, but his is on purpose, sexy. It softens his sharp chin and cheekbones. They stripped off his SWAT gear while doing his IV earlier. He still has on camo-green platoon pants and a drab T-shirt. His skin is golden, and I can see how toned he is by the vein up his neck and down his forearms. I look at him and feel a bit overwhelmed.

Not insecure. Shut up. I'm not.

I reach for his top button to undo his shirt, and he breathes in this staggered breath and looks away. I have time to think here. I suddenly remember pressing my erection into his waist and not feeling a corresponding bulge. I'm not questioning the man's physique, just realizing there are bits I'm overlooking.

I drop my arms to the side. When I speak, my voice is breathy with want. "What do you need?"

He doesn't say anything, but I remember the promise of restraint. I pull my tie out of my pocket and form a slipknot around both of my wrists and do my best to pull it tight with my teeth. I extend my arms toward him and am glad to see a bit of fire in his eyes. "Where do you keep the lube?"

I take a step backward and pry my shoes off, one heel at a time. I step on a toe of one of my socks and pull my leg out. Before I can do the other leg, he picks me up, just wraps his arms around my middle.

I try to lift my legs around him.

"No." He presses a kiss to my mouth as he walks us farther into the place, back to what I hope is his bedroom. "Tie won't hold you."

Which is true and makes me shiver. He dumps me on the bed and removes the tie. "Get undressed." I have no problem with that. I am naked, my dick straining and fully hard by the time he turns back from his closet with these long black ropes. I scoot up toward the headboard and spread my arms out to the edges because I think he'll secure me that way. He smiles, dumps the rope on my chest, and brings my arms together above my head. He strokes the inside of my arm, which has me senseless. He hasn't tweaked my nipples, hasn't stroked my throbbing dick, has barely kissed me, but I am trembling and can hardly remember how to breathe.

"Turn over."

"I want to see you." Yeah, it comes out whiny. The man has a gorgeous body; of course I want to see all of it.

He smiles, tilts his head so his hair falls forward. "You will."

I huff out a breath and flip over onto my hands and knees. He ties my wrists. The cords are as soft as silk. I find out that they are just as strong as I strain against them. He strokes the back of my thigh, runs the side of his hand up along the curve to my ass. The whole time I'm looking at him over my shoulder.

I like the way he licks his lips. He has full lips, and I'm imagining all the things he could wrap them around. He takes my ankle and strokes it a few times, then ties it to the bottom corner of the bed. It pulls me open a bit more and I moan. He then walks to the front of the bed so I can see him better—so considerate—and starts to strip.

It always pisses me off when the guys I sleep with take time to carefully fold clothes. One guy got undressed and put all of his clothes in the hamper before picking up my clothes and setting them on a chair. Like what? Tidy is more important than my dripping dick? It's not.

Longwei doesn't even unbutton his shirt, just pulls it over his head, the undershirt with it. He toes his shoes off while he opens his belt and pants and drops them to the floor. He is long, golden-skinned, and cut. All. Over.

"You'll do."

He laughs and lifts my chin up for a quick kiss, then places sucking kisses with that full mouth across my shoulders, down my spine, along the edge of each shoulder blade. He slots himself behind me so that his chest presses to my back. I arch into his skin and he wraps his arms around my chest. He sticks his chin just over my shoulder and starts

should be more careful? I get a bit pissed and think of the shittiest things imaginable to say to hurt him back. Because we both knew that's bullshit. Him questioning my certainty is just stating that he is unsure.

"I'm kind of glad you rushed into that burger joint."

I laugh and sag in relief, sinking further into the comfort of the bed.

"I'm going to keep you safe."

Hear that, motherfuckers? Because in that moment he isn't just saying it to me. He's telling those dicks down in the van who are monitoring us. It's a warning. A claim. His voice isn't sweet, it's deadly serious.

"Hell yeah, you are." I twist around and get my mouth on him, to get us both excited about round two.

Chapter 15

GENERAL KHAN was walking a very fine tightrope with this meeting. He knew that Franke was reassigning the Walker-Zumati pair. She could stick them processing interviews for the Judge Advocate General's office in Nebraska. Or, out of sheer spite, send them to some Podunk outpost like Gowen Field, Idaho. He had to convince her that they needed to work on Valhalla for him. Yet, if he worked too hard to convince her how important the pair was, she'd assign them to train her own pet projects.

Khan's secretary escorted Franke into his office. Khan saluted and received a quick reciprocal salute. He let her lead the conversation but made sure his body language suggested he was open and relaxed.

"We've received new information on the Dios Provee site in Trinidad. The task force would like you to take a look at the intel."

Khan tilted his head to the side and considered her request. It was odd to have a general in charge of a specialized training program like HAVOC kept in the loop about Army intelligence concerns. He had thought his move to overseeing HAVOC would mean more of a shelf position—political figurehead, his decision-making restricted and his impact low. Instead he often looked over the intel gathered and gave his two cents. So far he hadn't said anything their young tactical experts or even the CIA weren't saying. Yes, he had spent several years living among the early group that became Dios Provee, but his insider knowledge, if he had ever really had any, had expired.

"I could see them keeping a supply stash there, for water evacuation, but no personnel. Woodland wouldn't want anyone outside of his circle of influence."

They hadn't been able to confirm that Woodland was leading the radical group, but he'd been in charge when the United States had sent soldiers in to train the insurgents. Until they uncovered his body buried beneath Dios Provee's holy ground, Khan was keeping his crosshairs on Woodland.

Franke nodded. "You'll have a full report, but we'll also need you at the Mountain in a week. We'll have Lieutenant Colonel Ieti debriefed and the mission data analyzed by then."

"Yes, ma'am."

She crossed her legs at that point and rolled her fingertips over the top of her knee. Khan watched her look around his office. He had pictures from his years of service—pictures of his family and a few carefully chosen souvenirs, like a set of nesting dolls. "No pictures from your pinning ceremonies?"

"My wife keeps them in a scrapbook."

"How is Tiffany?"

What was Franke up to? Could she actually need to butter him up for something? "She's spending a week with the grandkids in Kentucky."

Franke nodded and then turned her gaze back to him. They were of an age, both military school graduates. Yet he didn't think asking after her husband, John, was appropriate. "I was hoping you were here to tell me that Walker and Zumati would be reassigned to HAVOC."

She snorted out a breath and shook her head. "Do you honestly feel it a good idea to leave Zumati as an active Hamask?"

"Last I heard, we don't have a way to turn the Hamask abilities off."

"There is always the option to put him out to pasture."

"Kill him. Let's say it how it really is."

"Sanderson has been clear that future missions could have the same liabilities with Zumati's high risk for sense memory. Walker is either unwilling or unable to put his Hamask in his place."

"Or perhaps unwilling to do it our way." Khan slid back from his desk so that he could lean back without his knees hitting the solid wood. He had had time to look back over the sensory testing. He had gone in expecting certain things—like Zumati initiating touch, Walker being silent—yet they had worked off each other without falling into those stereotypes. "I think the pair could benefit the military by being cadre, teaching those newly activated how to handle their abilities."

"Yes, Walker is quite good at handling us all," Franke said. She shook her head and rolled her eyes to the ceiling. "I think the pair should be split and reassigned. Under the Citizen Safety Act, Walker would be allowed to liaise with the FBI and Zumati could process back through until he finds a more suitable Vargr. That or he'd go dormant."

Khan did his best to breathe slowly and keep his body still. He hadn't found a better pair to lead Valhalla. Hell, the funding and project would be trashed, its budget absorbed, and his plans forgotten in the next fiscal year. He'd finally reconciled with the knowledge that Walker was out of his reach, and then the Ieti mission had raised his hopes. He was so close to getting the team he wanted in place.

You wanted to effect change out in the jungle? You had to start with hard truths in training.

He spoke in an even measure. "Walker would do well with the FBI. I'm sure Dr. Bur would sponsor his fieldwork." Khan nodded and tried to look thoughtful. "But he won't go without Zumati. They may act different from a traditional pairing, but I can attest to the fact that these men are bonded. Break that bond and they won't be able to function in a new pairing."

"We both know that sex doesn't equal a true bond. Plenty of active pairs don't require it. Minophen and Jones, our most experienced and decorated Hamra, often welcome a third into their bed."

Khan had heard the rumors but also firmly believed that being poly didn't mean you didn't trust and love your partner. Hell, it was probably an indication of a deeper bond. Who the fuck was he to judge? "They're not my pair, so not my business." He kept his tone light so she wouldn't hear his censure. "Walker and Zumati? They're friends. Only time I've seen that quick of a combat brotherhood was during the Ukraine Liberation. I don't think the Army wants to lose that."

She sat for a long time and just held his gaze. He blinked early, just to let her know he wasn't stooping to some childish staring contest. The air thickened as time slowed, and Khan tried to breathe with a bit of dignity.

"Well, the task force agrees." She uncrossed her legs and stood. Khan stood as well. "Looks like you'll get your Valhalla after all." She nodded and left his office.

Khan watched her walk out and tried to keep his victory fist pump low-key.

WHEN THE call came across the vid feed in their entry room, Rum was teaching Jamal to dance. The Commodity were singing about the hottest place on earth. Rum's face was promising all kinds of journeys as he sang loud and perfectly in key to the old words. Since that first training mission, they'd kept up the lessons, alternating between fighting skills—like the knives—and Jamal's recipe for the perfect pancakes. With three days and counting of being confined to their quarters, they'd taken the days as a much-needed vacation. Rum pulled Jamal close at the waist, stepping together hip to hip, turning and stepping away. As the song faded to "Everyday People" by Sly & the Family Stone, the music cut off and the video feed chimed the incoming communication.

Rum ignored it, singing about different strokes as he rubbed Jamal's bicep. He pulled them in close again and strained up to his toes so he could kiss Jamal's chin. Jamal gripped Rum's ass and pulled them even tighter together. Rum groaned and then disengaged. He squared his shoulders and then, instead of activating the call as it chimed a second time, reached back for Jamal's hand. Rum smiled and gave the general a left-handed salute when the hologram activated. The fact that it was the general himself and not a lackey was surprising.

"My office. Ten minutes."

"Yes, sir," they said together.

They pulled boots on and straightened each other's uniforms, then walked out of the quarters to find a transport waiting for them. They climbed in back, and Jamal reached automatically for Rum's hand.

The general was in his office alone. They saluted and waited for him to acknowledge them. Their wait was almost precisely the same length they'd made him wait before they answered the phone. A little petty, but probably well deserved.

"Sit down." The general stood and came around his desk. Jamal and Rum sat in the chairs facing his desk while the general leaned against the front of his desk.

Khan licked and then smacked his lips as he considered each one of them. He nodded. "The inquiry is over. There will be no further investigation into the bonding status of the Walker-Zumati pair."

Jamal took his cue from Rum, who was more experienced and could read people better than anyone Jamal had ever seen. Rum did not breathe a sigh of relief, and Jamal could almost smell the tension settle on his wolf's shoulders.

The general seemed to be waiting for a response.

"Thank you, sir," Jamal said.

The general nodded and then threaded his fingers in his lap. How would Rum read that gesture? As well as the sigh the general released next.

When Khan spoke, his voice was softer, lower. "Boys, we've got a serious problem with our Vargr."

Jamal's spine tightened at the base, and he felt his palms dampen. *Shit, what was going on?*

"For years we've acknowledged that Hamask had the dangerous possibility to go berserk or fury. But senior, unpaired Vargr also are in danger." Khan stared hard at Rum. "They often become paranoid, reclusive, and self-destructive. The death rate on a ten-year-unpaired Vargr is over 80 percent."

How many Vargr went that long without bonding? Wick, of course, was nearing that number and… Rum. He had said they'd activated at the same time. Jamal turned his head to look at him. Rum sat military precise, calm, blank. Was that where Rum had been headed? Was he safe now? It would explain his demotion. Hell, most people considered pulling Jamal from his fury a suicide mission. Why willingly step into a lion's den unless you were desperate?

"Vargr Walker, you are to be reassigned and placed in charge of a new program called Valhalla. Hamask Zumati will be your second-in-command. Valhalla's sole purpose will be saving these potential losses."

Rum said, "You're activating almost twice as many Vargr to the number of Hamask." He tacked on a delayed "sir" when Jamal nudged his foot.

"It was split fairly evenly until about seven years ago. We're trying to figure out why."

"Meanwhile—" Rum seethed. The general crossed his arms and tightened his mouth. Jamal could hear his heart speed up. When Rum continued, his tone was more respectful. "—you're activating them without them fully knowing the risks."

The general stared at Rum for a long, silent moment, then addressed his next words to Jamal. "The Secretary of Defense and the Minister of Special Warfare have designated Valhalla as a mating program."

Rum snorted, then crossed his arms and slid to a slouch in his chair.

"Valhalla will find out why we are activating so many Vargr. We will focus on the overall health and safety of unpaired Hamra and help them bond. You will be outside the line of command for the training cadre and will answer only to me."

Jamal blew out a quiet breath. This would be their new focus. If you can't play, coach. Wasn't that how the old saying went? There would be no more hoops to jump through; Khan obviously supported them. This was perfect. A giddy froth filled his stomach. He didn't bother hiding his smile.

"Sir, no, sir. I formally request to be discharged from service," Rum said, disdain dripping from each word.

"The fuck?" Jamal said.

Rum stared daggers at Khan. Khan shook his head and stared over their shoulders, possibly into space, searching for patience. He stood and walked back around to stand behind his desk.

Rum wasn't done running his stupid mouth. Jamal tried to use his eyes to pin him in place, but Rum, acting oblivious, ignored Jamal's second nudge of his boot.

"I will accept a dishonorable discharge if I need to."

"Shut up, Walker." Khan placed his hands on his desk and leaned forward. "The first Vargr assigned to the Valhalla program will be Wickham Ieti. You have a real chance to save that man's life."

Rum snorted and slouched even farther into his seat.

What, is he suddenly twelve again?

"Lieutenant Zumati, take your Vargr and talk some sense into him. You have six hours to return with a formal decision."

"I said—"

Jamal grabbed Rum's arm and yanked him out of his chair. "Yes, sir. Thank you for the time, sir."

"Six hours—" Rum sputtered and went to step forward.

Jamal fisted his hand in the back of Rum's uniform to keep him in place. "Ryan, shut. Up."

"Dismissed."

Jamal saluted and Rum just walked out. He walked not toward the privacy of their quarters but to the eco ground. Jamal's foster mom always called them "parks." This one had a couple of water features, several trees, grass, and benches. You could sit and watch the traffic in and out of the base.

Jamal worried for a moment that Rum would walk past the groomed yard to the gate and keep walking. Take that AWOL determination to the extreme and leave the base.

"Rum? You stubborn idiotic ass. Ryan!" Even now, Jamal could feel that deeper connection. It felt new but not fragile. Like a strong foundation, it would get battered but would be fine. He smiled, let the emotions well up inside him. They could make this work. Valhalla, their own saving grace. "Talk to me."

Rum spun around, eyes blazing and chest rising with each angry breath. Half an hour ago they were dancing, laughing. Now all this negative energy was just pouring off Rum. Jamal could hear the tension. "Intergenerational transmission of beliefs."

"WHAT?" JAMAL'S brows drew together.

"It's the idea that you believe what you're told, without question, by your parents and they by their parents. It covers almost everything. The perpetuation of abuse, racism, even favorite sports teams." Rum's body seemed stuck, his emotions and body vibrating on a high enough frequency that the tremors were invisible. Even with all his attention focused on this new issue, he couldn't quite grasp and hold all of the variables. He felt empty. His brain had finished shock, processed anger, set aside disbelief, and settled on hopeless. He would never escape their clutches. Even now he felt a sharp pressure on his chest, like scaly talons gripping around him.

He breathed out twice. Only Jamal's presence kept him from wanting to storm back in and pick a fight with the general so they would court-martial him.

Jamal had trusted Rum enough to tell him about his surrender. It was further proof that they were really building a relationship here. It felt so close, like this almost-perfect, nearly euphoric dynamic. A little bit more time and it would all fall into place, they could live happily together. But that very relationship was going to trap Jamal here forever.

"The Hamrammr program has been around for nearly a hundred years! And we still perpetuate dominance and submission in Hamra Pairs, rely on 'magic' processes to activate, and discard those who are broken. Those who don't meet the standard are put down. Sure, docile pairs are allowed to retire. They can even work in the private sector, like my parents. But the rest? Pairs like us? You can't deactivate a Hamra, so you keep them contained or you terminate them."

Jamal just continued to look at Rum. His dark skin glowed under the light of the sun. They'd forgone shaving that morning, yet Jamal's sharp cheekbones looked just as smooth as yesterday. He was enchanting. Definitely Rum's idea of the perfect leading man.

He needed Jamal to see his side in this, really understand where he was coming from. Rum realized in that moment that he hadn't talked about his college years. Being a kid, growing up with Hamrammrs as parents, he'd openly shared all of that with Jamal. Even the years since activation. But not the in-between years. "I've got a BA in Film from Wesleyan, including two semesters at the Beijing Film Academy. When I came to HAVOC, I'd just finished my masters in Fine Arts at the American Film Institute. AFI, man! Dianna Fogel teaches there. Are you hearing me? Like, I was there." He gestured with his hands. "I was going to… make a difference in the way people see Hamrammrs. Target-specific stigma change. That's where you sculpt future generations' beliefs by showing them the truths through movies."

Jamal held up a hand to halt his rapid words. "You lost me. Why did you go to film school if you planned to join the military? You were raised by a stable Hamra Pair." Jamal leaned forward and placed his forearms on his thighs. Before Rum could reply, he added, "Wait, Rum, back up. Are you telling me *Sesame Street* vids are a way to brainwash the next generation?"

Rum swallowed and rubbed a hand over the top of his hair, tried to breathe in a steady rhythm.

Jamal kept talking. "Of course, I assume people are bisexual until I know either way, because that episode with the gay trains. Shit."

Probably reeling from having his world blown apart mentally, Jamal ran his fingers across his short hair and looked off into the distance.

"I didn't plan on it," Rum finally said. "Joining the USHP, coming to HAVOC. Look at me." Once Jamal made eye contact, Rum gestured with his arms, dismissive. Rum knew his eyes were bright with anger. "I'm short. I could barely see. Not HAVOC material. Then they changed the physical requirements. You no longer needed twenty-twenty to enter the program, I had a ton of debt, and I had the most *idiotic* idea that I couldn't create something I didn't know firsthand."

"They activate you and you'll know personally what you're writing about? Makes sense." Jamal laughed. "That's why you can hide the accent so well. Acting classes."

Seriously, that was what Jamal focused on when Rum's world was crashing? "It was like I was a music prodigy and they were courting me hard. They probably think the wider requirements caused the issues with activation rates. Stupid bastards." He pushed out another breath. "Then, anytime I really step out of line, thumb my nose at the brass—"

"They use the Citizen Safety Act to keep you."

"I can't leave if they can prove they still need my skill set. They'll court-martial me and string me up one day. It's the only way I'm getting out. Khan just proved that in there." Rum's voice had raised back to shouting. He took a breath and shook out his shoulders to try and calm down.

"I won't let them hurt you." Jamal sounded primal, menacing.

Rum could track his Adam's apple moving the full length of his throat. It didn't help that they both knew Rum wasn't joking about being terminated.

Jamal took a deep breath. "This is your chance, Rum. Change it from the inside. If they give you carte blanche to do this Valhalla program the right way, you can make a difference." He scooted over on the bench and patted the seat next to him.

"You get a choice. I need to believe you still have a choice in all of this. I didn't condemn you to this life." Rum dropped down next to him, happy to let his body slouch. The bad posture was ridiculously satisfying. A little bit of rebellion.

"A life where I'm partnered with a brilliant soldier, fighting alongside a friend? Hard life, that. Three squares a day and you'd think I was serving time for being incredibly handsome."

Rum chuckled. Jamal hadn't touched him. Yet he felt soothed. "That you are. Handsome. And my friend." The strains to Barker's *Once More* soundtrack filled his head. He hummed a few notes to himself.

Rum laughed but then felt all the what-ifs flood his neural pathways again.

"Stop that. I had you mellow there for a minute. Don't fester over the worries. Share them."

Wow. Rum felt like a tadpole out of water, surprised and grasping to find his footing. He didn't realize Jamal could read him so well. And that shock-awareness gave him a full dressing-down. He loved this man so much that seeing it, finally, made him gasp and press a hand to his stomach. Then just waves of pleasant heat. *Huh.*

He'd told Jamal before that he was falling for him. Was Jamal there yet? Did he feel the same way for Rum?

When Rum didn't say anything, Jamal smiled and said, "Sounds like Khan's Valhalla program would let you do that. Have some say in how the military runs HAVOC."

"Yeah." It was way too good to be true. How fucked-up were their options if they were choosing to work with Rum on this project? How many more secrets were HAVOC hiding?

"Now you're thinking of all the problems and second-guessing why they'd choose you."

"What if I am?" Rum nearly crossed his arms and stuck out his lip.

"Just letting you know that I know."

Rum recognized that the angles weren't changing, no matter how many times they cycled through his mind. He needed to share the issue with Jamal. Another pair of eyes on the problem would help, plus Jamal would understand better than anyone else. "I can't do the program. When we were in that lab with Wick? I was one of *them*." He pointed back toward the general's office. "I fell back on procedure. I tried to use *regulations*." He shook his head, as if to unhinge it from his shoulders. "That cluster was *fucked*. It was this close to moving sideways." Rum didn't bother to demonstrate with his hands. "And it's not just me anymore. I'm going to probably thumb my nose, like before, but now it will hurt you too. Could hurt everyone involved in this program."

"You're getting better at working as a pair, as part of a team. We both are."

Rum reached out and rubbed Jamal's forearm. "Do you think Khan will actually give me that much say?"

"A lowly pair of lieutenants in charge of a multi-billion dollar, high-clearance program? Yeah. I think he was basically pleading with you to take the reins. Might let you skip forward to major. They haven't done battlefield promotions since World War II, so that would be cool."

Rum sighed and continued to hold on to Jamal's forearm. Jamal turned his hand over, and they both watched as Rum slid his fingertips down Jamal's tender flesh to his pulse point. Rum felt that flood of warmth, waves of it pushing toward his heart. He slipped his hand down the rest of the way to grasp Jamal's.

After a long moment—the song still cycling in his head—Rum said, "You know that scene in *Once More*, where Dianna Fogel sings with her dad's lover? I can give you the history clear back to James Brown in 1965. Original song title 'I Got You.'"

"Who?"

Rum turned to look Jamal straight on. "You've just sentenced yourself to an awesome weekend listening to Motown while your lover, who I might add, had six units on vocal performance in school, sings and dances."

"I got a trailer view this morning. Can this conviction include naked dancing?"

"You make me feel good." Rum smiled, and Jamal smiled back. Then it occurred to Rum just how they'd gotten to this point.

"What's that look for?"

"Do you know what this means? Khan let me wake you up for this very purpose." He let the laughter pour out. "I've been upstaged."

"Or we can say this was your plan all along." Jamal's rich brown eyes showed his relief and his pleasure.

"Yeah. My plan all along."

Jamal stood up, flipped Rum over his shoulder, and then ran flat out back to the general's office.

Rum laughed and reached down to smack Jamal's ass. Heavens, if an almost-botched rescue mission got them a promotion, showing this much bonding pleasure might get them knighted.

Chapter 16

HAVOC Class, 2098

ON THE third day of activations, Jamal entered the private quarters of female petty officer Davidson with Valhalla's activation team. They had activated one more Vargr than Hamask and were hoping this activation swung in their favor.

Jamal stood just inside the door and watched Rum greet Davidson with easygoing grace. No pressure and, thankfully, no nudity. Rum talked her through the process, and once she was ready—this brave lift of her sharp chin, eyes clear and determined—the doctor started the acupuncture. Rum stood back, and Jamal reached for his hand.

"You owe me," Jamal whispered. It felt a bit like talking in class, and it didn't matter that the other three Hamask present would hear despite the whisper. You were supposed to whisper in class.

Rum didn't say anything, his eyes sharply focused on the scene before him.

Valhalla had been given half of the potentials from the latest class to guide through the activation process. The idea was to have a control group to compare the results. When they got a fifty-fifty activation— Rum told Jamal he was confident in their success rate—they would take over the activation of all candidates. Half the class had headed to the shacks. The set they had handpicked was then led back to the initial lecture hall to be given full disclosure.

Rum continued to ignore Jamal's statement. Rum had been sure that if the potentials knew Vargr could self-destruct and Hamask could fury they would hesitate and a few would even drop out. So sure, in fact, that he'd placed a wager. No one changed their minds. Jamal didn't rub it in when Rum finally transferred the five-dollar credit to his bank on his smartwatch.

Together they had spent several weeks planning for these days of activation. Wick and three unpaired Hamask attended each one with

Jamal and Rum. Newly activated Hamask had never acted negatively toward each other so they didn't foresee any issues. Wick and the Hamask chosen had medical training so they could provide assistance if necessary.

Wick used a sponge to paint Davidson's skin with quick efficiency. Jamal stayed completely present, with not a single spike to any of his senses. He could tell that Rum was keeping an eye on his body language, looking for any change or agitation.

Hamask Ensign Kramer scurried like a small bird around the giant alligator that was Wick Ieti. Despite the several painful inches Kramer had grown after activating, there was still a serious size gap, not to mention the age difference. Kramer had his eye on being paired with Wick. Jamal had another five on that particular outcome.

Jamal caught Rum staring at him again. Jamal smiled to let his wolf know he was handling everything just fine. He squeezed Rum's hand. Yesterday morning, Rum had stared at him across their new kitchen table, and Jamal often woke in the morning to find Rum scrutinizing each breath and stretch as Jamal's body greeted the day. Perhaps Rum was waiting for the second boot to drop.

It would be just like Rum to second-guess this position *because* it was so perfect for him. He knew which candidates to encourage and which ones needed to prove themselves before activation would be a good idea. He had weeded out a pair of bullies from the cadre ranks who were terrorizing the candidates. He was a director of a large production, each Hamask and Vargr currying for his favor. It was perfect.

So why the long looks? Jamal and his abilities were useful too. He was teaching and supporting Rum. Yet, as he stood looking at Rum, Jamal realized why Rum had been so concerned—because he was making sure Jamal was happy with their new place in life.

As Hamask Davidson came online, Jamal nudged Rum forward to welcome her to Valhalla and help her establish baselines. Rum worked seamlessly with the activation team. Wick and Kramer would help the newbie move into the Valhalla housing. They were a team, and it felt good finally to see Rum depend on more than just himself.

Rum took Jamal's hand once again and turned to leave Davidson's quarters. "I say we take the evening off. No more case studies to read. Just us, a pint of ice cream, and *What's Up, Doc?*"

"We can't."

Rum groaned. "Someone else can play matchmaker for a few hours."

All unpaired USHP active military had been assigned to Valhalla. Even if they worked in other units, Rum received their records and together he and Jamal had built a database of who wanted and needed pairing. Jamal joked that it was like going through a Jewish matchmaker. Rum shouldn't have shown him *Fiddler on the Roof*.

Clearly Rum had lost track of time. Jamal pressed a brief kiss to the top of Rum's head. "We're about to have visitors."

Bur, Brad S., PhD,—Personal Journal, Returned 2098, HAVOC.
Keep your hands off my journal, you damn dirty ape.
Page 37

JUST TO be clear, I wasn't exactly on board with bringing the pinhead and the hothead into this investigation. Upside, we've been stationed in Havana, putting together international charges against Woodland and Dios Provee for months. Downside, this means political maneuvering. President Santmosa of Columbia, who, lah-de-dah, was once head of the South American Union, has agreed to let the United Nations help bring Woodland to justice. Awesome. Even better, the UN was all, like, "All right, FBI. Go in and get this guy."

Personally, I think they should have asked us and we could have gone in all sneaky and snatched the bastard. Instead they staged a press conference and demanded he turn himself in. Then they issued a warrant for his arrest. Now we've got expats and mercs trying to get our man before we do. It's not like there is a bounty out for his head. Yet it's taken on a big-game-hunting frenzy.

HAVOC looks like a military base. What? I'm not spending a page describing boring-ass cement. It's gray. Moving on. Major Ryan Walker and 1st Lt. Jamal Zumati stand at the edge of the tarmac and watch the helicopter descend. Jamal has noise-canceling headphones on, despite this bird being pretty damn quiet, new technology and all. It's powered by a bloom engine. Look it up. Pretty tight. Besides the two of them there are a few other men and women. Longwei is considerate and tells me the ones he recognizes before I can get a good look.

We step clear of the helicopter and someone I don't recognize tries to welcome us to the base, blah-blah.

"Make sure this gets to our room." I toss my duffel at this stick on legs, some young lieutenant. Wick Ieti snags the bag out of the air, which makes me smile. "This could be fun."

I especially like how pissed off the kid is that Ieti steps in.

Rum thanks the greeter and steps forward to shake our hands. I'm having none of that. I pull him into a hug, stick my nose right in the crook of his neck. I give great bear hugs. Pop always says I'm likely to break a rib, to which I always reply, "Only ribs of fragile old men." Damn, I miss him.

Longwei pulls me off him, shakes his hand, and presses his forehead to Rum's. Rum got USHP off our backs. We haven't been monitored in over a year.

He goes to introduce us and I shush him. "Jamal Zumati?"

"Dr. Bur." Zumati extends his hand, all quiet confidence. I like that in men.

Rum is still doggedly going on with the introductions. I know that when I need them, the names will come to me.

The greeter leaves us in "good hands." He hasn't stepped more than two feet away before I'm telling Jamal that he needs hazard pay to be anyone's "good hands." If they're giving out hand jobs, I want one.

Ieti volunteers to take our kit and Longwei is all superpolite with the thank-yous. Stick goes running along behind him, carrying one of our bags. Poor guy is panting at the wrong heels. I even say so. "That'll never happen."

Rum sees where I'm looking and looks pleased as piss. Jamal is shaking his head. "Don't listen to relationship advice from this Casanova here." A pretty weak dig, even with Jamal's sarcasm.

Rum indicates our direction. "Dr. Bur, Agent Longwei, if you'll follow us."

"You can call me Haruki," Longwei says.

I don't know what the hell he is thinking. I don't even call him that. I'm not jealous or anything. Okay, I am. Shut up.

"Pop that ego, Major," I tell Rum. "It doesn't mean he likes you. He just thinks you might actually be able to pronounce it correctly."

Longwei takes my hand. He laughs, maybe at me. Whatever.

Let me set the stage a little. Rum is like that superhot guy in school on the wrestling team. You know. His features are a bit average, except for the killer blue-green eyes, and his body is compact and muscular.

Jamal has dark skin for miles, full lips, cut cheekbones. They're both ridiculous. The fact that I took so little notice of Rum before, that just means he was messing with my head back then.

It's just the four of us walking across the compound, past hangars and toward wherever our destination is. And I'm thinking about Rum playing his "aw, shucks" routine with us. So I just go for it. I ask him about New Tokyo, adding, "Don't shit me this time. Seriously, you went into a Triad compound without permission?"

"First of all, it wasn't unsanctioned. My commander agreed to my plan. He was completely drunk on rice wine, but"—he pulls the door open and holds it for us to pass him—"I'd spent time in my younger years in Beijing. I speak excellent Mandarin. I'm short. With a little costuming, I didn't need to sneak in."

"So it's just a tall tale?" And it's Jamal asking this. Like what, they didn't have this out day one? Course, if I had a couple of young things like them at my dick and balls, I'd spend plenty of time not talking. I must be smirking or looking like that lewd nut that parks by the eco ground to watch the twinks walk by, because Longwei pinches my side.

I swipe a hand over Rum's head. "I think that pun went right past him."

Longwei yanks me close. "Try not to get us kicked out."

I turn the innocent eyes up to a four. That's as high as they go. Longwei snorts out a laugh, even presses a quick kiss to my mouth.

Rum continues. "Nope. It happened, just gets bent in the retelling. Once I took out the hostiles, I figured I'd let the Hamask loose and it would be like a frag grenade in a china shop. Turns out he actually has a surprising amount of control. By then, Cooper's team—Peytlyn was still team lead then—is at the front door wreaking havoc."

Nice one. I'm going to wait until just the right moment and use that one myself.

We enter one of the larger holo rooms. The table has power stations for smartwatches and field tablets. There are several pitchers of water and glasses on a side cabinet. Water is always a sign of a really long meeting. "Joy."

I hate long meetings. Just gives me more time to mess things up.

Rum explains that we're waiting for Colonel Gelbrit and General Khan. Which means I've got time to be bored. Never ideal.

"Is it true what they say about black guys?" Yep, I say it just like that. But see, the way I'm thinking about it is if this guy is going to 'roid out during the mission, then I don't want him anywhere near it. We've worked this case too long and too hard to see it get flushed because we put our trust in a Pair that isn't functioning.

Jamal tries to call my bluff. "That we're well hung?" He makes it clear he isn't impressed with me or my attitude. Not so much pissed off or anything, more just finds my antics juvenile.

"Must be, to land a size queen like Walker here. No, what I heard was that black guys are just like all other guys."

"It's true," Longwei says. When he decides to play along with whatever I'm stuck on, he can really do it up right. Gets superserious and becomes all dignified assurance. I'm telling you, very sexy.

"There's no pissing this guy off." I indicate Longwei with my thumb. "I've tried." I start working on the vids we'll need for our sales pitch. My field tablet connects to the table just fine and I enter my security code, swipe my identification card, and let it scan my face. "Idiot thinks I'm adorable."

Rum tilts his head, bats his eyelashes, and sighs deep enough to rattle his chest. He puts on this Southern accent and everything, plays it up real well. "That's because you get all sappy-eyed when you look at him." It has me laughing.

When I get my breath back, I say, "Of course I do. The man is perfect."

Longwei shoves me aside and starts to manipulate the data to bring up the correct images. Don't mistake the action for any real censure. He looks pleased. I stand by my assessment.

My body is twitching a bit, like the buildup of excess energy ready to jump like static electricity. "Bored." I say it to both whine and also to give Longwei the heads-up. Sometimes he comes back with a well-deserved "Tough shit. Suck it up." The other half of the time he distracts me with something.

This time he chooses to ignore me. He's focused on the HoloPoint. We've got sweet holos, complete 3-D imagery of the compound and the surrounding area. I watch it pop up on the table, like if I could just shrink down, I could walk into it. That'll never get static. I'm super jazzed about getting Rum's opinion on Woodland. I've brought field vid from Woodland's days in the military. All those politicians that pushed for drone evaluation out in the field will have a poster boy after we build this profile against the Dios Provee leader. One of the actual times drone footage will be used to take out the bad guy instead of building criminal cases against soldiers and cops.

"Okay, so let's start without the rest. I don't mind talking twice."

"Evidently," Longwei says.

"Obviously," Jamal adds.

Rum wants to give them both a high five. I can see it in his face. Makes my stomach feel all warm and burns off a bit of that jittery energy.

"You've got four weeks before the next Indoc class starts. Instead of going on some lame vacation, the FBI is requesting your assistance. You'll get the details here in a minute, but short version, Dios Provee compound outside of Bogota? We infiltrate and kick ass."

"We're not doing field missions."

At this point Jamal reaches for Rum's hand, but it's more of an unconscious gesture, to show affection, rather than needing Rum to center him. So far everything I've witnessed has put me at ease. I'd done a few subtle things to test Jamal since walking out of that helicopter. I've read his file and know about the foster homes. He has a very low tolerance for bullies. I've also turned up the pheromones. Walker may have gotten the jet-speed reflexes with his Vargr activation, but with mine, I can turn my pheromones on and off as needed. Pheromones aren't just lust; they can also induce anger, fear, doubt. So far Jamal acts like he's just hanging out with his pals. His older, cooler pals.

"Yeah, that would be crazy stupid. Let's stick the raging hothead into a compromised situation. Brilliant."

They're both leaning against the side of the table, watching Longwei do his thing. With my words, Rum steps toward me, eyes all intense. Not an easy target now, are you? Like I said earlier, this could be fun.

Except Longwei is there to keep my ass from getting kicked. He speaks quickly but isn't all defensive, more like he's just clarifying my point. "Which won't be a problem. We'd use you two specifically in Command Central."

Yes, they recognize their own limitations. Hell, we all have them. And rather than quitting outright, Walker found the perfect job for them, running Valhalla. It was probably this epic manipulation going on months before they were assigned to the program. I'm not capable of planning that far ahead. See, limitation recognized.

I explain why we chose them. Rum has worked with me and Longwei before, and we trust him. Jamal is the icing on the cake, because the man has serious skills, even working remotely. Them and WREAC T6 are the only ones we're reading in on this mission. We want a tight lid. No leaks, clean op.

Rum looks at Jamal and raises an eyebrow. Seems they're speaking in code, because Jamal just says, "Chakosky is bitching to the colonel about one of the testing cadre. He'll be a few more minutes. Khan isn't in the building yet."

"Hm," Longwei says. Which means he's impressed.

So they've established we've got a pocket of time. Rum walks to the cabinet and pulls out a box wrapped in bright blue paper with a silver bow. If you're going to give, make a statement, right? I doubt the base store has a huge selection of wrapping paper, so extra effort. But whatever. He tries to hand it to me, but I ain't taking foreign shit until I've checked with Longwei. At least not anymore. Longwei just looks curious. That means he doesn't smell or hear anything concerning. I rip the paper apart to get to the box. It's fancy, even has a lid rather than just being taped closed.

Rum talks this whole time. "I wanted to send you and Longwei a bottle of scotch as a thank-you. I'd read your research on navigating the fury state and then saw your success." He means with Longwei. I can be all articulate and insightful when I want, and that research is some of my best moments. "It gave me the guts to help Jamal."

I pause just before I lift the lid. If this gift needs a speech like that, I don't think I'll make it past the feels. I'm gearing up to say something particularly bitchy, but I see Longwei shake his head at me. I scrunch up my mouth and open the box. "I take back all the times I called you a pinhead… and lame and mouse and—" I'm actually aiming for nice, but it sounds defensive.

"None of which I've heard you actually call me." Rum crosses his arms.

It's my journal. This journal, the one I'm writing in right now. Browning and his goons had taken it, along with my research, field tablet, smartwatch. All of it. I recognize that they were following procedure, but holy hell, that had sucked cow dung. I had backups of the research and the FBI issued me another watch, but this… I pull the journal from the box and flip to the last entry. There's a bunch of labels indicating it's been processed as evidence. The last label is recent. I read it out loud. "Keep your hands off my journal, you damn dirty ape?"

"Movie reference," Jamal explains.

"And oh-so appropriate, my furry friend. There is a difference between letting your hair down and letting yourself go. Manscaping is your friend."

Longwei takes the book out of my shaking hands. "Thank you," he says because he can see how much I like the gift.

"Yeah, what he said," I manage. Longwei nudges me, so I come back with, "What? You think oral would be a better show of gratitude?"

Jamal turns to look at the door and then says, "Colonel finally ditched Chakosky. I think he is using his watch to notify the general."

Rum indicates the box. "I hope you enjoy the scotch."

Yeah, he isn't being subtle. This never happened. Anyone listening will think he really has given me a bottle of scotch. Even the movie quote can be attributed to a greeting card. I'm feeling more in favor of this whole joint effort. These guys know their shit.

Longwei puts the book back into the box, closes the lid, and sets it carefully out of sight.

"Thanks." Ma would be so pleased with my sincerity level on this one. I pull out the pastor voice. "No sarcasm." I have to pause and take a breath before I can continue. "This really was a decent gesture."

Rum nods. "If either of you ever need anything, just let us know. You'll always be welcomed in Valhalla."

He walks to the door just in time to open it for Gelbrit. He's professional and polite, and the colonel has no clue he's being handled. Super fun to watch. No longer bored.

Chapter 17

A FEW days later, Rum and Jamal were back in the same holo room receiving a report from Browning about the latest activation's progress through their individual MOS training. Browning looked to be nursing a hangover. Next to him were his three top training cadre. It felt like sides were being drawn, so Rum brought Wick and Lisa to the meeting to even out the numbers. The two Vargr—Lisa and Wick—got along like siblings, ones that liked each other. Neither had gotten frustrated with the other's overbearing protective side. At least not yet.

From Browning's report, it was clear all activated Hamrammr were handling their new abilities. There were a few injuries to report as they purposely pushed themselves to find their new limits. Happened with every class; someone needed to test their new boundaries. It was the main reason all Hamrammr bases were dry. You didn't want to get supersoldiers drunk and set them loose.

Davidson had filed a request to pair with Sylvia Baker. If Baker was in agreement, it would be Valhalla's first match and the first double-female pair since McCarthy-Ladd. Which might have been Browning's reason to drink. Rum could imagine the anxiety of the situation. How do you describe double maidenheads in reports? Though maybe Rum was being too harsh. Since the start of Valhalla, Browning had supported their efforts. If Rum read him correctly, Browning was relieved.

They'd made it through about half of the individual cadets when Jamal suddenly slid his chair back and stood, looking at the door. One of the cadre, also a Hamask, stood as well, even took a step toward the door. This immediately had the rest of the room on its feet.

Clive Cooper entered the room and saluted Browning as senior officer.

Browning returned the salute and barked, "Report."

"The helo carrying Dr. Bur and Agent Longwei back to Havana lost contact over the Gulf of Mexico." His words were rushed together, his eyes intense.

Browning and the cadre didn't know, beyond base gossip, about the planned operation with the FBI. It wasn't scheduled to start for another two days. FBI Director Kimball had wanted to wait until the president had agreed to the action.

Lisa said, "Fucking hell." She dropped back to her seat and buried her head in her hands.

Cooper was already continuing. "Walker, Zumati, they want you on deck. They're sending us in now."

Cooper seemed off. Shouldn't he have asked to speak privately with Rum? Rum turned to Browning and said, "Colonel, thank you for meeting with us. If you can send us a copy of the minutes and reports on each serviceman." Browning simply nodded and led his team out.

"Cooper," Rum said to indicate he should proceed.

"T6 will be going to the compound with the FBI Critical Incident Response team. We're leaving now. We'll be in place in just under eight hours."

Rum's head buzzed with necessary changes to the plan without Longwei and Bur in place, but then he saw Jamal looking at Wick. Wick stood with his fists on the table, head hung down between his shoulders.

"Are they sending in a different Hamra Pair or…?" Rum let his voice drift off under all the details of what he needed to alter in their plan.

The compound definitely needed a pair to guide the men past booby traps; it all hinged on that. Rum's brain finally caught up with the full impact of Cooper's message. A sharp pinch gripped the top of his spine and his hands started to tingle. His stomach dropped. Jamal wrapped an arm around him and told him to breathe.

He had a lot of respect for Bur and Longwei. Hell, they had fast become friends. To lose them like this felt so hollow.

"Minophen and Jones are going in. They were prepped as backup, so they know the mission," Cooper said.

At that point, Rum's brain engaged enough to take note of a few things he had been ignoring. Cooper had closed the door behind him and stepped around Rum and Jamal. Rum thought for a moment that his eyes, intense and expressive for the first time Rum had ever seen, were trained on Lisa. Instead, Cooper stepped up to Wick. He pulled the big man's arm to get him to turn toward the WREAC team leader. Then Cooper wrapped his arms around Wick. Maybe you could say it was two buddies saying good-bye, except Wick raised an unsteady arm to embrace Cooper back.

Then Cooper was gone.

Well, crap. How long had that been a thing? Was it serious? Was that why Wick ignored all the baby Hamask running around his ankles?

Rum looked at Jamal. Jamal's eyes were unfocused as he stared off into space. "What is it?"

"I don't know," Jamal whispered. "Just a feeling."

Rum considered teasing him; Jamal had seen that embrace too. But that pinch continued to spread down Rum's back. "What kind of feeling?"

"They're not dead. It's too soon for them to discover any kind of wreckage. When they do…." He shook his head. "I just…. We shouldn't rule them out yet."

RUM BURNED through six hours of sleep while the assault teams were in transit. He was standing at his kitchen counter, eating apple pie from the mess, when Jamal stopped midsentence and walked to the door to let Lisa in.

Lisa didn't act surprised that Jamal would know she was coming. She was in full uniform—Rum doubted she owned any other clothes— and she looked wrecked. Her long straight brown hair had come loose from her braid, wisps framing her face. Her breathing was uneven, and whatever else she was emitting had quickly wound Jamal up like a top.

"Can you double-check?" she asked Jamal.

Jamal didn't get insulted. Instead he took Rum's hand and closed his eyes, letting his senses amp up to scan the area. Occasionally he tilted his head. Rum softly tapped his fingers against the counter in a long-delay pattern. Sometimes it was the repeat of sounds on recording devices that Hamask would hear first.

Currently, Rum was working on the theory that Jamal could use his hearing so well because he tied it to his sense of touch, not touching Rum, but feeling the frequency at which things vibrated. Jamal described his hearing with visuals, able to place with strong precision the location of what was causing the noise. He opened his eyes, the pupils pinpoint tight, and he blinked several times until they adjusted. "We're good."

Lisa held up her mini field tablet. "When Dr. Bur was here, he asked that I show him how to send information to a specific IP from his smartwatch."

"Does anyone actually still use the IP system?" Jamal asked.

"Cell phones still have them as a backup system to the main, like a generator. He said that last year the knowledge would have come in handy. But what good is that going to do him if he can't spend five minutes typing it all in?"

Rum nodded to encourage her. Whatever she had to say must be important enough to come in person rather than just sending him a message or video calling him.

"So I created an app that acts as a type of panic button. He activated it an hour ago."

They are *alive. We can save them.* The relief pressed a harsh breath out of Rum's lungs. He felt light.

But wait.... Rum took in her fierce eyes, her makeup-free face, and her adamant grip on her cell, which she still raised in the air. Lisa had been active and unpaired for a long time. She impatiently brushed hair out of her eyes. No, this wasn't just paranoia or wishful thinking. This felt very real. And though she hadn't been officially bonded, ever, she had been paired with different Hamask for the majority of her activation.

"Audio recording?" Jamal asked.

"Yes, and limited visuals."

"What else?" Rum asked.

"The doctor said there was someone on the inside."

"Brad talked to you?" Rum wiped his mouth on a napkin and went to the couch to fish his boots out from underneath. He made quick work of getting them on.

"No, he is talking to his captors. Almost running commentary but subtle."

She unpaused what must have been a live feed. Rum could hear Brad telling someone that he would never break, that his captor was a pissant bitch. That was definitely Brad's voice. Whatever Jamal could hear had him pressing a hand to his mouth and swallowing.

"But we have a signal, which means the techs can trace it back." Rum stood and tugged at his pant legs to straighten them.

"No." Lisa was resolute but not crazy-eyed. "We are keeping this between us."

Rum recognized that she was right. Not a single Ghost Chinook had ever been shot down. They couldn't be tracked by satellite and had anti-targeting equipment. Someone would need to know where they were and when they were coming, and have the right jamming devices and visuals.

If Wick really had been moved that many times because of an insider, then who had given them the information? Who hadn't known that Franke's unit was coming? As the radical leader, Woodland was former Marine Raiders and still had United States citizenship. Wick gave the FBI and the United Nations the necessary details they had needed to finally press charges.

"Plus I've already traced it." Lisa started to pace back and forth across their living room. "They're using some type of dampening, which won't let me transmit to the phone or ping its GPS."

"But the signal has to come from somewhere." Jamal stared at her cell, tracking its movement across the room. His eyes were wide and dull.

"Right, but only *one* somewhere. You need three to get a specific lock. Hell, two would be doable, but one teltom tower?" She shook her head.

Jamal reached out and took her phone, pausing the feed. "I can hear his blood dripping." He took a couple of shallow breaths and Rum rubbed a hand across his back. Jamal continued. "Rum needs to go to the command deck and help with the mission to take the compound. If Bur and Longwei are there, then we need to make sure they aren't taken out in the crossfire."

Jamal was now lit up with a stony determination. Rum hadn't felt this level of passionate determination coming off him since Jamal had told him about his surrender.

"Me and Lisa will go to a holo room and work on any verbal clues Bur might be relaying. Maybe if we boost the signal, we'll get another tower in play."

"They're not at the compound. That teltom tower? It's Cancun. Even max range of the watch, which is 160 kilometers, no way is it picking something up all the way from Columbia."

Mexico? How far were the Bahamas? Even Cuba, where they had been headed, had to be hundreds of miles from Cancun. Would there be a place that had a low enough population that a crash would go unreported? Any populated place would have shown a crash on social media.

Jamal gathered Rum up in his arms and tucked him underneath his chin. It felt good to be pressed against Jamal's solid heat. His strong hands pressed just the right spots on Rum's back to line their bodies up as he liked. It felt like home and welcome and safe. "Stop. All those what-ifs you are puzzling? Lisa and I will do that. They need you clearheaded and on deck in—" He checked his watch, "—ten minutes."

Lisa nodded. "We'll be in holo room 4."

Rum turned his face into Jamal's chest and took a deep breath. "Let's do this."

JAMAL PULLED up mapping and weather as well as specs on the Ghost Chinook and its flight crew. The flight plan looked standard and there weren't any weather issues along the trajectory. He did mental calculations based on speed and planned elevation and the time they had been told the bird went down. No SOS had been sent. Jamal pulled up commercial flights and overlaid them. He calculated wind buffer from the sonic wash of the two private planes with flight plans in the area. It narrowed down some land options, but "Lisa, has the signal fluctuated at all?"

She had been working on setting up the holodeck so that Jamal could walk through the image they did have. "I hadn't thought of that." She gestured to her head. "Too much noise sometimes. Especially without Travers."

"What happened?" Jamal had noticed she'd been going solo lately, but he figured once it became his business, it would be because Lisa asked Valhalla to set her up with a new Hamask. If she kept to her normal pattern, she would pick a freshly activated male Hamask. They called her "the cougar" for a reason.

"Travers plans to submit a request to work with Bennet."

"I'm sorry." The few times Rum had talked about being reassigned, Jamal had felt like his head had been stuffed in a plastic bag, as if he couldn't gather any oxygen and the thin plastic walls were pressing against his mouth and nose, strangling him.

"I'm not." She hadn't once paused tapping and swiping at her field tablet. "Okay, signal has remained the same."

So probably not a boat or moving vehicle. Good. Great, even, because they were going to save Bur and Longwei. Jamal could feel the truth in the way his knees shook and his arms tingled.

Jamal left his list of possible locations up on the screen. The holodeck came up, blue lines representing the solid state the watch could see and green lines for what might be there. "Shit."

The watch was in a box and had only gotten a limited view of one wall and the ceiling before being put there. Jamal used his hands to rewind the projections to when it was activated. "Is there any memory before the panic button was pushed?"

"Yes, but not that we'll have access to."

"Would it have synced at any point on the journey? Like towers it may have passed?"

"Ah, I love you." Lisa chuckled, snapped her field tablet to the closest console, and started typing with a new frenzy.

Jamal played it from the start, listening over and over to those first five minutes. "Longwei is the one who pressed the button."

"How do you know that?"

Jamal held his hands up in a universal stop motion to pause the feedback. "Do you know about echolocate?"

She paused her work to turn and look at him.

"Like bats and sonar. I can not only hear the sound but how it bounces off the walls. Brad is a good five feet from the watch when it's activated."

"Maybe it isn't even his. I assumed it was because his voice is what you hear, but… maybe Longwei copied the app?"

"How does that help us?"

She took several deep breaths and straightened her spine. "I was looking for Bur's unique identifiers. If I switch to include Longwei's—"

"Do that. I'm going to give Rum a sitrep."

Jamal typed a message on his watch's interface.

Lisa and I have narrowed it down to three possible movie genres. We'll let you know when we pick one so you can recommend a specific movie.

It would let him know they were still working. Jamal had purposely limited his senses to the problem at hand, but he took a minute to let them unfurl. He was looking for any general feelings of alarm.

"*Stop it*," Lisa hollered from across the room. She took several steps toward him, a bundle of raw energy focused on him.

"What?" Jamal could feel the pressure at his eyes that signaled the beginning of a headache.

"If you get too far, I can't bring you back. Keep it close."

He sighed. She was probably right. He'd only purposely used his senses while in Rum's presence. Sure, he could do a lot without physical contact with his Vargr, but there was a lot of research that indicated it was attached more to his sense of smell. He had stopped reading all the "official" commentary after the Chakosky mission. Rum and he didn't fit that, and Jamal was okay with it.

Yet now that Lisa had told him not to check his perimeter, his senses itched. He could turn them up just a little. Past the cleaning equipment running in holo room 2… beyond the buzz of the coffee machine on the second floor just above them.

Lisa knew what he was thinking. "I am monitoring base communications. I even have a bead on the command room Rum is working in." She brought up a video, audio muted, on the wall closest to her. Rum was talking over a headset, directing the room at large to specific intelligence. All the man needed was a bullhorn and a director's chair.

Jamal smiled to let her know he was pleased. "How do you—?"

"I'm the best cyber tech in the USHP. *The best*. I can get access to pretty much anything."

Hell, if she really was able to guard her own perimeter, it would explain why she had gone as long as she had without needing a Hamask. Dr. Bur had explained his new research to help Valhalla's success—Jamal stopped his thoughts there. That prickly bastard's life was precarious. Even with the feedback paused, Jamal could recall each sickening *thump* and *crunch. Shit.*

"Well, all right. Got anything I can use to draw the rest of this room?" He gestured to the hologram around him.

"Yes. Then what?"

"We get as much data as we can and we check with Rum. If they're done with the compound, we can send in T6 and Minophen and Jones. If not…." Jamal took a minute to look at the locations on his list. "Franke could send Milo and Scott with T3."

"Can she be trusted?"

"I think so. But we'll feel her out. I know a Ranger Unit that would love the chance to rescue a Hamra Pair. They are definitely the closest team to these three locations." Lisa handed over a long stylus pen. He pressed to activate the drawing wand and etched where he felt the door was and where Brad seemed to be hanging from the ceiling in chains.

He rubbed a hand over his face and gritted his teeth before activating the feed. Then he could hear a meaty fist connecting with someone's torso. They needed to hurry, but he wouldn't botch this by bringing his B game. Bur and Longwei were getting his best.

Bur, Brad S, PhD—Dictated Report, Evidence in Case 892231-Woodland.

I KNOW why I'm still alive. It wasn't luck, that's for goddamn sure. It also wasn't some noble gesture from that bastard. What Woodland had on the pilot of the Ghost Chinook will hopefully come out during the investigation. I don't know what it is. Sure didn't know it when the helicopter landed and the pilot was killed.

It was early enough that the sun had just started to crest the horizon. The orange-red glare of the sunrise turned my vision down to, like, a two. That and general lack of markers during the flight meant we had no clue that we weren't landing in Havana. The gulf looks like the Gulf.

With the pilot gone and us highly outnumbered, we didn't have much of a chance to escape. I'll be adding flying helicopters to my knowledge list next.

We resisted. I'm not saying we didn't. I know for a fact that Longwei snapped two of their necks before they Tasered him unconscious. High enough current and even Hamask can't stand on their feet.

This last twelve months or so I've lived with anxiety. I wouldn't call it fear, exactly. Not enough racing-heart panic to be fear, but still bad. I described it to my ma about a month ago. Want to know what she said?

"Brad, when you were a baby, I would check on you every night, sometimes several times a night, until you were four or five. I was afraid you'd die in your sleep."

Normally she doesn't talk about my older sister who died at fourteen months of a brain aneurism, so my ma going down that road stuck with me. I can see her sitting in the living room, crocheting some obscene thing like a pecker warmer or rainbow gloves for the PFLAG fundraiser. Pop always rolls the balls of yarn. Then she says, "It's okay to be worried. That's normal. You had some great times with Daire. Just don't waste time with Haruki because you're protecting your heart."

So what do I do? I wait a whole fucking year until death is imminent to try and do right by Longwei. I'm a work in progress.

I know I'm rambling. I'll edit this private shit out later.

The room they took us to looks like a large mudroom. You know the type. Usually next to or part of a laundry room, has a drain in the floor and a commercial-size sink. Only this room is bigger. Commercial-grade mudroom. The walls have rust lines down them from water damage, which means we're in some type of a sublevel and the water contains a high percentage of metal. I've spent this time gathering information because that's a fuck better way to spend my time than hyperventilating or yelling at my captors.

Don't believe me?

Okay, yeah, I was talking. I don't remember it all. I keep turning my pheromones up and down, hoping it will jar Longwei into consciousness. They strip us down to our briefs. Easier to mark up our skin if they actually have access to it. They toss our kit into a case in the corner. I'm thinking I'm going to get us out of here, so clothes will come in handy. So nice of them not to get our stuff dirty. You know?

They think Longwei is still out when they toss him against the wall but I see him catch himself to minimize the impact.

Then they strap my wrists into cuffs hanging from the ceiling. I have no illusions. These chains aren't just for me, so I'm working with trained sadists.

You'll have the vid feed and transcript, so let me just give you some of the logic I base my verbal blows on. The pudgy Latino in charge has serious inferiority issues. The hostile with the overly puckered lips wants to strip Longwei the rest of the way. The young guy is empty-headed. The other three leave the room, speaking Spanish and chuckling and smacking each other on the back.

See, Ashley was a quiet kid. Yeah, I'm talking about my sister again. See what shit pops into your head when you're recalling how you almost died? She didn't cry. Hardly spoke. Mom was determined I would be the opposite. Loud, boisterous, opinionated. And growing up in a small town, it wasn't a big deal to be a bit strong-willed and blunt. Hell, I didn't even realize other people might have a problem with it. Ma and Pop debate issues with me. We have wicked discourse. You hearing me? I learned in high school to hold my tongue. Mostly.

I remain silent while they hook me up—I don't struggle with that shotgun pointed at my gut. Plus silence seems to be what they are hoping for. Quickest way to lure someone in is give them what they want. Then, *kerpow*, *bang*. Upper cut.

Columbia has an ancient history of ransoming prominent businessmen and politicians. It peaked in the 1980s but regained fashion ten years ago. I'm telling myself all this to keep my head level. If they find out we are Hamrammr, we'll be dead. Being an unsanctioned civilian pair, though, means we aren't designated ID-wise other than as FBI agents. Any intel these guys have on us doesn't include our Hamra status.

My hands start to tingle from the blood flow being fucked. They stretch me to the pads of my bare feet. My stomach rolls and clenches, and I try to roll my head to get a better look at the room. That's when I see Longwei gesture at his ear and then his bare wrist. It's our signal that we are being listened to. Lisa's panic button. God bless the boy-loving cougar technogenius.

I start giving Pudgy lip service. "The Geneva convention forbids cruelty. No state of emergency justifies the torture of prisoners."

I lay on the insolent tone and even manage to cock my hip. I tell him with everything at my disposal that he is insignificant. Worse, incompetent. *How dare I tell him what to do?* Yes, this gets me punched. He hammers away at my chest and face until I lose my footing. I feel my shoulders pop and worry about them dislocating. My hands are numb and swelling, the chains purpling bruises on my wrists.

At some point Longwei must raise hell because once I have my footing again, my breathing shallow, I see them strap him against the opposite wall. "It's a good thing he can't get loose. He'd kick your puny asses."

I say it to remind Longwei not to get loose. He could snap those cords with enough effort. But we've got a cover to maintain.

I laugh. "You should wait until the man in charge comes. Put on a show like the puppets you are." I don't know why shit like that works. Yet Duckface is laughing and Pudgy is sputtering about answering only to God. He calls me things like heathen and sinner or whatever. This is how many fucks I give. Zero.

I drop into unconsciousness with his next punch. When I come around, it is to the sound of Longwei spitting blood out of his mouth. He doesn't look good. The healing will kick in, that isn't the issue, but he's about to snap.

I saw that look in Chicago. It's not a look easily forgotten. Being restrained must summon memories of his days with the USHP. Probably conjures up fear and anger over being forced. Shit. Take that part out too.

My man is a survivor, and this time he has me to help.

"You call yourselves men? You're just bullies."

It isn't my best line, but add the tone and aggressive body language, and they leave Longwei alone to come over and yell in my face. Longwei's breathing evens out. At some point the young guy leaves. He comes back in with a bucket of water that he uses to drench me. Pudgy and Duckface jump out of the way, yelling at the kid to watch out. It stings a bit but also helps me wake the rest of the way. I still think the kid was trying to help us. He takes a cloth and presses it into a slit in my eyebrow. I was wrong about his eyes. They aren't empty. They're scared. Wish we'd gotten that kid out of there.

Woodland comes in at that point, and I start laughing at Pudgy and Duckface because they are posturing like fucking peacocks. It's obscene.

Woodland looks like a Texan. He has a bushy mustache, a small gut, and a non-chin; the kind that goes from mouth to neck without any real pause. I'm not saying Texans have weak chins. The Texas comes across in the thinning hair, cowboy boots, and Western-style suit. Far as I know, the man has never lived in Texas.

He asks me straight out, "Do you believe in God?"

I know it won't make a difference, so I tell him the truth. "Yes, sir, I do."

What? Faith and science do not need to be a separate thing. Hell, how awesome is God that he can create the world within the limitations of physics and chemistry? Pretty damn awesome.

Woodland just rolls over my words. "God created man in his own image. Yet man is conceited. He sins by rejecting God's word, by desecrating his creations. Changing men into abominations."

He turns quickly and hits Longwei in the face. He breaks Longwei's nose. Blood spouts out. I try to take back his attention. "Tell me, Bishop Woodland, what must we do to repent?"

It works for a while. He lectures us on how some sinners taint the nation and can never be washed away. Blah-blah-blah. Check the feed. I look attentive, but I'm just giving us time. That is until he brings up how we made it into this shithole.

"Elder Ohad is striving for God's forgiveness. Yes, the man brought you here as part of his penance. One day God may grant him the peace of death for his service to the cause."

Before he can launch into more scripture—seriously, it's been over forty minutes—I ask him, "Where is good old Ohad? I think we need to thank him."

Woodland laughs. It creeps me out that he doesn't sound evil; a bit wheezy but not sinister. "Ohad Chakosky told us of your flight back to Cuba. He has shared many truths with our cause. Perhaps God will bless him." I don't recognize the name, but I can see from Longwei's response that he does.

The kid reminds Woodland of the time and all but Duckface leaves the room. Duckface checks our bindings, lingers over Longwei until I'm spitting threats at him. He laughs as he walks out.

I know that Longwei will listen until they're clear before speaking. I stretch up to my toes to relieve some of the strain on my hands, and I flex my fingers.

"You're doing really well, Brad, drawing this out."

He means keeping us from being killed too soon. I just nod and stare at the door a bit. I try to rest, but my hands have gone numb and I'm worried I'll lose them even if we make it out of here. Guess it's a good thing I can dictate these entries.

Longwei tries to bolster my spirits. Maybe my silence worries him. He says, "It's been a few hours, with them transporting us here and you out for a while when they were working me over."

"Don't. Don't do that." I can't stand to hear him trying to reassure me. Like what? Someone is going to save us? I know Lisa's panic program is doing its thing, but I can't let hope in just yet.

"We're going to be okay. They'll come back and we'll get us switched so your hands can rest."

"Stop." If he says "don't worry" or worse, "we'll make it out," I'll be really pissed.

"You're so brave, Brad." I've seen this in vids, that speech between comrades or estranged lovers just before certain death. If you can't say those things every day, how true could they be? You're just saying them to make yourself feel better. It's all just a bunch of bullshit.

I blink my eyes a bunch to draw tears to the surface and lay it on super thick. "Haruki, I just want you to know"—I let my voice hitch with emotion—"it's been a privilege to work with you and—"

"Shut up. That is not what I was doing." He smiles and then winces when his lip splits back open.

"It feels false, like a good-bye. Like giving up."

He nods and looks toward the door, just listening. Except then the emotions really are at the surface. I bite my lip and stare really hard at his beautiful face. I've been fortunate to wake up every day to that face. I pray. The actual words are between me and God, but it includes a lot of thank-yous.

Then I start talking to Longwei and, apparently, Hamask Zumati. "Don't laugh, but I've been learning Japanese. Working in Central and South America, maybe expanding my Spanish skills would have been smarter. But nope, Japanese."

Longwei does this cute eyebrow scrunch as he considers what I just said. "I don't speak Japanese."

"I know that. Realized after a couple of months of serious study." I stretch up to my toes again. "It's not a total loss. Your parents will think I'm amazing."

He smiles. He thinks I'm adorable. They probably don't speak Japanese either. That's what I get for trying to be the good guy, the keeper. He gets a real kick out of this next part.

"I wanted to be romantic when I asked you to come home and meet my parents. When I told you"—his pretty eyes go all soft—"*aishite imasu*, Haruki. I love you."

"I love you, too." He says it quick, like a valve popping, like he has wanted to say it for months.

I watch his mouth as he speaks. I can't wait until he says those words to me, with our mouths pressed together.

"Hell yeah, you do."

Chapter 18

THE SNEAK and grab required a lot of look-over-here and wasn't really all that sneaky.

Rum stood at the center of the room. They had the stats of each team member on the wall screen to his right. The live video feeds from Minophen and Cooper were split on the screen at the front of the room. The compound and pictures of Woodland and his officers were up on Rum's left. The pinch to his spine had eased a bit, yet his hands itched to grab up his knives and shadow Minophen into the places evil lurked.

In turn, the feed from the command room broadcasted to General Khan—who sat in New York with officials from the UN Task Force—and Major General Franke at Fort McCoy. Operation Holy Fury had taken a higher profile with the recent unconfirmed deaths of Bur and Longwei.

Rum got the attention of one of the techs. "Jankovic, does each camera have the IP system?"

Jankovic swiped around his field tablet. "Yes, sir."

"Let's get those up and running. It'll fill in any gaps for the main vids." Plus, if they had similar equipment to wherever they were holding Bur and Longwei, they might lose the main feed midmission.

Jankovic nodded. Rum pressed his earpiece to connect him to his FBI counterpart. "Agent Mendoza, we'll have IP feed as well. We've received reports that teltom feed-suppression equipment is on the black market."

"Agreed" was the terse reply. The man wasn't rude, just direct.

T6 had quietly taken out the guards patrolling the back perimeter and then created a ruckus to draw more from the house. They used a funneling technique with controlled fire in two different quadrants. They had created realistic soundtracks and were playing them in designated areas to give those rushing in the idea that guards were fighting with enemy combatants. FBI sharpshooters picked them off as they entered the kill zone.

Longwei had asked about the tactic during the planning stage. Rum had simply replied, "I saw it in a movie once."

Rum watched as Minophen's feed paused in a hallway; a hand in view tapped a small closet door. Rum pressed a different button on his headset. "That's supposed to be the water main."

There were three quiet *click*s on Rum's side to indicate acknowledgment. The water main wasn't essential to the mission, but Rum trusted Jones's instincts in bringing it up. Either someone would log it as weird commentary in a report later or they wouldn't. Rum alerted the sharpshooters that the east-side sensors had been triggered. Best thing about taking over your enemies' security system was when you could use it against them.

Minophen and Jones had eliminated each threat that arose—silent kills done with efficiency. Leaving men alive was not an option inside the compound. It would make their backs vulnerable until they could find and arrest Woodland. They'd walked through enough of the compound so that Command could cross-reference heat signatures from the drones flying overhead with the actual locations of targets. This would provide a digital map of the building.

"Upper floors clear," Minophen said.

"Seven disabled in back of compound. We'll bag them ready for transport," Cooper said.

Good. It would give the FBI the option to question Dios Provee. It didn't look like Woodland was on site.

FBI flooded through the building, tagging evidence by zone, scanning rooms with portable holo devices for later re-creation. They were working with solid intel that a second location had strike commands if this building was ever compromised. The ultimate trip wire that would decimate the building rather than allow an enemy to escape. There was a limited window before missiles would be sent to destroy the whole place.

"No sign of Woodland."

"Proceed to extraction," Agent Mendoza said.

Rum stared at the compound mapping again and checked their time. "Jankovic, we got anything registering on the waves?"

Any incoming ballistic would register on early-alert sensors. "No, sir."

"What you think, Rum?" Jones spoke in a very soft voice. He sounded young, timid even. That impression had cost many people their lives.

Having finally seen the layout through the video feeds, Rum figured out what felt wrong. "The other three locations had basements."

"That water closet is in the wrong place." Jones again.

"Heading there now," Minophen said.

They stopped in front of the door and did their Pair thing. The cameras couldn't see it, but Rum had witnessed it in person. Both spoke fluent sign language. Not a skill set most supersoldiers possessed. They always angled the cameras away so that only the two of them would see.

Jones opened the narrow door and shined a light into the corners. The water heater and pipes swung back to reveal stairs.

Jankovic took that moment to give a time update. "Two minutes."

"Hear that, guys? You need fifty seconds to get to the extraction point." Rum rolled his shoulders and did another scan of the path out, looking for complications.

"Plenty of time," Minophen said and led the way down the stairs.

"Jankovic, mark the time in ten-second increments."

"Yes, sir."

A second text came across Rum's watch.

Have found location and lead actor. Can you recommend best support?—Jamal

"Is there a problem, Vargr Walker?" Khan had switched to just his Hamrammr title to downplay Rum's recent promotion to major.

Five minutes, he sent as he said, "No sir."

"Sixty seconds," Jankovic said.

"Minophen, Jones, time's up."

Neither responded. *Stubborn.* Yet, Rum knew the feeling of wanting just a few more minutes to gather every possible lead, to truly make sure nothing and no one was left behind. "Leave a room scanner hooked to the video on Minophen's hat. It'll transmit even after you leave."

"Fifty seconds." Jankovic's tone had changed.

The tension in the whole room amped up. Still silence from Minophen and Jones.

"Do I need to come in and get you?" Rum made it as threatening and full of censure as he could.

Jones flipped the camera off as he left it on what looked like a lab table. Both agents activated their smartwatches. "Smells like that stuff they activate Hamra with."

Shit. Dios Provee's whole religious rage was over the Americans' manipulation of genetics and the natural order of things. They saw the Hamrammr program and the whole USHP as an abomination. Rum had hoped that Wick's imprisonment and the research he had been doing was a false ploy. He had thought that Wick was given the task to create bombs or drugs for Dios Provee to sell. It was naive to think Wick would use subterfuge to hide his real work on purer solutions and easier ways to make the activation compounds. Rum had wanted to believe that, to leave the information there.

Yet, two labs in different locations could only generate the most ominous scenarios. "Notify us when you've cleared the building." Rum pressed the original button on his headset. "Agent Mendoza, is your unit clear?"

"Affirmative."

"Cooper?"

"Clear and accounted for, sir. Plus the seven detainees."

"Twenty seconds," Jankovic countered.

Then one of the other techs spoke. "Drones have picked up incoming—we've lost the drones."

They lost all data feeds from the site, including personal smartwatches.

Rum whistled shrilly to regain the attention of the room. "Keep it together, folks. Jankovic, I want make and trajectory of that missile—"

"Short-range ballistic missile," Agent Mendoza interrupted. "Less than six-hundred-kilometer range. Sending you possible trajectory."

Rum's chest tightened and he gripped his hands at his sides. The communications had been disrupted by the blast concussion, yet the devices would switch from local to satellite relay. That just caused a time delay. Ten agonizing seconds before Cooper said, "MJ accounted for."

MJ, short for Minophen and Jones. Happy chatter and several deep sighs of relief turned the still room into busy energy.

Rum's stomach pitched forward in relief and he squeezed his eyes shut for the briefest moment. His watch chimed. He knew what it would say without looking, but he still felt Khan and the task force perk up. "Jankovic, you and the other techs head to holo room 2 and start breaking down the data. Everyone else clear the room."

When they didn't move quick enough, Rum added, "Now."

Once Rum had the room to himself, he looked at General Khan and General Franke over the vid feeds. Hell, even the president could be listening to this moment. He checked his watch and sent back a message for Lisa and Jamal to join him. "Sir, I know that WREAC Team 6 and the FBI Critical Incident Response team will handle the return without our management."

"Agreed, Vargr Walker." Khan wasn't emoting any concerning tells. "We've also notified the Columbian president of the missiles so they can work on containing any damage to the immediate target. Luckily it is an isolated area."

Jamal came in to the room and stood next to Rum, saluting in the general direction of the feeds. Rum just raised his eyebrows.

"Vargr Naylor is securing the communications," Jamal said.

Securing communications? Is she worried about them being wiretapped?

"Done," Lisa said as she entered the room.

Khan might have been taking this all in stride, but Franke appeared very displeased.

"General Franke, we know the location of Woodland. We know his location because he captured FBI Agents Bur and Longwei," Jamal said.

"Hold," Franke said. She stood suddenly and the camera showed only her stomach.

The feed was muted. Jamal used one of the consoles to bring up the building and room he had created.

Holy impressive Toledo. Most of it was in brown lines, which meant Jamal had drawn them. He had speculated that he could use echolocation, but on this scale?

Before the rush of ideas on all the practical applications, Rum took a moment to dwell on the pride he felt. He reached out and stroked a hand down Jamal's forearm. Jamal turned and smiled, but his eyes were distant. *Shit, this has cost him.* Not only did he look drained of energy, but he also looked haunted, damaged. It reminded Rum of how Jamal had looked when he pulled him out of the coma. Waxy, frail. He hadn't known just how frail until Jamal's full strength had returned.

Rum looked away, back to the holo rendering. Jamal even had the general size of each person in the room.

When Franke came back on the feeds, it was without the rest of the task force. "Walker, we are going to have a long discussion about proper channels of command."

Rum held back his eye roll, but it was a near thing. "Yes, ma'am."

"WREAC Team 3 was in standby for this operation. Send us the data you've—"

"Ma'am," Lisa interrupted. "There is a unit of the 75th Rangers less than fifteen minutes to the location. They've already received ready codes."

Rum was impressed by the ballsy and dissident move.

"How the fucking hell—?"

"Ma'am, you have a chance to save these people. Please, ma'am," Jamal said.

Khan said, "Franke."

Rum didn't know if it was Jamal's hollow eyes or Khan's threatening tone, but she pulled out her personal phone. "They're going in blind."

"No, ma'am. They have full holo rendering of the building and precise location, including all combatants," Jamal said. He lifted his head as he spoke, as if a heavy yoke lifted off his shoulders.

They heard her speak to the Rangers. She gave them the go code and directed them to bring back Bur and Longwei, whatever their condition.

Jamal whispered, feather soft, "They're still alive." His tone was fiercely determined, as if Jamal knew to his core that Bur and Longwei would make it out.

God, Rum loved him. Loved watching him sleep, content and still. Loved watching him talk or read while he ate. Hell, Jamal had probably caught him staring half a dozen times lately, but Rum just couldn't help it. It made him feel so complete. Jamal was Rum's proudest success.

Franke took a moment, after ending her call, to glare at Rum and Jamal. "I'll be there in the morning." She disconnected.

Khan was looking over the data Jamal had sent him. Rum could see a miniature of the room and surrounding building Jamal had painstakingly created. Khan shook his head and glanced up at the three waiting in the control room. "I'll be there in three hours or less. Keep me apprised en route."

As soon as both lines disconnected, Jamal pulled Rum into a hug. Jamal shook, racking trembles rolling down the muscles of his back and arms.

Lisa worked at one of the consoles. She cycled through several data screens on multiple walls. "Hoo-rah. Just got confirmation from Cooper that Minophen and Jones have only minor injuries from blast debris. No other friendly casualties."

Rum didn't bother trying to follow any of it. He felt warm. Like wrapping up in a heated blanket, letting the heat press into his muscles until they unclenched.

"Hoo-rah," Jamal whispered.

"I want to apologize. For using Jamal," Lisa said.

Rum couldn't be bothered to move just yet. "What are you talking about?"

Lisa huffed out a breath and shook her head at Rum. "For someone who is so observant of others, you can be pretty obtuse about yourself. Hamask and Vargr, that's a symbiotic relationship. Their chemistry keeps us level. The two of you churn out enough to keep the whole base happy as cats in a sunlit window." She used her fingertips to rub her eyebrow. "Normally I'd keep my distance, wait for a new Hamask to become available, but Travers was getting too attached."

"So you've been getting high off Jamal?" Rum snorted his disbelief and felt a corresponding rumble in Jamal's chest. "Does that make me your dealer?"

"You don't realize you even do it. Dr. Bur said you didn't, but I didn't believe it. I learned how to turn it off by watching you."

Okay, sure. Rum wasn't really listening to her. He threaded his fingers in Jamal's bigger hand and stepped back to really look at him. Jamal had his head tilted to the side. Rum realized in that moment that Jamal was trying to decipher Rum's look.

"Lisa, can you get us a pizza from the mess? We can eat while we wait for the Rangers to report in." Jamal cupped Rum's cheek, stroked his thumb across Rum's eyebrow.

Lisa must have left, but Rum didn't put any effort into verifying that.

Jamal cleared his throat. "I thought you were worried about me."

Rum shook his head. "No more than typical worry. I knew you could work on the panic feed without my help."

"No, I mean these last couple of months." Jamal stepped back, guiding Rum to stay close to him until Jamal could lean back on one of the command stations, lowering him to Rum's eye level. He pulled Rum between his warm thighs and rested his hands on Rum's hips.

"Did I need to be worried?" Jamal had really nice thighs.

"No." Jamal laughed for a moment and pressed the sweetest kiss to Rum's mouth. "I'm really happy. Sometimes I see you checking on me, like just now."

"Actually, I'm thinking 'How did I ever live before him?' I love you."

"Yeah, is that what you were thinking?" Jamal smiled, all his passion gleaming in his eyes. "I love you. Man, that feels really good to say."

"Feel free, anytime. I love you." Rum softened his voice with each word and then started pressing kisses to Jamal's eyelids and cheeks. "I love you. I love you." They got lost for a bit in each other's arms.

Finally, Rum stepped back and took a deep breath. "Let's check on those boys. See if the Rangers are bringing them home."

Before General Khan made it to the base, they were able to confirm the rescue of Bur and Longwei. The Rangers would have an extra swagger, intentional or not, for a while. Bur and Longwei were getting treatment at Fort Hood's extensive medical facilities in Texas. Longwei had a few broken ribs and Bur needed surgery for a broken wrist. Yet they were under the best care. The government paid their medical staff extremely well and the system was highly competitive. No doctor would want to lose reputation by the loss or mistreatment of a Hamra Pair.

Woodland escaped, but Operation Holy Fury had seriously affected his forces and resources.

Wick and Browning oversaw Chakosky's arrest and were taking turns watching him until JAG could escort him to Leavenworth, Kansas. Neither would leave the Vargr alone with the MPs. The FBI wanted the chance to interrogate Chakosky. Normally Rum would be interested to see how they maneuvered that joint effort. Instead he was just blasted grateful that neither he nor Jamal needed to be part of that process.

Once Khan had received all immediate and pertinent information, Rum and Jamal headed for their sanctuary. They slept, and people wisely left them alone.

IN THE morning Jamal stroked Rum awake. He kissed along Rum's jaw until Rum twined their legs together and smiled.

Jamal cupped the side of Rum's face, brushed a thumb across his bottom lip. "I love you, Ryan Walker. I'm going to proudly work by your side until we've changed the world." It didn't matter if that sounded sappy. They had found each other. What could be more miraculous?

"I think we might actually do just that." Rum kissed along his cheekbones and slid his hands around to Jamal's back to pull him in closer.

Jamal loved the way Rum fit against his bigger body.

Rum lay quietly for a while, letting Jamal do all the work of getting them both languid and aroused. He gripped Jamal's shoulder for leverage as he thrust his hips in Jamal's grip. They came in quick succession, long, stretched-out, easy orgasms.

Rum pulled back enough to look into Jamal's eyes. He let all the vulnerability he felt show on his face. Then Rum whispered, "I love you."

Jamal felt like he was waking up from his hibernation all over again, stepping into the heat of that day long ago, his muscles quaking from emotion rather than disuse and feeling the effects of their recent victory rather than the drugs in his system.

Rum's Southern drawl wrapped through the neurons of his starved and lonely brain.

Yeah, well worth the wait.

Stay tuned for an excerpt from

Rinse & Repeat

By Amberly Smith

After reliving the same day sixty-two times, Repeater Peat Harris is about to give up on his latest case: saving Jake Schwinn. In the past, Peat has solved some seriously twisted crimes, caught the bad guys, and kept an emotional distance. But this time, his heart's involved, a definite must-never-do on Repeats, and he can't just walk away—even if that means putting himself into the bullet's path.

A year ago, Jake's best friend was gunned down, and Jake has been playing bait to catch the killer. But now a wicked-looking hottie named Peat is warning Jake that he's about to die—again—unless they can catch the shooter. *Yeah, right.* Then Jake starts to remember the previous Repeats and how he and Peat hooked up….

www.dreamspinnerpress.com

PROLOGUE

JAKE SCHWINN had plenty of first-person, hands-on, defining-moment levels of experience with funerals. When it came to saying goodbye to the dead, he'd seen it all. Unfortunately. But this one felt different.

Looked the same: flowers, crying people, conservatively dressed funeral director. Even the rows of uniformed police officers, supporting one of their own in his time of need; been there, seen that. The mourners, mostly college students, wore somber faces.

Was the difference the person who had died or the people he had left behind? And what the hell was the matter with Jake today if he couldn't even think of his best friend's name? Had to refer to him as the person, the departed, his loved one?

But Geo's name had always been powerful, just like the man himself. People would argue that at nineteen he wasn't a man yet. Wrong. George Noble, or Geo, hadn't been a kid, not really, since his mom died.

The speaker finished his talk and turned away from the podium. No applause. The church thought it disrupted the spirit. The bishop had spoken of Geo's commitment to serve his church. That he'd just received his mission papers to serve in Brazil, that he was a righteous brother. Minus the gangster slang on the last bit.

The bishop spoke about eternal families and Heavenly Father's promise that they would all be able to see Geo again. It gave comfort. That was the difference. Maybe.

At Grandpa Johnson's funeral, Jake'd only thought of the past. At Grandma Sara's, how there would be no future. And at Uncle Nik's, Miss Karen's, and Granddad Max's, he'd just been angry. When his sister Eugenia had died, he felt denial and despair.

It was Jake's turn to speak. It said so on the printed program. He stood up, feeling the theater-style seat flip up behind him, and took the necessary steps forward to look at the crowd, more than two hundred people packed into wooden pews and standing along the back wall. He began to sweat. His heart spun like a loose wheel, wobbling about his chest, ready to fall off its axle.

They didn't approve of him standing before them. He wasn't a member of their church. He was that "faggot" friend who'd corrupted Geo.

A mechanical buzz sounded as the podium rose, lifting the mike closer to Jake's six-foot-four-inch height. Geo would start his talk with a joke: Gee, Bishop Oliver, how short are you? Except Geo wasn't as tall as Jake. Hadn't been as tall.

Jake swallowed.

He cleared his throat and looked down at the open casket in front of the stage, then jerked his head away from the sight. He felt the moisture gather at the corner of his eyes. That would so help this situation. To look like an emotional drama queen in front of these people.

"Geo once explained to me about Heavenly Father. He said it was God's other name. Like Santa Claus was really Kris Kringle. Of course that was when we were just kids. Fifteen or sixteen." They might have smiled or chuckled at his attempt at humor, but he didn't hear it. He zoned a bit, still talking but immersed in his memories.

"The last funeral I was at was for my Grandma Frankie. Geo, being a good friend, he was…." He stumbled over, paused at the word, so final. "Everyone's friend, he came with me. And I got all crazy Texan, and he asked me what was wrong, and I said that the speakers had gotten it all wrong."

"Grandma was Catholic and that priest didn't know her from Eve. He asked me that day to speak at his funeral. I said he'd be seventy-five and his grandchildren would need to talk. That the people from his mission would travel across the world to speak on how he'd saved them."

Jake's voice broke. The bright lights of the Sacrament Hall blurred and elongated as he blinked back the tears. His chest ached, and he wanted to press his hand over his heart to keep it in place, make sure it didn't become a projectile weapon as his body splintered from the pain. "He said he wasn't going on his mission to save people." Jake swallowed, sniffed as quietly as he could, and found a box of Kleenex pushed at his elbow. "Thanks." Jake took a few and held them in his fist.

"He said he was going on a mission to share the gospel. And I said, 'You can do that here.' And he said, 'I do do that here.' He explained it was like sharing a musical talent, or art. He'd been given this amazing knowledge that made him happy, and he'd share it. Baptisms or not."

He snorted at the memory, then swiped at his nose. "Then he was, 'So will you do it?'"

Jake had joked back that, no, he wouldn't marry Geo, but that type of humor wouldn't be understood here. "'Will you talk at my funeral?' And I said absolutely not. I'd stand up here and bawl, and his family would pitch me off the stage." He saw a few smiles this time. Either his idea appealed to them, or they understood how Geo would dig in and make him promise, determined, as always, to get his way.

"Geo was a great student. Not only because he got good grades; lots of people do that. But he liked school. Liked challenging himself and his teacher to make every class an opportunity to be better. He was a great example. Morally steadfast. He was a decent skateboarder, and he could kick your—" Jake caught the word and altered it with little disruption "—butt at Guitar Hero."

Jake had written all that down and said it easily because it was prepared. The next came from his gut. "He didn't agree with my choices." He let that stand. Either people would understand or they wouldn't. He didn't say it for them. "But he didn't judge me." He closed his mouth, shifted his chin, trying to keep the tears back. "I was his friend and that friendship was unconditional, both ways." Jake turned his head and blew his nose. He turned back to the mike.

"Geo died because of hate. Because someone put a condition on his further existence. You're not allowed to live unless you live my way. They killed him thinking he was different." Were you allowed to say gay in a place like this? "Geo was straight, he always did the right thing, and had a great capacity to give.

"Not because it was required of him. Not because it was easy or expected. But because he was happy. It felt right and good and made him happy."

Tears dripped down Jake's face, and he knew squelching them would make his face red and blotchy, but they made him vulnerable, so he locked them back. Locked them in. "He's in that Celestial Kingdom he told me about, hunting down all the recent arrivals from Brazil, and teaching them how to be happy. I know it's true because Geo wouldn't settle for anything less. Stubborn."

Jake folded his hands into fists, a slow curl inward. How to end this speech? The church said, "Amen." Like they were finishing a prayer, and he couldn't say it. He wasn't a hypocrite. Jake believed in God and in heaven and that love was forever. He knew that love for him would be with a man, and God would not only understand, he would rejoice.

"For George." He returned to his seat. He nodded to Officer Noble, Geo's dad, or rather the grief-stricken, stone-faced man who had lost both a wife and a son. A man who had no one else to sit beside, hold him, grieve with him. The sight cut at Jake's stomach, and he swallowed back the hysteria, the wail of longing for his best friend. He, at least, still had family, was still alive, and he'd keep reminding himself until the despair dissipated, until he could breathe again.

He knew why this funeral didn't feel like the others. Geo had been murdered.

CHAPTER
ONE

Monday, September 7.

OF COURSE the man had a name, but suffice it to say, names didn't come into play when saving a life. At least not the first couple of times Peat Harris saved them.

Peat rammed the minivan into the side of the speeding truck. Once again the truck's brakes were out, and it was about to slam into a wall. Major crunch and goodbye driver. The van absorbed the impact that the wall couldn't.

The first time he'd saved the guy, Peat had prevented the brakes from being cut. But now he realized that hadn't been the correct solution. The crime had to be committed so the perp could get his sunny day in prison. Or three to five years for attempted murder. Whichever.

As a Repeater, Peat relived the same day until he got it right. He wasn't looking for perfection, wasn't out to get the girl or to improve himself. He helped people, all kinds of people. Sometimes, like today, Seattle bankers.

The airbag exploded, smacking Peat in the arms and upper chest. Mental note to self: disconnect the airbag. The seat belt tightened painfully into his gut, and he kept his foot on the gas, spinning the truck and finally pushing them both into parked cars along the north side of the street. More air bags, and a few car alarms. Peat's airbag started to deflate. He flicked open his knife and slashed it to hurry the process, released the seat belt, and tried to get out. His driver side door was mangled and he had to push with both feet to get it open. Or rather the minivan's door. It wasn't his vehicle. Something he hoped to avoid, explanation-wise. The door swung out and tilted down like a drunken, boneless body.

Peat's arms hurt, and his chest hurt, but if he didn't stop, his body wouldn't figure out who hurt the most and award the prize of unconsciousness.

Seattle's monorail rattled a block away and tall, white buildings shadowed the street. Every viable square inch of the buildings had windows. All the white helped with the dreary, bleak, rainy days but the windows were beacons of hope. Hope for sun. Like today.

The driver sat, white-knuckled and red-faced in the blue truck like a patriotic statue. "Mister? Are you okay, mister?" Peat said.

The windows had broken as the body of the truck twisted and contoured around the minivan. Though the damage was extensive, American steel workers countrywide would be proud. The two fiberglass compacts the truck had pushed into were crumpled in shame.

Had Peat hit him too soon? Would the man know today that Peat had saved him? It sucked when he got his timing off. "Sir?"

"My brakes. They weren't working."

Not too early then. "Are you hurt?"

"What?"

"Are you hurt? I saw you trying to stop, and I was hoping you wouldn't.... Are you hurt?" Peat said.

The man turned his eyes toward Peat and blinked. "What?"

Peat surveyed the damage around him. He counted the cars involved and sniffed the air for a gas leak. The owner of the car alarm came running, his arms up and yelling. Yeah, good indication that the cops had been called. Hopefully the irate car owner had thought to ask for a paramedic as well. A matter of priorities.

He almost apologized, the proper course of action. His British parents would approve of being proper, polite. But he couldn't promise to never do it again, and the housekeeper would say that meant he wasn't really sorry.

Peat reached in and touched the man's throat. It felt like modeling clay. Cold, smooth, gray. The man's heart raced. Shock.

Peat didn't have anything to help with that, no blanket or jacket. The temperature was in the eighties and for once the Seattle skies were clear of all clouds. "Mister, are you hurt?"

"I'm okay," the driver said to himself. He flexed his hands on the steering wheel. "I'm okay."

"Can you move your legs?"

"Yeah." He looked as he said it to double-check.

Okay, so this had some real potential. Peat just needed to cinch that noose around the perp's throat, and Peat would be on his way. "What's wrong with your brakes?"

"They weren't working. I tried to stop at that light back there. Ran right through it. Thank God I didn't hit someone." He released the steering wheel and ran a hand over his face. "Shit. I could have died."

Peat could hear sirens. Time was up. He used his belligerent tone to push the issue. "You should take better care of your car. Shit. What's it been, five years, since you had your brakes replaced?"

"No. I got new ones last month…." Peat could see the change in the man's face, the raised eyebrows, the change in tone. Perhaps the idea, still vague, circled his subconscious. The firefighters were the first to arrive, hoping for a jaws-of-life situation. Not today, boys. Maybe tomorrow.

Until the clock struck twelve and it became Tuesday the 8th, Peat wouldn't know if his actions today were successful. Midnight could come and, with a massive shift of time gears, it would be Monday. Still.

"Could it be foul play?" This part was hard. How much did you push and still stay out of the way? But the guy needed to get the rest of those clues without Peat spelling it out for him. That would mean answering questions, and Peat needed to get back to college, not testify at a trial.

The man looked at him again. He'd looked at his legs, flexing them. He'd looked at his truck, body shaking. He'd looked at the street they were on, thanking God. But when he looked at Peat, it was with an absent jerk of the eyes, not registering him. Until Peat said foul play.

Then he focused. "You saved my life."

"That's why I'm here."

Tuesday, September 8
Four days later.

PEAT KNEW he was in the right place. His hands vibrated like tuning forks. They didn't visibly shake but the fibers under his skin were alive with first sense.

He'd been relieved when Seattle had been a fairly quick turnaround and the day didn't repeat. Monday went, and Tuesday started, and he answered a few police questions, mapped out his journey home and took in some shopping. But as midnight approached, his hands grew restless.

The skate park in this small city surprised him. Perhaps it was a Northwest thing. Skaters back home skated illegally, and signs of "No skateboarding" were vandalized. But here they had a clean, maintained-by-the-city, cement, metal, and wood park dedicated to skating.

Peat tipped the cab driver. It had been a short ride from the bus stop, but the cabbie had been full of useful information, and he hadn't taken offense to Peat's sudden, "Stop. Stop here."

Never before had his first sense been so precise. This Repeat had been like that, though. When Tuesday happened for the second time he woke up knowing he was going to Boise. Not a, gee I think Idaho is my next stop, which he got on occasion, but a sharp conviction of what came next. Most Repeats were blind fumblings along the chicken coop floor.

The minor psychic ability, or heightened sixth sense came first in his decision making. When he used it, it was his only sense, his first sense. It muted sight, hearing, touch, taste, smell.

Peat walked into the park with his backpack on one shoulder. A skater did a complicated twist midair and landed with a stuttered smack on a ramp.

The boarder stopped at the top of the tall U-shaped ramp and yawned, puffing out white steam and rolling his shoulders. A white cloud in September? Go fig. California never got this cold. And though it rained in Seattle, it didn't feel like it would snow before November. Of course maybe Idaho got snow by Halloween.

A fence separated a warehouse alley and the park's basketball court. Peat leaned against the chain-link fence, his ankles crossed, his shoulders pressed back, enjoying the view of the sexy skater.

The blond pushed his long bangs out of his eyes and looked over at Peat. Peat nodded once in greeting, not expecting a response. His gay little life didn't make every other man gay.

He realized the guy was about his own age, twenty to twenty-five. Even from this distance the man's eyes looked intense. Dark. In sharp contrast to his golden skin and sun-lightened hair.

Hello, Mr. Hottie, something's come up, and I need a helping hand. Stand over here with your board and look sexy. Peat's heart did a dance in his chest.

The skater flipped the board, planted his feet as it headed down the ramp and sailed at a dizzying speed straight at Peat. Aggressive and intimidating, his kind of man. Peat maintained his ground, and the guy did a sharp turn to skate past, then did a board-wheelie or whatever it was called to come back.

Surely Peat had time to flirt, be himself, until he found his next damsel or dude in distress. What would a little extended eye contact with a man whose very presence made him smile and warmed his blood harm?

"Hey."

Peat just smiled and nodded. He felt his dick stir in appreciation, and he resisted the urge to adjust.

"New?"

"Just got into town," Peat said.

"Do you board?"

"I'm thinking about learning." Oh yeah, he was thinking about it. About the tight ass on display as he moved with his board, about the masculine, arousing scent of sweat and the heady drug of laughter as they joked around.

The guy smirked and gave Peat the once-over. He had this slightly crooked, adorable grin. Ah, his heart would be reading more into that look for many days to come. "Get a board, and I'll show you the basics."

Without waiting for a reply, the hottie serpentined back toward the U ramp. The first gunshot pushed him off his board. The second gunshot knocked him down to a knee. The board rolled to a stop against a metal rail.

Peat just stood there. What? What was happening? Neither his body nor his mind could process it. The edgy dullness of shock flushed his skin. No warning. No sign.

He'd seen more than his fair share in the three years since he became a Repeater. He'd seen the results of death, a few times self-induced. He'd seen sickness and despair. Human depravity. Houston, two Repeats ago, had been the worst. But this?

Please say this isn't my next Repeat. But please God, let me fix this if it is. No more Houstons. No more letting the right thing happen because it was destiny.

Peat felt the guy's pockets for a cell phone. He didn't remember walking from the fence, only shaking loose from his trance as he knelt. He pulled out a shirt from his bag and pressed it to a wound. The guy grasped Peat's hand. Peat didn't speak, not even to hush the gasping pleas for help. He couldn't speak. Couldn't think. Knew he should get them out of firing range. Knew he should get help, the police, something. React, do.

The hand in Peat's went slack and the ragged breathing stilled as the guy died a fourth time. Four Tuesdays. It had taken Peat two days to get here and the initial day before it repeated. How many more before Peat found the right combination of events? How many more before he stopped the loss of this beautiful, young life?

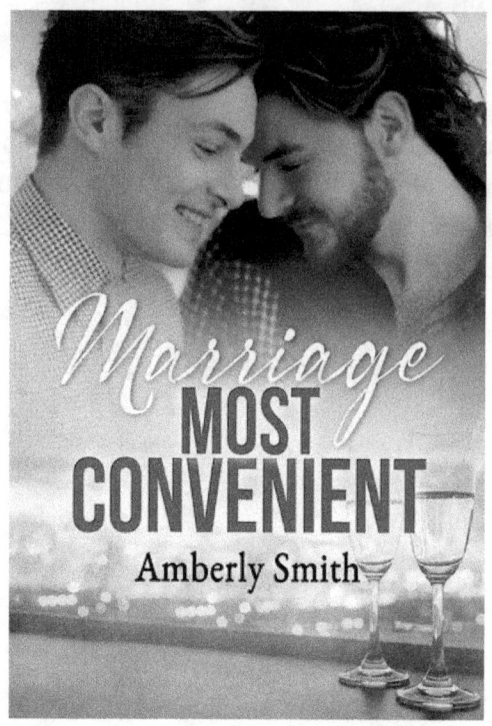

No bank is going to give a nomadic thrill seeker a loan, even if Tom Flynn wants to develop and run a retreat for disabled kids. Good thing he's finally old enough to pull from his trust fund. However, it would mean settling down—because accessing the money requires him to be married—so he asks his best friend, Luke, to marry him.

Luke Marten's goal is simple: don't go on one more crazy adventure with Tom. Knowing how successful he has been in the past, Luke has a backup plan: don't fall in love. He's a goner when Tom not only proposes but confesses to one seriously hot kink.

For their friendship to survive this marriage, they'll need to face DOMA, conservative judges, and long-held beliefs about each other. Talk about getting caught by the short hairs.

www.dreamspinnerpress.com

AMBERLY SMITH struggled with reading until the fourth grade, when she was placed in special tutoring. At eleven she read her mom's romance novels, pausing every other page to have her mom read an unknown word to her so she could memorize it. Back then, authors were mythical creatures and like unicorns, only existed in people's imaginations. It never occurred to her that she could be a writer.

Amberly lives in the Northwest with her husband, two children, and two cats. She has a bachelor's in communications and does freelance editing for other writers. Life has given her plenty to write about, including breast cancer, friendship, love, bomb threats, dysfunctional families, sexuality, and hope. It's been a weird journey.

Still on the lookout for those mythical creatures, Amberly prefers to write about relationships and the power of love.

Connect with Amberly via her website (www.amberlysmith.com) or on Facebook, Twitter, or Pinterest.

www.ingramcontent.com/pod-product-compliance
Lightning Source LLC
Chambersburg PA
CBHW060103260626
47160CB00005B/1781